William Van Zandt Cox, Milton Harlow Northrup

Life of Samuel Sullivan Cox

William Van Zandt Cox, Milton Harlow Northrup

Life of Samuel Sullivan Cox

ISBN/EAN: 9783337333515

Printed in Europe, USA, Canada, Australia, Japan

Cover: Foto ©Raphael Reischuk / pixelio.de

More available books at **www.hansebooks.com**

LIFE

OF

Samuel Sullivan Cox,

BY HIS NEPHEW,

WILLIAM VAN ZANDT COX,

AND HIS FRIEND,

MILTON HARLOW NORTHRUP.

With Illustrations.

M. H. NORTHRUP, PUBLISHER,
SYRACUSE, N. Y.
1899.

To the

Employes of the Postal Service

and of the

Life Saving Service

this biography of their champion

is respectfully inscribed.

PREFACE.

Samuel Sullivan Cox occupies an unique place in American history. Precisely his parallel has not been known. As was well said by Dr. Talmage, at his obsequies: "It will be useless to try to describe to another generation who or what he was like. He was the first and the last of that kind of man." His distinguishing characteristic was his versatility—his many-sidedness. He had a marvelous faculty of adaptation. It is difficult to conceive of an emergency to which he would not have proved equal, or a situation in which he would not have made himself quite "at home." He was unquestionably a genius; but, unlike most men thus gifted, he was an indefatigable worker. He had an unquenchable thirst for knowledge, and would hesitate at no exploration in search of it. Men marveled not only at the extent and diversity of his knowledge, but even more at its thoroughness and profundity. He confounded the savants themselves, who could not understand when he had had the time or where he had found the opportunity to delve so deep into the mysteries of the sciences or philosophy. His public life covered half his years; and yet if we eliminate from the calculation that entire public career, we shall still have, in his charming books of travel and other literary ventures, enough left to establish his title to an enviable niche in the history of his country.

His service in Congress, aggregating close upon three decades, covers a memorable period, or rather three memorable periods, in the nation's history; the first, the period immediately before the war of the rebellion; the second, the period of the war itself; and the third, the period of reconstruction.   In all three he was a conspicuous figure. The stranger entering for the first time the gallery of the House of Representatives, and asking to be pointed out the men of note on the floor below, was sure, any time in those thirty years, to inquire, among the first, "Which is Sunset Cox?" His speeches, always breezy and brilliant, were sure to fill the vacant seats in the Hall, from the adjoining cloak-rooms and lobbies.   It was, however, in the heat of debate that he shone the most vividly.   In repartee he had no superior, if equal, in his day.

Mr. Cox's energies as a legislator were rather on humanitarian than strictly political lines. One of his eulogists, of a race which had been the victim of prejudice and oppression in many lands and for many centuries, characterized him as a "strong and wise defender of the oppressed of all climes and of all faiths."   His humanity was broad and deep.   Wherever was persecution, the first to spring to the front in the American Congress to do away with it, was Samuel Sullivan Cox.

Of none of the achievements of his public career was he prouder than of those which justified his title of "Father of the Life-Saving Service," or the "Friend of the Letter Carriers."   And yet, in his elaborate volume, "Three Decades of Federal Legislation," he modestly refrains from making even passing allusion to those crowning triumphs of his legislative life. Those, however, whom he so ably served will ever keep his deeds in grateful remembrance.

In the limits set to this volume it was not possible to go beyond a mere outline of Mr. Cox's memorable legislative experience. His many notable speeches in Congress and public addresses outside of that body would make a valuable volume, sparkling in thought and expression, and evincing ripe scholarship and profound study. He touched no subject that he did not illuminate and adorn. Generations hence, traditions of Samuel Sullivan Cox will be on the lips of the men who shall serve in the halls of the American Congress.

CHAPTER I.

ANCESTRY.

For Virginia the claim has proudly been made
that she was the mother of States and Statesmen.
The Old Dominion has a rival in the State which
lies between the Ohio River and Lake Erie—the
only State of the Union which, in the days of slavery, touched the borders of a slave State on the
one side and the Canadian line on the other. With
the record she has made before her, Ohio may
justly contest with Virginia the honor of being
the mother of statesmen.   Especially since the
outbreak of the civil war, in 1861, the State of Ohio
has, through her gallant sons, cut a conspicuous
figure in American history, in both field and cabinet.   Every Republican chosen President of the
Republic since Lincoln—Grant, Hayes, Garfield,
Harrison, and McKinley—first saw the light in
Ohio. Here also was the birthplace of those great
military chieftains, Grant and Sherman; of great
administrators such as Chase and Stanton; and
statesmen foremost in the halls of legislation, like
Ewing, Hendricks, and John Sherman.   In this
last named group belongs also another name,
equally illustrious, suffering naught by comparison, a man for over thirty years conspicuous in the
country's service—Samuel Sullivan Cox.   With
the zeal of his service he blended a keen political

foresight which history has vindicated, in the triumph in recent years of the conservative principles for which he so ably contended.

The secret of the prominence in national affairs attained by these sons of Ohio, the product of her virgin soil, is easily found by those who would seek it. Largely it is a matter of heredity. The early settlers of Ohio were sturdy representatives from the best families of New England, the Middle States, and Virginia, and if we examine the family history of any one of the distinguished representatives from Ohio we shall find that he was a descendant from some one of these brave pioneers. The truth of all this is demonstrated with more than ordinary force in the case of Samuel S. Cox.

Of his ancestors on the paternal side the first to come to the New World was Thomas Cox, who, with his wife Elizabeth Blashford, of Marshpathkills, Long Island, settled in Upper Freehold township in the Province of East New Jersey in 1670. The family came from Herefordshire, England, and were people of means, as is shown by the fact that the name of Thomas Cox is included among those of the twenty-four original proprietors of the Province. Their son James (born August 18, 1672; died October 18, 1750), was born in Monmouth County two years after their settlement in New Jersey, and he became a large land owner. His estate included some of the most valuable lands in the colony and from its richness was called "Cream Ridge," a name handed down to posterity by a postoffice in the immediate vicinity, at which some of his descendants

GENERAL JAMES COX.
(Grandfather of S. S. Cox.)

still receive their mail. He lived to the age of
seventy-eight.   The next in descent was Joseph
Cox (born August 18, 1713; died April 17, 1801).
He was a farmer in easy circumstances, of whom
it was said that "he always contended for the
equal rights of man; that he was opposed to all
oppression and injustice; that he honored no man
because he was rich; that he was never ashamed
of honest labor, and readily put his hand to any
work to be done on his farm."   In early life
he married Mary, (born May 31, 1715; died November 24, 1800) daughter of Thomas Mount of
Shrewsbury, N. J., and the last years of these two
good people were spent in comfort and ease on the
fine old farm in Upper Freehold. One of their
grandchildren often referred to the happy hours
spent in their rooms listening to the Bible which
this venerable ancestor delighted to read aloud to
his wife.   He lived to be eighty-eight years of age
and survived his wife by one year; she having
died in 1800, at eighty-five.

James Cox (born October 16, 1753, died September 12, 1810), was the ninth child of the foregoing.
As a young man he was noted for his mental and
physical vigor and activity, and these qualities
stood him in stead in the stormy times so soon
to occur.   When the war of the Revolution began
he promptly enlisted as a private in the First New
Jersey Regiment.   He was soon elected first lieutenant of his company, of which he was frequently given command, and participated in the battles
of Germantown and Monmouth, the latter of
which was fought within a few miles of his home.
To illustrate his courage when under fire the following story was related to his son, David Jones

Cox, by an Irish soldier from Delaware, who served under him: "In the battle of Monmouth, be dad, the bullets flew thicker than hail-stones, and 'Jammy' right in the midst of them—indade I never ixpected to see him alive if he did not flee— but the divil a bit of flight was there in Jammy and he did not even get hit by 'em. Och! your father was a blue hen's chicken, indade was he." His patriotism was so intense that even after the war was over he persistently held aloof from those who had remained loyal to the crown, as the following anecdote will show: One day while at work in a field he discovered the residence of a neighbor to be on fire. He at once hastened to the spot, accompanied by the farm-hand who was at work with him, and by great exertion, even at the risk of his life, succeeded in extinguishing the flames. This service excited lively expressions of gratitude and elicited a confession that this same family had often attempted to have his house burned during the war. But no permanent reconciliation took place. General Cox still looked upon these neighbors as enemies of his country and they for their part never ceased to regard him as a rebel against the King.

Soon after the Revolution Mr. Cox was made a major in the militia and later he was chosen by the legislature brigadier-general of the Monmouth Brigade. He was also called to various civic offices of trust, such as assessor and town clerk. In 1800 he was induced to become a candidate for the State legislature but was defeated. A year later he was elected a member of the General Assembly and held his seat in that body for seven terms. In his third year he was elected speaker of the Assembly and he continued to hold that position so long as he was a member of the Assembly.   In 1808 he was elected a Representative in Congress.   He had served two years in that body when his career was suddenly cut short by apoplexy which terminated fatally in September, 1810. General Cox was known as an earnest Christian gentleman.   His generosity and hospitality were famous, so much so indeed as to prevent any great accumulation of property.   His son, the Rev. Samuel J. Cox, wrote on this point: "The large size of his family; the great number of visitors; and the natural desire to make an appearance in accordance with his station and the company he kept, prevented much accumulation of property." Besides this, he was induced by his pastor to purchase Kentucky land, the title of which proved worthless.   He was also prevailed upon to become security for a man engaged in the same land transaction, which he had to pay. During the time he was making payments he promised to deliver a load of leather on a certain day.   On his way, he heard that the purchaser's affairs were in a critical condition; but he went on.   Before he arrived he passed the residence of Rev. Dr. Staughton, who hastened out to stop him, and informed him of the state of the case.   General Cox replied, "I have promised, and what can I do?"   After some further conversation, Dr. Staughton lifted up his hands and exclaimed in the language of Dr. Watts, "And though to his own hurt he swears, still he performs his word"——"Go on, and may the Lord bless you!" This circumstance shows how rigidly he regarded the obligation of a pledge.

He was a rare conversationalist and his anec·
dotes were spiced with wit and humor. He was
very popular among his neighbors by whom it was
related that he never asked any person to vote for
him, and that from the time of his nomination till
after election he scarcely ever left his own farm.
In appearance and manners he was dignified and
commanding, and he was a general favorite with
both political parties. It was from this ancestor,
apparently, that his distinguished grandson inherited some of his choicest traits. In a speech
made in Monmouth county in 1868, Mr. S. S. Cox
said:

"The Tories never loved my grandfather Cox as
a whig in the Revolution. They hated him as a
Democrat after. For years he was a member, in
fact, the Speaker of one of the houses of legislation at Trenton. He died as the Democratic member of Congress just before the War of 1812. He
was an honest, just, courteous, courageous, and
fearless Democrat champion. He was the warm
friend of Jefferson and the devoted advocate of
Madison. He believed in the Democratic rules of
interpreting the Constitution. His hatred of re-
straints upon personal and soul liberty; his di-
atribes against the alien and sedition laws; his
steadfast dislike of Englishmen and English policy have been handed down as heir-looms."

To disregard the maternal line in considering a
genealogical record would be to ignore a most important influence in moulding life and character.

Anne Potts (born February 13, 1757; died March
21, 1815), the grandmother of Samuel S. Cox on
the paternal side, was the daughter of William

Potts of Burlington, N. J., who was the grandson
of William Potts who arrived in the New World
in 1678, having with his wife and children come
over in the "Shield," the first ship that ever dropped anchor before Burlington. Her mother was
Amy, the youngest daughter of Joseph Borden.
the founder of Bordentown, N. J.   The Borden
connection is one of special interest for the reason
that Richard Borden, the grandfather of Joseph
Borden, who founded Bordentown, was the only
New England ancestor that Mr. Cox had. Richard
Borden was a resident of Portsmouth, R. I., and
served as an Assistant in 1653-4; as Treasurer in
1654-5, and as Deputy in 1667-70. Although only
collaterally related it is interesting to note that
Col. Joseph Borden, who was the son of the founder, was an ardent patriot, being a member of the
Stamp Act Congress in 1765, a Delegate to the
Provincial Congress of New Jersey in 1775, and
subsequently to the breaking out of the war of the
Revolution, a Colonel of a Batallion, and Quarter-
Master of the State troops.   His daughter Mary
married Thomas McKean, member of Congress
from Delaware in 1776, and a signer of the Declaration of Independence. Subsequently he became
Governor of Pennsylvania.   Another daughter,
Anne, married Francis Hopkins, also a signer of
the Declaration of Independence from New Jersey.
Joseph Hopkinson, the author of "Hail Columbia," was his son. The marriage of Anne Potts
with James Cox, the grandfather of the subject of
this biography, took place on February 29, 1776,
a few months prior to the Declaration of American Independence.   We may be sure that she

shared with her newly wedded husband his strong
love of country; indeed, it may have been her po-
tent influence that induced him, leaving his bride,
to join the Colonial army. Mrs. Cox was long remembered as a devoted Christian and an excellent
mother to her thirteen children. She was described by one who knew her well as "an almost
peerless woman." While on her way to pay a
visit to one of her children, in 1815, she was
drowned in the Delaware River by the capsizing
of the packet boat on which she was a passenger.
The simple inscription "Mild, benevolent, and
pious, few lived more beloved, or died more lamented" engraved on her tombstone in Trenton,
is a truthful epitome of her character.

Speaking, in the campaign of 1868, at Mount
Holly, New Jersey, Mr. Cox indulged in some reminiscences of his family connection with that
neighborhood. "Fifty years ago," he said, "my
father emigrated from this neighborhood, where
his father lived before him. He carried, on a pack
horse over the Alleganies, the old Ramage printing press. He was a pioneer printer. His father, a
descendant of the proprietor of East Jersey, was
Gen. James Cox, one of the heroes of Germantown,
Brandywine, and Monmouth. My grandfather was
married at Mansfield, in this county. My great
grandfather was Mr. Borden: Bordentown per-
petuates his good name. Some of these good people were Baptists, whose motto was, 'Let us have
war,' while war was flagrant; and some Quakers,
whose motto was, 'Let us have peace,' when peace
was needed."

An old water color still in the possession of the

"BOX GROVE," CREAM RIDGE, N. J.

Home of S. S. Cox's Grandfather, Gen. James Cox.

family shows the old homestead—"Box Grove" as
it was called—near Imlaystown.   General Cox
stands in the doorway of the picturesque home
clothed in his military uniform of buff and blue
with cocked hat and knee breeches.   His devoted
wife, Ann Potts, is by his side dressed in the plain
garb of a Quakeress. In the foreground is his
handsome son, Thomas, also in knee breeches and
with a very long tailed coat. Thomas is greeting
a young lady wearing a quaint short waisted
white gown, who is said to be his fiance. To the
left by a grape arbor are Amy and Mary, twin sisters, dressed in the style of that time. The pride of
a parent, in those days, was in his family; and in
this respect General Cox was abundantly blessed,
being the father of fourteen children. Of these
the twelfth, and father of Samuel Sullivan
Cox, was Ezekiel Taylor Cox (born in Upper Freehold May 25, 1795; died in Zanesville May 18,
1873.)   Ezekiel as a boy was given such limited advantages of education as the country then afforded. A cousin by marriage was James J. Wilson of
Trenton, a man of extraordinary talents, editor of the "True American" newspaper. Wilson,
whose wife was a daughter of Samuel Cox, an elder brother of General Cox, held in his time many
offices of public trust, including that of United
States Senator. Concededly he wielded the largest
political influence of any man in New Jersey. It
was Ezekiel Cox's good fortune to become associated with Senator Wilson, in the publication of
his newspaper. "Wilson," wrote the Rev. Samuel J.
Cox, brother of Ezekiel, "was very intimate with
my father and his family, and a strong attachment

both political and social subsisted between them.
This, probably led to my being placed in his family and in his office, where at a subsequent period,
my brother Ezekiel was also placed, for the same
purpose."

Young Ezekiel found himself in a congenial environment and he improved every opportunity to
educate himself. His studious habits, probity, and
great aptness were appreciated by Senator Wilson
who soon grew to depend on him and placed much
of his private business in his care. This was performed with such satisfaction that the young man
was given an interest in the "True American." He
rose to be State Printer of New Jersey, by appointment of the Legislature, of which his father,
Gen. Cox, was speaker. The west in those days was
still new, and opportunities for fortune-making
presented themselves to such as were willing to
brave the hardships of a frontier life.

"Westward the course of empire takes its way."

Wildernesses soon became fertile farms, settle-
ments grew to towns, and towns gave way with
equal rapidity to large cities. Ohio was an Eldor-
ado fifty years before California claimed that ap-
pellation. Strong with an ambition to succeed in
life, Ezekiel T. Cox disposed of all his belongings,
save alone his Ramage press and type with which,
packed on the back of his horse, he turned his face
to the west. Behind him were strong family and
local ties. In front of him was an unknown land.
But firm in his faith of ultimate success he per-
sisted and overcame the trials of a long journey
through the wilderness and over fastnesses of the
Alleghenies until at last he reached the promised

land of Ohio. He stopped at Zanesville and the natural advantages of the place appealed so strongly to him that he determined to build for himself a home on the banks of the Muskingum. About this time the "Muskingum Messenger," one of the earliest of Ohio newspapers, having been established in 1810, was for sale. Mr. Cox made an offer for it, which was promptly accepted, and in February, 1819, he became its publisher and editor.

Party feeling even at that remote period gave rise to bitter animosities, but with an experience gained in the best school, and with rare tact, Mr. Cox was soon master of the situation. His ready pen, combined with an excellent stock of information, made the "Messenger" the most influential Jacksonian organ in the state. A writer referring to the trials experienced by Mr. Cox in conducting his paper said: "It was no ordinary effort—at that day—when everything, from rags to cord wood— everything but cash—had to be taken for subscriptions and jobs, to make a paper successful." The success of the "Messenger" shows that it was edited and managed with ability.

In 1821 Mr. Cox, having demonstrated himself a successful editor, was chosen a clerk of the Court of Common Pleas, and so satisfactorily did he perform the duties of that exacting office that he was also made clerk of the Supreme Court and Recorder of Muskingum county. These offices he held for many years, so discharging his duties as to receive the commendation alike of judges, attorneys, and clients. In 1831 he was elected to the State Senate, and while a member of that body secured an

appropriation for the slack water navigation between Zanesville and Dresden. In general affairs
he was also active, among his achievements the
most important, perhaps, being the establishment,
in 1833, of a steam paper mill—said to be the first
paper mill west of the Alleghenies—in Zanesville.
The mill was destroyed by fire in 1837, and soon
after he disposed of his interest to his brother,

After years filled with activities of many kinds,
came the natural desire for rest; and one by one
Ezekiel relinquished his different offices in order
to retire to a farm of some forty acres which in
1840 he purchased in Springfield township. Here
for a decade or more he made his home, while he saw
around him his large family growing from childhood to maturity. In 1850 he returned to active
journalism, and with his son Alexander purchased
the ' 'Gazette," which was published in Zanesville.
It has been pointedly said concerning this new
venture that: "It showed more than his early efforts in the same vocation, that the graduate of
the poor boy's college, the printing office, was worthy of his education."

Public office again claimed him, and he was
made United States Marshal for that section of
Ohio in which he lived. An incident occurred
while he held this office which will illustrate the
character of the man. He had received instructions to apprehend a runaway slave. Bearing in
mind the sacred obligation of his oath of office, and
not to be deterred by angry threats, he determined
that he would arrest the negro at all hazards, even
at the risk of his life. This he did, not however
without sacrifice of standing in his church. As

penalty for performing a most disagreeable duty he was expelled from the Market Street Baptist Church, in which he was a deacon, losing also, of course, that honored office. Although opposed to slavery he was not a man to flinch in the execution of any duty connected with a public office that he held, or to resign his commission in times of emergency.

In 1866 his children having for the most part settled in life, Ezekiel Cox determined to give up his farm and settle in a city. Accordingly his son, Samuel, secured for him from President Johnson the nomination to be Pension Agent in Columbus, Ohio. The Senate refused to confirm him, on the ground that the candidate was a Democrat. However, he went to Washington and was associated for a time in a large claim and brokerage business established by his son Alexander. Longing for his old friends and his old home, he returned in a few years to Zanesville. He celebrated the golden anniversary of his wedding at the old home (then the property of the widow of his eldest son, Colonel Thomas J. Cox) on April 8, 1872, and a year later on May 18, 1873, he died.

Senator Cox was an uncompromising Democrat. of the Jackson school. In the family archives is extant an old letter signed by twenty or more leading Democrats of Ohio, and addressed to President Andrew Jackson, introducing Senator Cox. The letter is dated Columbus, O., 20th February, 1833, and reads thus:—

"General Andrew Jackson—Dear Sir:—Our esteemed fellow-citizen, E. T. Cox, Esq., of Zanesville. at present a member of the Senate of this State, expects to visit Washington, and for the first time

to make a call on the President while in the city.
Mr. Cox stands deservedly high among his friends
and acquaintances in Ohio, and for many years has
stood identified with the democracy of the Union.
From his character and standing among us, he is
worthy of all confidence. It is with much pleasure
we introduce him to your acquaintance, and beg
leave, through him, to tender you, as the chief
magistrate of this nation, our kindest regard and
salutations."

A newspaper obituary said of him: "Whether
we regard the deceased as a pioneer citizen of
this place, as an early and constant friend of its
improvement, as an officer and legislator, as a political and social friend, as a kind, indulgent
father and affectionate husband, whether as an
adventurous printer and editor in the wilderness
of Ohio, combatting with untried difficulties, and
not only accomplished at the case and the press,
but in clear, technical, and accurate style of writing, or as a faithful, well-informed and attentive
officer of the court, courteous to judges, jurors,
witnesses, suitors, and lawyers; or as a Christian
man of just views and honest conduct, refined by
extensive reading and reflection, and a constant
communion with his Bible and his God, his name
will be remembered with honor. It reflects credit
upon his children, as well as the city and state in
which he lived."

Such was the father of Samuel S. Cox as he appeared to his neighbors.

The mother of Samuel S. Cox was Maria Matilda (born March 16, 1801; died April 3, 1885), the
second daughter of Judge Samuel Sullivan and
his wife Mary Freeman.

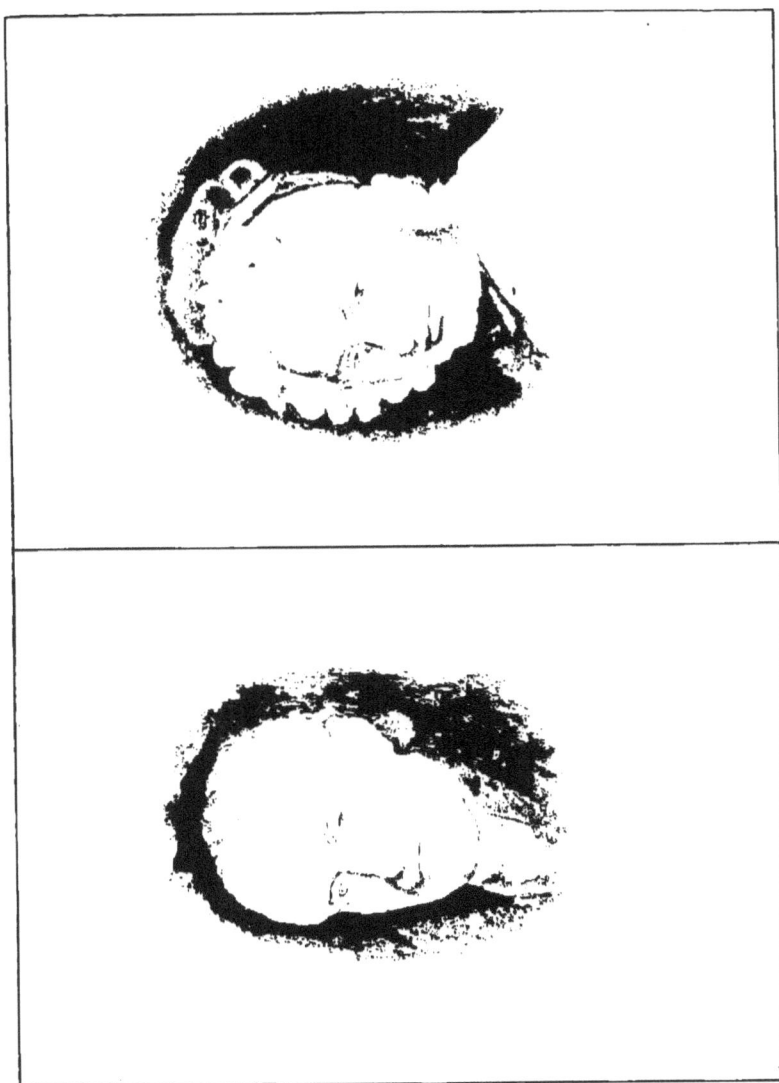

JUDGE SAMUEL SULLIVAN.　　　MARY FREEMAN SULLIVAN.

(Grandparents of S. S. Cox).

The Sullivan family is of Irish origin, tracing its
line to one Fingin, a son of Aod Dubh, King of
Munster. Its first ancestor in this country came to
America with one of the Irish colonies sent by Lord
Baltimore for the settlement of Maryland under
the charter granted by Charles June 20, 1632. The
intolerance of the Old World is in great contrast
to the broad tolerant spirit of the State Constitution of Maryland, framed by these refugees of the
Roman faith.

The Sullivan family was scattered through various parts of Maryland, Virginia and Delaware,
and from that branch that settled in Delaware the
present line of descent is derived.

Samuel Sullivan, son of David and Jane Sullivan, was born near Wilmington, Delaware, April
10, 1772; and died, October 15, 1853.   The early
death of his parents, the misappropriation of the
family estate and bad investments by the business
partner left the three young boys dependent upon
strangers and the labor of their own hands.

As was customary in those days, they were ap-
prenticed, and Samuel's lot was to serve as a potter in one of the factories on the banks of the Delaware river, below Philadelphia. This factory
was among the first of its kind in the New
World. The knowledge here acquired was "stock
in trade" for the young man when his fortunes
drifted him into the Middle West. He discovered
and utilized the fine clay banks in Ohio, and was
the pioneer manufacturer of fine wares of which
the Muskingum Valley and other parts of Ohio
boast to-day.

There are specimens of this early, yellow orna-

mented ware made by Samuel Sullivan still in the
family.

Samuel Sullivan was scarcely of age when he
married in Philadelphia, Mary Freeman, daughter of Samuel and Elizabeth Freeman. Mary Freeman was a native of Delaware, born August 25,
1773. She lived to the great age of ninety, dying
in Zanesville, Ohio, December 27, 1863. In 1804
Samuel followed his two elder brothers, David and
Aaron Sullivan, to Ohio and after spending some
years in the Scioto Valley, and in St. Clairsville,
he finally settled permanently in Zanesville, then
the Capital of Ohio. Identifying himself with the
general interests of Muskingum county in 1816 he
was elected a judge of the Court of Common Pleas.
Later he was sent to the Ohio Senate and then was
chosen by the Legislature State Treasurer, a post
which he held for a year. Finally from 1827 to
1831 he was postmaster of Zanesville.

The last years of his life were spent on his farm,
where he devoted special attention to horticul-
ture. He planted two orchards, the last after he
was seventy-five years of age. When asked how
he could interest himself in labor, the fruits of
which he could not expect to live to enjoy, he gave
the philosophical reply that: "We were not working for ourselves only—that we are serving as
stewards for others; and that if our predecesors
had been governed by the restricted views indicated in the inquiry, the world would not now be
covered with good and pleasant things."

Judge Sullivan was a self educated man, well-
informed, and of affable and genial manners. He
was never charged with a wrong to anybody.
Recognizing the full measure of his responsibility

in moral duty, he was rated by those who knew him best as eminently a just man. He died in Zanesville in October, 1853, in the 82d year of his age.

Reference has already been made to the decision of Mr. Ezekiel Cox to settle in Zanesville. Among those who urged this action was Judge Sullivan. The young editor became a visitor at the home of the Judge and showed every evidence of enjoyment in the society of his senior and the visits grew in frequency. An account of these visits taken from a family record tells the story so exactly that it is quoted: "The Judge's idea of Mr. Cox's platonic feelings, however, received a rude shock, one day when he asked for the hand of his daughter, Maria Matilda." Consent followed and on April 9, 1822, Ezekiel T. Cox and Maria Matilda Sullivan were made one—the Rev. James Culbertson performing the ceremony.

Through his mother, as has been stated, Mr. Cox traced his lineage to one of Lord Baltimore's associates in the settlement of Maryland—the grandfather of Judge Sullivan. In a reminiscent mood Mr. Cox, in 1885, wrote to an old friend: "I have heard my grandfather say that he remembered his grandmother counting her beads. These Quaker-Methodists of Northern Delaware and early Ohio were three generations before devout Catholics. But the change of faith never swerved the ancestral integrity."

Judge Sullivan gave to his grandson and namesake his fullest confidence, choosing him among several sons and sons-in-law, as his sole executor.

In his last will and testament Judge Sullivan

charged his own and his children's children to remember that "their inheritance was the result of
Democratic institutions." and that he expected
his namesake and executor, Samuel Sullivan Cox,
"to sustain those institutions in their democratic
form and tenor with ballot and with bullet."

The mother of Samuel Sullivan Cox was born in
Philadelphia. As a child three years of age she
accompanied her parents on the tedious journey
over difficult roads, across rapid running streams
and mountains that were high and hard to climb,
until the great fertile Scioto Valley was reached.
Of the wanderings that followed until Zanesville
became the permanent home of her parents, Mrs.
Cox retained a vivid recollection, and many incidents of that portion of her early life she was
fond of relating to her grandchildren.

She frequently recalled the cutting down of the
"nice grape vine swings" that were removed when
the bridge was built across the Muskingum river
at Zanesville. It was on the banks of this river
that she spent the happiest hours of her young
girlhood. Here it was that she and the children
of the early settlers romped and played—often
with Indian children from "Wapatomika towns."
There were no schools in Zanesville in those days
and she received her education almost entirely
from her parents, but being very bright and a
quick observer, she shared with her sister Sarah
the reputation of being "the best informed young
woman in the neighborhood."

While in her teens she accompanied her father,
when elected Senator, to Columbus, no longer
"the spot opposite Franklinton," but now the

MARIA MATILDA SULLIVAN COX.

(Mother of **S. S. Cox.**)

Capital of Ohio. By her ready wit and by her clearness of repartee, she became a great favorite, and many of the state officers were willing to become more than "my lady's most devoted admirer." Among these suitors were two, one of whom became a governor of Ohio and another a president of the United States.

As a wife, she was devoted to every detail of her husband's career, watchful of his interests, and happiest in his presence.

In one of her letters while her husband—the father of S. S. Cox—was in attendance at the Legislature she writes

"I hope you will soon be with us," * * * * "we put off all pleasure until your return."

As a mother, she was careful, tender, and watchful of her children, most of whom she saw grow to maturity. For more than fifty years the unbroken thread of her married life continued. It was a happy gathering, that at the old homestead on April 8, 1872, to celebrate the fiftieth anniversary of their marriage. Their children and their children's children were there to render filial homage and respect. Here and there from the group was a missing face, and perhaps most of all in this hour of gladness the aged couple thought of that first born* who in the time of his country's need had left home, like that ancestor of old, to fight for his country.

Few parents have lived to see such a company of descendants as were gathered on that occasion

---

*Thomas Jefferson Cox, born March 7, 1823; died, September 17, 1866. He tendered his services to the Government, and on June 11, 1862, was appointed by President Lincoln, Captain and Assistant Quartermaster. He was promoted three times, and died at his post of duty at Nashville, Tennessee.

and they had a pardonable pride in their reflection
that not one of them had brought reproach upon
their care and teaching.

In a few months came the death of the husband,
and more and more as the years advanced the venerable widow came to depend upon her second son,
Samuel Sullivan, named for her own father, and,
as events proved, the stay of her widowhood and
her old age. Twelve years she survived her husband. In April, 1885, her distinguished son, then
about to embark for Turkey, as United States Minister, was summoned to his venerable mother's
bedside, reaching it just in time to receive her conscious blessing. She died April 3, 1885, aged 84.

CHAPTER II.

Of such honorable lineage came Samuel Sullivan Cox, in whom were happily blended the best traits and characteristics of his ancestors. The second of a family of thirteen children—of whom eight grew to maturity—he was born, in Zanesville, Ohio, September 30, 1824. His father was at that time clerk of the Supreme Court of Ohio and the family residence was on Third street. Surrounding the home which welcomed the little stranger were well kept grounds, abounding with flowers and shrubs, which were the pride and special care of the boy's mother. Not far distant resided Judge Sullivan, and his honored name, the parents decided, should be bestowed on the grandson. So they called him Samuel Sullivan.

The future statesman's advent into the world was in the midst of an exciting presidential contest. The administration of President Monroe was drawing to a close and with it the "era of good feeling." General Jackson was waging his first campaign for capture of the White House. It was a quadrangular contest, his rivals being Henry Clay, Wm. H. Crawford, and John Quincy Adams. In both the popular and the electoral vote the hero of New Orleans was first in the race, but, notwithstanding, he failed to secure the glittering prize.

A plurality was not in this case a majority—there was no choice in the electoral college, and, in consequence, the election went to the House of Representatives. That body chose the son of the second president, who then was nearing the close of his eventful life in Massachusetts. While this crisis in American history, culminating in the election of John Quincy Adams to the presidency, was going on, Samuel Sullivan Cox was an infant blissfully indifferent to the storm of passion which was raging without. Indeed Ohio, three quarters of a century ago, was practically as distant from the Atlantic seaboard as is Alaska today.

The steam engine, on the iron rail, had not yet come to annihilate space; nor the telegraph to girdle the earth and annihilate time and space. Weeks must elapse before the mails, carried by lumbering stages over rough roads and across the mountains, could convey to the frontiersmen of Zanesville the news that, not Jackson but Adams, had been elevated to the chair of James Monroe.

Little Samuel grew and flourished. He early became the pet of the neighborhood. He is described by one of his neighbors as having been "bright, sunny, genial, fond of fun, sparkling with wit, always truthful, fearless, and generous, never hesitating to confess a fault of his own, and ever ready to defend the weak and oppressed." The child was father of the man. In the village school he was known as an exceptionally bright scholar, always ready, however, to help any who lagged behind him in the race for learning. A cousin of his was fond of relating how he was taught his

RESIDENCE OF EZEKIEL T. COX, ZANESVILLE, OHIO.

(S. S. Cox's Boyhood Home.)

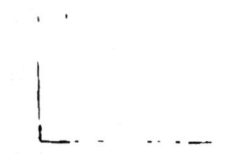

letters by this boy, who, having reached the mature age of six, was ambitious to elevate his playmate, his junior by six months, to a level with his own advancement.

He had hardly learned to read before he developed a special love for books of travel, devouring eagerly every such book he could lay his hands on. Visions of travel filled his boyish imagination, and he used to tell his mother that some day he, too, was going to visit the Holy Land; that he would go to Russia; see the Sultan and the minarets of Constantinople; that he was going to the North Pole, or at least near enough to it to see the sun go 'round without setting. These childish fancies were no idle dream; he lived to realize them all, and, moreover, to make word-pictures of the wonderful scenes he witnessed, which were to be the delight of thousands. A brilliant career for the preternaturally bright boy was freely predicted by his teachers.

A sample of his precocity as a child is shown in a letter written by him when he was eight years of age. The letter is to his father while the latter was absent at Columbus. Mrs. Cox, who was sending a letter to her husband, from "Lonely Mansion," January 30, added: "I shall fill the vacancy with Samuel's letter, as he is at school but has it written on the slate. He says:

"Dear Father: I take the liberty in writing in Mother's letter to say that we attend to our school, that we study our tables in the evening and I believe I know mine pretty well and what do you think of that? Don't you think I deserve a News gift. We had a fine time on Christmas. We

barred the master out and he had to treat us to
some cider, apples, cakes and nuts. We were all
sorry at the loss of Turk. Thomas attends to his
little cow. She is fat and gives us plenty of milk.
Mother has made Thomas (then ten years old) a
fine green hunting shirt.   He looks quite like a
backwoodsman.   Samuel S. Cox.' "

Two other literary ventures of young Samuel
are extant, being compositions in the form of letters addressed, one to his mother, the other to his
father, when the boy was ten years old.   They
are written in a neat hand and read as follows:

"Zanesville, Ohio, April 25, 1835.
"Dear Mother:
"It is now spring, and the blossoms and the cher-
ry-trees are out, and I expect we will have some
cherries, and other fruit; we had no fruit last
year. When summer comes the boys go in a swim-
ming; they go a fishing, and catch fish, and sell
them.   And then comes autumn, when the leaves
fall off the trees.   And then comes winter, then
you will have to wear mittens or gloves to keep
your hands warm; in very cold weather the river
freezes over, and the boys bind skates to their feet
and amuse themselves with skating.   I skated
last winter, and was much pleased with the exercise.   Your affectionate son,
                "Samuel S. Cox."

"Zanesville, Ohio, April 25, 1835.
"Dear Father:
"On Beasts—The lion is called the king of the
beasts, the tiger is a fierce animal of the cat kind,
the elephant is the largest animal in the world,

he is very sensible, he will carry boys or men on his trunk. In India they carry large burdens; in some parts of the world there are white elephants. The rhinoceros is a large animal. I saw one in a menagerie in this town; they had a log chain around his neck, sunk ten feet in the ground to keep him from getting loose; the zebra is striped; it is of the horse kind and is very handsome; there are many other beasts, but I have not time to describe them. Your affectionate son,

"Samuel Cox."

The boy was sent to the academy at Zanesville to prepare for admission to the Ohio University. The academy principal was Professor Howe, a well known and somewhat distinguished educator of those days, a man of learning and cultivation. "Samuel," says one of his townsmen of that period, "was always full of his boyish pranks, even venturing sometimes to play tricks on his dignified father, for which it is said that his eldest brother, Thomas, used not infrequently to receive the reproof and punishment rather than betray the real culprit, to whom his self-sacrifice would be all unknown. But he was a diligent and enthusiastic student, who won and kept a high place among his classmates. Before he had passed out of boyhood he was appointed deputy to his father, who was then serving as clerk of the Supreme Court and of the Court of Common Pleas. Even at this early age he was so thoroughly conversant with all the business of the office that a great part of it was safely intrusted to him."

The official documents leading to the appointment of this boy of fourteen to a court clerkship follow:

"The State of Ohio, Muskingum County, ss.:

"To the Honorable Judges of the Court of Common Pleas of said county, at their May term, A. D. 1838:

"From the experience and capacity of my son, Samuel S. Cox, I hereby nominate him as my Deputy Clerk of said Court, and request your Honors to ratify and confirm said nomination, pursuant to statute. By this appointment I am well satisfied that the public interest and convenience will be subserved.

"Given under my hand this 31st day of May, 1838.

"E. T. Cox,
"Clerk of said Court."

(Appointment made.)

"The State of Ohio, Muskingum County, ss.:

"I, E. T. Cox, Clerk of the Supreme Court of Muskingum County, hereby certify that I have this day appointed my son, Samuel S. Cox, as my Deputy Clerk of said Court, and request that said appointment be approved and confirmed.

"In testimony whereof I hereunto set my hand and affix the seal of said Supreme Court, this 30th day of October, 1838.   E. T. Cox, Clerk."

The following incident has been preserved as showing his interest in current affairs even when a mere child:

During the Black Hawk war supplies and blankets were being collected for the use of the volunteers and those having the matters in charge came

OLD COURT HOUSE, MUSKINGUM COUNTY,
Former Capitol of Ohio.

to Mr. Cox's house late one night.   Samuel over-
heard the conversation from the head of the stairs
and running to his room pulled the blanket off
from his bed and threw it over the balustrade with
the exclamation, "Here, mother, give them this
one.   Hurrah!"

His patriotism did not cease with this incident,
and a few years later his elder brother, Thomas
J. Cox then at college in Granville, writes him as
follows, under date of July 20, 1839, at which time
the younger brother was fourteen, the elder being
sixteen:

"So you read the Declaration of Independence
to the Sabbath School.   I suppose you read it
well, for a boy who can read the minutes of the
Court before judges and lawyers ought to read
the Declaration of Independence a great deal better where there are only a parcel of children—and
besides a boy who professes to be such a great
friend to his country as you do ought to have it
committed to memory."

If he had not at that time committed this precious document to memory he certainly soon followed his brother's advice, for it is well known
that as a boy he learned by heart both the Declaration of Independence and the Constitution of the
United States.

"This," writes one of his relatives, "is the first
authentic statement that I have been able to find
locating definitely when he began making patriotic addresses, although it is claimed that he
made, when much younger, speeches that were lit-
erally stump speeches, for his only audience was
the trees of the neighboring woods."

The reference in this letter to the fact that he "read the minutes of the Court before judges and lawyers" corroborates statements made by the successor to his seat in Congress, the Honorable Amos J. Cummings, that "at the age of eleven he was a valuable assistant to his father in the County Clerk's office at Zanesville. There are men living," he adds, "who saw the boy swear jurors and witnesses, issue writs, and make up journals. He performed all the duties of an expert clerk before he was thirteen years old."

Years afterward when addressing an audience in Black's Music Hall in Zanesville, Mr. Cox said:

"When a boy I was sworn in yonder Court House—as an assistant to my father, then County Clerk—to support the Constitution of the State of Ohio and of the United States. Since that time I have wandered all over this country and in many climes, yet I have never wandered from my oath to support and maintain the Constitution of these United States."

Meanwhile he continued his preparation for college. Among his teachers were Messrs. Mears, Hobby and Fulton. He also studied under the Rev. George C. Sedgwick, a Baptist minister, who had his school in the basement of the First Baptist Church on Sixth street, and under Professor Howe of the Market Street Academy.

He was a diligent and enthusiastic student, and yet he was by no manner of means a mere student, for it is well known that he was full of boyish pranks.

Old residents of Zanesville still recall the picture on the streets of "Sam Cox and his pony,"

as the one on the back of the other dashed into
town at full gallop, from the boy's country home.
In connection with that same quadruped and his
boy rider. the mother of Mr. Cox used to tell with
evident relish, this story: One day as she sat in
her parlor window sewing, chancing to glance out
of the window she saw little Sammy galloping up
the country lane towards the house. The next
moment both rider and pony were attempting to
make their bows of obeisance to her ladyship
from the hearth rug, in the parlor, where, the back
door being opened, the youthful scion, having rid-
den into the house, thought to give his maternal
a surprise party! "You, Samuel!" was the star-
tled greeting—but the jolly laugh that followed
ended the reproof.

One of his early schoolmates, Rev. S. D. Clayton
of Dayton, Ohio, has written:

"He and I went to school to Mr. James Fulton
opposite the west end of the Market House. We
all and always called him 'Captain' and such he
was from the time he was six or seven years old.
He was very small of stature at that time, but a
born leader, small as he was. He was not quar-
relsome, rather the reverse, but he would fight
like a tiger if he was imposed upon, or if he saw
any one wronged, he would pitch into a boy twice
his age and five times as large. His fighting qualities were magnificent. It stirs my blood to recall his combats and his victories. There was
nothing low or base in his nature. There could
not be, for he had good blood in his veins, and a
more chivalrous soul was never champion for the
weak, or struck stronger blows for his friends."

It is more than likely that the title of "Captain" was a surviving memory of a short military experience when he and others of his comrades organized the Zanesville Lancers, "in which," to quote a surviving member, "Sam was Orderly Sergeant."

Of his boyhood schoolmates more than one has become famous, among them Justice William B. Woods of the United States Supreme Court, the Rev. Dr. William Aschmore, an eminent Baptist Missionary who spent his life in China, and Dr. James M. Safford, the State Geologist of Tennessee.

"His memory," says one, "was marvelous. As a Sabbath school scholar he easily committed to memory the entire book of Romans, and it is said he knew the old twenty-ninth volume of the Ohio Laws by heart, and that, later on, he could draw up any pleading without consulting Chitty." An Ohio Congressman, in his tribute to his memory, tells us: "Mr. Cox was popular from his earliest boyhood; he was a natural orator, possessed of an eloquent, pathetic manner that never failed to captivate the audience he addressed. He was singled out in his school-boy days to be the orator on each occasion that required a speech."

In 1842, at the age of eighteen, he entered the Ohio University, at Athens. He ranked with the most brilliant of his class. It is related that during his stay in the State University a law suit between the college and the town was decided in favor of the latter, much to the displeasure of the students. Party spirit ran high, and the divisional lines were as marked as in fights between "townsmen and gownsmen" in an English university

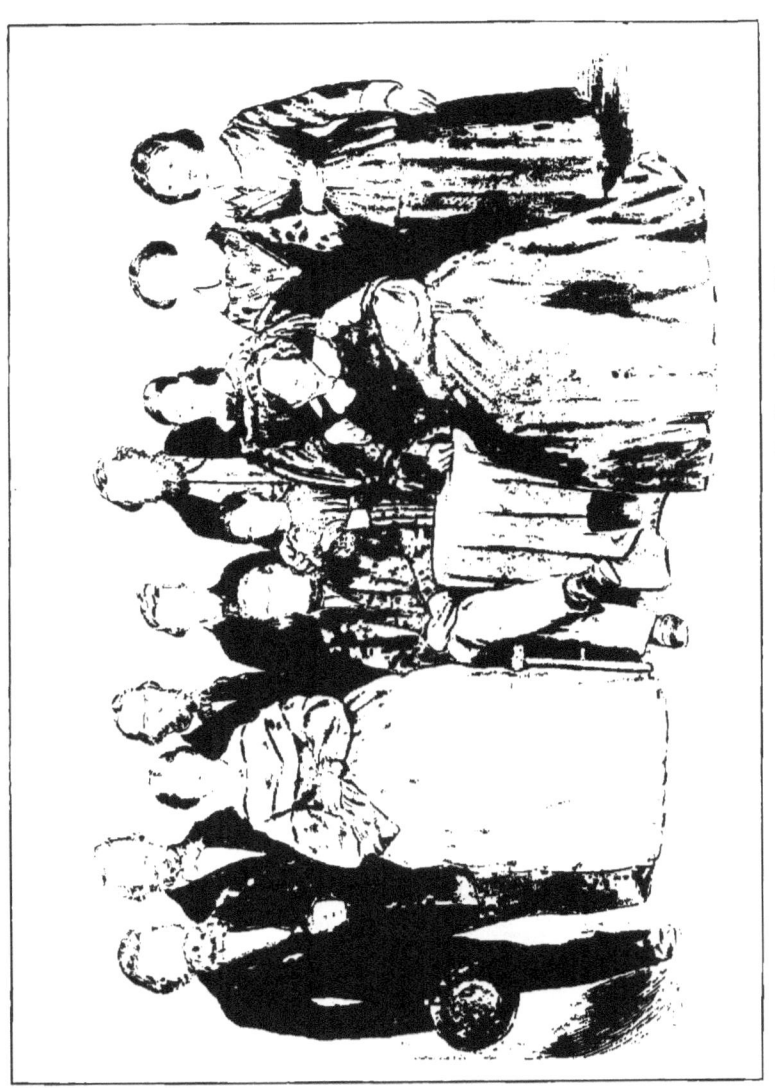

EZEKIEL T. COX, WIFE AND TEN CHILDREN.—FROM PHOTO ABOUT 1850.

S. S. Cox Third Man in Group on the Left.

town.   A celebration most distasteful to the college was   decided   on;   a bonfire was to be built,
speeches made, and a cannon fired.   The bonfire
blazed, the speeches were made, but the boom of
the cannon was not heard, the "great-gun" of the
town, a 6-pounder, having been prudently spiked
the night before by a daring college boy.   It was
not known till long after that the youth who so
effectually   silenced the voice of   the cannon for
that and for many succeeding nights was S. S. Cox.

CHAPTER III.

The distance from Zanesville to Athens in the Hocking Hills is not great according to our modern idea of locomotion, but in 1842 there were no railroads in that part of the country, and for convenience as well as for economy's sake the future statesman made his way from home to college on the back of his horse.

He was now duly entered as a Freshman in the Ohio University.

Several letters addressed to his father are extant, throwing light on his life in that institution. In one of these dated January 30, 1844, he writes:

"I endeavor to improve every particle of time. A person cannot know how valuable time, an hour, or a half, or a quarter, is until they are situated properly to improve it, and then every moment of it is in demand. From daylight to sunset there is one continual going if you are regular in your studies, and it seems the very regularity acts as a preservation on the health by keeping the mind active and awake."

No longer a child, but now a full fledged college man he was, as usual with Collegians, oppressed by the weight of his own knowledge. He unloads a little on his father, after this style:

"I read a good little work on the 'Philosophy of

Living,' which I want you to read. It is written by Caleb Ticknor, A. M., M. D., etc. It is no piece of quackery. It condemns in toto your whole system of doctoring, dieting, studying your own diseases, and shows the remarkable affinity between the mind and body—it scouts at the ultraism of the day both in politics and morals as well as in diet. What were the good things of the world placed around us for? Would God tantalize us? Thus he reasons, but moderation nevertheless he enjoins, and he agrees with your views in everything as to exercise, etc. But I will not review it further. I wish you would read it, it is in the Athenaeum."

The value of money had evidently begun to dawn upon the student, for he writes:

"As to 'Domestic Economy' I think that from my former habits and associations I was not inclined to value money as much as the filthy lucre should be. Yet, I know, that I have done the best down here. You are not aware and couldn't be till you were here, how easily money goes without, too, a single useless thing, or without that which is necessary. Now, I left my umbrella at home, and would not buy any for three weeks, but there is such continual wet weather that I must have it. There's coal, too, and the bill for the horses at General Brown's, and society expenses, paying for my bureau in advance, and all those little things summed up I find my $10.00 gone almost imperceptibly, and yet I know I have not paid out money except when needed." Hardly an exceptional experience.

But he was growing restless and casting about for a change. To his father he writes:

"Although I wrote you yesterday, circumstances have occurred which require I should write again. Do not think I am troubling you too much about my future course. It is not a very trifling matter where I am to pass the remainder of my collegiate course, and it should receive a degree of consideration, you will admit, correspondent to its importance.

"I wrote you I had determined on leaving Athens. I can spend my time profitably by reading, studying for debates, etc., and can easily enter junior at Cannonsburgh. If I trouble you too much, I have a tolerably good reason, you will admit, and I hope you will give me credit for wishing, at least, to do the best with the least inconvenience and expense. But I am perfectly at your will in regard to my future course."

During a temporary absence from class duties at Ohio University one of the faculty of that institution wrote to the young student's father:

"Allow us to express the hope that your son will not be detained from his studies longer than necessary. There is not a youth of his age in the institution at this time doing better than he, and it is very important that he should not lose his standing in his class. He is as zealous and successful in his studies as any parent could wish, and if he continues in the same course in which he has commenced, your expectations will be most fully realized."

The student, for the remainder of his course, was casting his eyes eastward. To his father he thus reveals his hopes and aspirations:

"I trust and hope you will be enabled to send

me the remaining time at an Eastern Institution. I prefer Dartmouth, though Brown would probably be as well. I am resolved to get an education, and I don't want to do it half, if you only encourage me and assist me by your means. The education is for life, that I know; it is, too, the means of life, and these means will be great in proportion to the education, that I know. Will you not give me the right encouragement? I know you will. Some fathers, I know, would glory in having their lazy, hanging-about, doing-nothing sons go to college, even should they go through as a drag and come out asses."

His purpose to go to Brown was approved by Professor Mather, a member of the faculty at Ohio University, as this letter shows:

"I mentioned Brown University to Professor Mather and he told me that he was there himself, at about my age, twenty years ago. He intended to graduate there and was in the course when he received his West Point appointment. He speaks highly of it, as it was then, and some few years ago, on a visit, he said, it had increased greatly and materially. In fact these institutions which are endowed are always the best, and those institutions in the East are constantly on the increase in order to keep up with the go-ahead age. He concluded by saying there was not a more desirable Instituiton for thorough scholarship in the country, and he is a man who understands the colleges of the country. Perhaps on account of his being a Baptist he speaks so highly, which is natural, you know."

In regard to his progress he says:

"I am getting along very well here, kept very busy; all my leisure moments I take to exercise, and sometimes I woo the Muses. I have finished my poem for Spring Exhibition. But there is not much encouragement here to literary attainment. It is a pleasant little recreation sometimes to scribble a little poetry, it not only refines the imagination, but a good set of wares can be garnered up in the store-house of the mind. I do it more to give my writing in general an easy flow, a smoothness. I know I have no talent for it, but I can do something as well as others. I contribute weekly to the paper here. Sometimes poetry and sometimes prose. I send mother rhymes on 'A Moment'—The Value of 'A Moment,' doubtless I have learned from her maternal advice—how I practice in regard to what I write, mother is dubious, I reckon. The first piece I wrote I signed 'M. P.' (Maternal Poetry) the last 'D'—the gossips here have been comparing the merits of their respective authors. I look on and grin. The least thing of that kind excites talk here in this scaly vale of mud."

Politics had not been forgotten, and he adds:

"I would have no particular objections if my Democratic grandfather (Samuel Sullivan) or some other Democrat would so far contribute to the youthful aspirations of a young Democrat like me, as to send me Duff Green's new paper started lately at New York and called the 'Free Trader.' I saw a number of it. Oh! but he is a scorcher, he lashes with no uncommon virulence."

In a letter to his cousin, Miss Julia Cox, of

Zanesville (Mrs. A. W. Perley), written contemporaneously with the letters just quoted, he says:

"I am reviewing all my former studies in order to enter Brown University, Rhode Island, where an indulgent father intends me to go, in order to put a finish, or rather rub off the rough corners of his son's education—It makes me feel four cubits and a span higher than I ever was (and you know, I am not remarkably tall)."

He has but little faith, if any, in the University in Athens, for he writes:

"Going East! Think of that Julia, that's some recompense for sticking to Athens as long as its soul and body could hold together — For understand me, the College is the soul, — Athens, minus the college is the body—when the College goes the way of all the Earth, as it probably will, after this season, it leaves Athens, the body, defunct."

The town itself is uncongenial to him. He describes it as: "A murky, cloud-covered, uncomfortable outpost upon the confines of Barbarism."

Mr. Cox's wonderful power of description, often illustrated in later years, crops out in the following, one of his letters home from Athens:

"The wind whistles without—the blackness of darkness shrouds the College,—O! how it roars amidst the old sycamores over Hocking; now it comes in gusts, fierce, scowling, piercing—slam! bang! bang! goes the doors of the empty rooms—rattle—rattle—goes the windows—whiz-z- goes the shrill winds—merrily dances my fire in the stove—merrily dances my pen on the paper."

Another quotation must be given from an Athens letter for it is significant of his appreciation of the value of mental training. With reference to one of his friends at home he says:—

"Does he still retain his reputation as one of the leaders of the Fashionable world? * * * I would not care three straws how I dressed, what I eat or drink, provided I could revel sufficiently in my own thoughts. One can by a little training make a little world of their own thoughts, and place himself as regent over them. He can then shut himself in his room and say with Crusoe, 'I am lord of all I survey'—and not be tormented with a wish besides."

A few months come and go and he is in Providence, a student in Brown University. Under date of June 25, 1844, he writes to his father:—

"I have now been here two months, and have fairly tested the college and the land of the Yankees, and I cannot but say, that I am still satisfied. Indeed, I came with the intention to be satisfied, and that is the great secret. * * * Although I have had not a little to discourage me, which I thought proper not to write, although there are numerous disadvantages and mortifications, always attendent upon entering into a strange land, more than most persons would imagine, yet I still get along swimmingly."

His reference to "Domestic Economy" in an earlier letter already quoted from, finds its counterpart in the present communication. The question of finance is always an important one, and especially so to a college student. The details mentioned are not without interest as showing the expenditures of students in college half a century ago. He says:—

(FIRST PAPER MILL WEST OF ALLEGANIES)

STEAM PAPER MILL.

E. T. COX, & CO.

PAPER MANUFACTURERS,

ZANESVILLE, OHIO.

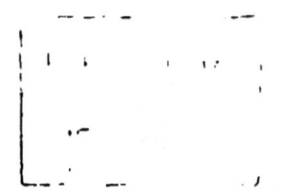

"I had paid all my money, which was $10, before you wrote, to the tailor, shoemaker, and booksell-er, I had not money to pay my postage, or for my boot mending. But after paying the $10, which I borrowed, $1.00 to the shoemaker for my boots, $1.00 for a covering for my caput, and some other little fixtures, I have left about $7.50, my sum total in hand. The expenses will cost me more than I anticipated. My clothing, etc., which I always ob-tained at home, increases it considerably. Stu-dents here say that with the utmost parsimony, you cannot get along (on) less than $250 per year, after buying all necessary preliminaries. It is ex-pensive here, I know, but to go to a college, re-quires money. The money ($7.50) I now have, will barely suffice to pay my washerwoman and other expenses at the close of the term."

In the choice of a Greek-letter fraternity, the new student from Ohio gave the preference to the Delta Phi, whose invitation to become a member he accepted.

In a letter to a sister, dated Brown University, Providence, November 25th, 1845, Mr. Cox gives his unique experience as a temperance lecturer. He was then in his Senior year. He writes:—

"There was to be a grand temperance oratorio (about 40 singers), after the speaking (at Me-chanic's Hall), and the house was densely crowd-ed, mostly with females. The aisles were full— some 1,500 or 2,000 people present. I did not in-tend to speak—was standing up in the aisle with some students looking at the girls; when someone came pushing through with a little trunk in his hand, declaring he had to speak and must get through. 'Oho! Buckeye,' says I. 'Hallo! stranger!' says he. 'Bear, or I am no Buckeye,' says I. 'Right, young man—give us your hand—see this cane? John N. Bear on it.'

" 'Cox is my name,' says I. The Buckeyes embrace—push through the crowd, Cox in the lead. Everybody staring. I told the president of the meeting who was present. He had heard of me, and said I must speak too, and introduced the Buckeye Blacksmith. Well, I was stirred up—made a speech of 20 minutes — introduced Bear with a gusto. He made a perfect roarer of a speech, astonishing the people considerably. He got up a little respectability for me, after I had soft-soaped him—told about my taking him with a habeas corpus or something in his intemperate days—said I was Clerk of the Court at Zanesville, etc., etc. Last Monday I had a special invitation to lecture. I signed the pledge, and as the doctor was away with Dr. Judson, I prepared myself well; spoke 40 minutes to a very refined audience —was nicely complimented by the president--but that is my last one for some time. Our exhibition comes off Saturday. We have been practicing all the afternoon, and the way we are drilled!" In the same letter he more than once expressed a longing for pumpkin pies, such as he had at home. "I must say," he writes to his sister, "if I have a failing, it is pumpkin-pieward."

Of another college experience he writes:—

"I made my debut here on the stage—spoke a part of my Fourier speech, which the Professor did not like as to the sentiment, but which brought down two rounds of applause from the students. I never felt so elated in my life, my manner of speaking was so different and I put all my soul in it, (as I had written it myself and consequently felt what I said) and there was so much of the free and easy, Western stump-speech-manner about it that it took. The Professor told me not to speak any more such things as Fourierism, but said he saw some fine promises in my way of speaking. He did not know I wrote it, and as we are required to make selections from others till next term, he supposed it somebody else's. The students wanted to know where I got it, as there was considerable fun and novelty in it. I stopped once in the middle, having forgotten the next sentence, and they commenced stamping, and it put me considerably out—and some, most fellows, would have been abashed and took their seats, but I stood it and at last got through. So much for my Entre! They think here I am an odd genius, I don't visit any body—stick to my room—mind my own business —walk as straight as a lightning rod, and as independent as a woodchuck.   I can put on all kinds of airs, and they will lay it all to Western manners and characteristics. They generally suppose we are mostly heathens out West, without refinement and taste for literature—and the specimens of Western students here, are by no means flattering."

His classmate Mr. Frank W. Anthony of Mattawan, Mich., describes this incident as follows:—

"The class had been trained for nearly two years by our prim and precise Professor of Rhetoric, Professor Gammell, into his peculiar and polished style of speaking and writing.   S.S. had doubtless

had triumphs at the cross roads schoolhouse of the
West. You can imagine the effect of his first
speech in the college class upon Professor and students. It was the first stump speech any of us
had heard. We all tried hard to control our risi-
bles. It was impossible after a few sentences. I
see now the determined look that came into the
new student's face as the laugh grew louder and
longer. It said, while he completed his speech,
'laugh if you will, the power is in me and you shall
yet respect it.' When completed he leaped from
the platform, regardless of the steps, and made for
his seat. As soon as Professor Gammell could
control himself and the uproar, he said, 'It is customary, Cox, for the student to pause at the foot
of the platform for criticism. We will excuse you
this time. Next.' "

Another class mate, the Rev. James C. Fletcher,
writes:—

"Cox liked to take a hand even in his student
days in addressing a crowd; and on one occasion
he made a stump speech to the assembled Democrats in Providence, R. I., in connection with
Thomas W. Dorr, who in 1842 endeavored to
change the old government of Rhode Island by
forcible means—for which Dorr, being overwhelmingly defeated at the polls and elsewhere, had to
suffer for it in prison. The Democrats as well as
the old Whigs were overwhelmingly against Dorr.
Nevertheless when agitation began in regard to
liberating Dorr from the penitentiary, 'Sam' (as
we called him), with the pluck that always characterized him, took the part of the small party, demanding the pardoning of Dorr, and, actually, to

the chagrin of the faculty (all Anti-Dorrites)
'Sam' addressed the 'unterrified' in the streets.
'Sam' always took the part of the 'under dog' in
the fight."

Dr. Charles R. Cullen of Gaines Mills, Va.,
writes:—

"We sat beside each other three years. While
we were at Brown the Liberty party was forming
and the Garrisons were in full blast. In the Meth-
odist Church (the only denomination at that time
very radical) Abbey Kelley, Abbey Folsom, S. S.
Foster and Wendell Phillips were to speak. They
abused Dr. Wayland, who was carrying on the
controversy with Dr. Fuller, on the subject of
Slavery, but could not tolerate the Garrison set.
The doctor advised the students not to attend the
meeting, as he knew they would commence by
abusing himself, calling him anti-slavery hypo-
crite, etc. This made the whole body of students
decide to go and take possession of the meeting—
to allow the Abolitionists to speak fifteen minutes
and the students thirty minutes—to hiss them and
applaud the students. Sam made a rousing speech
—so did Dr. J. Wheaton Smith, now of Philadelphia. Philips was severe on the students and told
them they might be as silly as geese or venomous
as serpents, he would speak if they staid till midnight. We generally did for several nights."

Cox freely gives his opinion of his associates.
He says:

"They judge of a fellow's respectability greatly
by his dress here. * * * There are some monstrous mean fellows among the Yankees. Again
there are some fine fellows—good—open-hearted

—warm-hearted students—in my class. Some of
the best families of N. E. and the Union are my
classmates. A grandson of General Greene; a son
of Com. Morris, of Washington, D. C., Dr. Wayland's son; Professor Goddard's two sons."

It will not be out of place at this point to contrast some of the foregoing with opinions of his
classmates on the young man from the west. It is
true that they are of recent date and perhaps have
been somewhat influenced by the lapse of time,—
still they are of interest.

Judge Franklin J. Dickman of Cleveland, Ohio,
writes:—

"I have a most distinct recollection of his per-
sonality, as we entered Brown University almost
at the same time, just before the Sophomore year
closed in 1844. Entering as we did at that late
day in the college course—he coming from Ohio
and myself from Virginia—we were naturally
drawn together as two interlopers, and in a short
time became exceedingly well acquainted with
each other. From his first entrance in college, he
showed a marked proclivity to politics and political studies, and it was anticipated that he would
have a distinguished political career. In the Literary Society to which he belonged, he at once
took rank as a leading debater, and always enlivened the debate by his overflowing wit and humor. His mind worked with uncommon rapidity,
and he was thereby enabled to find much time for
general reading after preparing for the exercises
of the class room. While his scholarship was
creditable in the Greek and Latin classics, he
stood especially prominent as an English belles-

lettres scholar; and in the Junior and Senior years,
he was awarded the first premium for excellence
in English composition.   But while he was endowed with great quickness and versatility in the
acquisition of varied knowledge, he did not forget that there is no excellence without much labor.
No one ever saw him idle during study hours.   He
was a constant attendant at the University Library, and his chief pleasure seemed to be in gathering stores of information for future use."

Judge Thomas Durfee, who, for many years was
Chief Justice of the Supreme Court of Rhode Island, says:

"I knew Cox very well when he was in College.
I think he did not enter until in the Sophomore
year. He quickly made a strong impression. He
was a superior student in the regular course of
studies, but did not limit himself to those studies,
but pursued a wide course of reading outside of
them.   He wrote several prize essays, and was
always successful in taking the first prize, I think,
whenever he competed. He excelled especially in
writing and oratory, and was even then an excel
lent ex-tempore speaker and debater.   His mind
had already turned to politics and his aspirations
were for a public career, such as he subsequently
pursued.   He was much sought after whenever an
address was to be made.   He was also very com-
panionable and popular in a social way; very
witty and ready in anecdote and   repartee.   It
was generally felt, both by his classmates and
others, that he would attain distinction."

Of his career at Brown University, Prof. Francis

Wayland, who now fills the chair of jurisprudence in Yale University, says:

"Active in mind and body, capable of earnest and continuous study, yet delighting in fun and . frolic, wholly unconventional in dress and deportment; a pronounced political partisan but not offensive in his frequent utterances—for he was always 'on the stump'—'Sam Cox' became, even before the close of his first college year, the most prominent member of his class. His favorite field was the college debating society, from the meetings of which he was rarely absent. Probably none of his comrades so often joined in the discussions. Undoubtedly in the Saturday afternoon debates at the 'United Brothers' he laid the foundation of that familiarity with parliamentary procedure and that readiness in impromptu address which characterized his long and distinguished congressional career. All who knew him well during his college course—and his warm friendships were by no means confined to his own class—predicted for him a brilliant future."

Dr. August Shurtleff of Brookline, Mass., writes:

"Cox joined our class in the Sophomore year, and won our hearts at once. He was one of the most genial kind-hearted and witty men I ever knew. The Professors all liked him, and when he asked funny questions sometimes, never reproved him. I think he was about medium as a scholar. certainly not less. He was always talking politics. I have a class-book in which my nearest friends wrote a sentiment over their autographs —It is before me now. He says, he has always been celebrated as an unterrified Democrat. That there was a tradition in his family, that when he was born a scroll of fire was seen extending around the top of the bed-posts on which appeared the legend 'Vox populi Suprema Lex.' He looked like and always reminded me of Dr. Oliver Wendell Holmes and like him showed his under teeth when he laughed, which was about all the time. He was a dear good fellow."

It is clear that he was a favorite with his classmates, and at the same time that his sterling qualities were appreciated by the faculty.

Writes one of his classmates: "A persistent questioner of President Wayland in recitation in intellectual and moral philosophy, sometimes consuming half the recitation hour in this almost mutual debate."

Another has this testimony: "He was not only liked by his fellow students, but by the faculty, and I know that Dr. Francis Wayland thought very highly of him."

President Wayland's regard for his pupil was thoroughly reciprocated. Indeed in after years, Mr. Cox gave full credit to his preceptor for the methodical way in which he prepared his speeches and books.

Col. William Goddard, a well known merchant of Providence, R. I., and subsequent to 1888 the Chancellor of his alma mater, says:

"When he came under the personal instruction of that great teacher, President Wayland, he displayed such intellectual gifts and such originality of thought that Doctor Wayland was much drawn towards him and loved to lead him into discussions upon the questions before the class."

Writes Reuben A. Guild, Librarian of Brown: "Mr. Cox's subject on graduating was 'Hero-Worship.' I remember it to this day, and how eloquent he was on the stage."

As to his literary methods, Mr. Cox said to a friend:

"Some of my work I have to write with my own hand. I find that when I have an elaborate description to make or some very careful matter to prepare I can do it better by writing it myself. I do not begin my work until I am ready for it: and as you ask me the secret of my doing so much work I will tell you that it all lies in method and system. I went to school at Brown University and there came in contact with Dr. Wayland. The Doctor was a great advocate of thought analysis, and he trained his students to make an outline of everything they took up. In this way we were trained to think analytically, and I find that the moment I take up a subject the thoughts begin to fall into their appropriate places. In making a speech on the floor of the house I can see the end before I begin. Here in this book I made the skeleton before I wrote a chapter. I then outlined the contents of the various chapters, and I am now filling in the flesh and polishing up the skin by dictation."

A few statements concerning his class rank must be added. Dr. J. Wheaton Smith of Philadelphia writes:

"We were members of the same societies and near neighbors as to rooms at the University. He was a witty, genial fellow, but also a close and industrious student, almost the only man I remember of my college friends who objected on principle to light reading as a waste of time. Several of his vacations were spent in writing essays for college prizes, quite a number of which he captured."

On the other hand Mr. Frank W. Anthony writes:

"He had apparently no ambition for high class standing, no taste for mathematics, and sought every opportunity to make speeches on any and all subjects. * * * * Speaking and writing were his especial pursuits. General scholarship in these lines rather than the college ruts. When he wrote his prize essay on the 'Fairy Queen' in his Junior year all conceded first prize to him from the start. So had he impressed his merits upon his classmates in a year from his entrance."

Another classmate, Col. William Goddard, writes:

"He came to Brown University to get an education and he got it. He made upon his classmates the impression of a very brilliant man and he was considered one of the ablest members of the class. In debate he was facile princeps. His essays and orations were truly original and brilliant. * * He graduated with honor and his name is always mentioned with respect by the few classmates who have survived the half century which has elapsed since we parted."

The Rev. James C. Fletcher sums up his college career under the following four heads:

"He was an earnest student, and stood well up in

the first half of his class. Excelled in rhetorical studies.

"He was exceedingly popular with both faculty and students.

"He was cheerful, bubbling over with fun, but he impressed me most by his seriousness.

"He was a man loyal to his college friendships, and was always full of sympathy."

Honorable James B. Angell, president of the University of Michigan and lately Minister to Turkey, who entered Brown as a freshman, just as Mr. Cox was entering his Senior year, gives the following full and interesting account of his college career:

"As my college room was near Mr. Cox's, I soon had the pleasure not only of making his acquaintance, but also of being admitted to his friendship. This was a privilege which I greatly prized. He was then regarded as one of the most eminent writers, and by all odds as the most brilliant debater, in college. His style was already mature. It was terse, sparkling, and epigrammatic. His wit illumined his most weighty and serious speeches. It was always so free from malice that his opponents in debate could share in the enjoyment of it. As I was a member of the same debating society with him, the 'United Brothers,' and indeed largely through his influence was induced to join it, I frequently had the pleasure of hearing him take part in discussions. He was a regular attendant on the meetings, and rarely failed to participate in the debates. He improved every opportunity to train himself by practice in the art of public speaking. He readily accepted

invitations which came to him from outside the
college to address audiences on matters of public
interest.   On the fourth of July, 1846, he gave an
oration before the college, which was considered
one of his most successful and brilliant discours-
es.   He did not study for class rank, though his
general scholarship was good.   But no student
worked more industriously.   He gave most of his
time, however, to the study of English and American history and political economy.   He was, I
think, much impressed, as most students were, by
the instruction he received from President Wayland, especially by the free trade doctrines set
forth in the President's work on Political
Economy.   He seemed to be preparing himself for entering on political life.   He gave
full promise of all he subsequently accomplished in his public career.   When he left
college, we all confidently expected that he would
attain to great eminence in public life.   His attractive social qualities made him a great favorite
in college.   He was brimful of innocent fun.   He
had considerable skill with his pencil in carica-
ture.   He was an agile participant in the sports
of the ball ground.   Wherever one met him,
whether in athletic contests, in social life, or in intellectual tournaments, there was an abounding
vitality and effervescent good nature in him,
which made him a most stimulating and enjoy-
able companion.   I am sure that all of his con-
temporaries in college have cherished, as I cherished, the most pleasing recollections of their
companionship with him in the days of his student life."

The month he completed his twenty-second year
found Mr. Cox a graduate of Brown University
with high honors. Both faculty and students predicted for the young alumnus a brilliant future.
He returned to Ohio to commence the real battle of
life.

CHAPTER IV.

Samuel S. Cox's early experience in his father's office seems to have influenced him in his choice of the law for a profession. In a letter written home while he was a student in Athens, he says:—

"Yesterday I wrote my Inaugural as President of the Athenian Society. My subject Law. There is nothing like fixing beforehand one's course of life. Everything great and little which will subserve the interests of the particular profession, will almost unknown be treasured up. I know a little more about the general principles, tendency, etc., etc., of Law (taken in its general sense) than I ever supposed. I am perfectly at home in it. It's my delight, I love it, and my every energy shall be bent toward it."

It was during his college course that he actually began his law studies. With that systematic habit of making every moment tell, using time when others would waste it, he saw the possibility of employing a portion of one of his vacations in the active study of legal text books. In that connection Judge Dickman writes:—

"Between the close of the Senior year and the Commencement day in September, 1846, there was an interval of over two months in which the graduating class was relieved from academic duty.

During that time Mr. Cox would not seek relaxation, but entered enthusiastically upon the study of law; and before Commencement day he told me he had read Blackstone's Commentaries, and a large part of Cruise's Digest. How thoroughly he could have accomplished so much reading in so short a time, it is not necessary to inquire. But it is evidence of the zeal he manifested in preparing to enter his chosen profession, through whose portals he desired to pass in achieving that political distinction of which he was ambitious."

In this connection it is interesting to mention that even in his law studies he gives credit to President Wayland, for he says:—

"When I studied Blackstone, by the aid of my training in analysis I found that I could repeat almost the whole of it in my own language, and since then, throughout the whole of my life, I have found analysis of the greatest advantage."

On returning to Ohio after graduation he continued his study of law, at first with Judge C. W. Searle in Zanesville, and then with Judge Convers of the firm of Godard & Convers, in whose office Mr. George Hoadley, afterwards governor of Ohio, was also a student. Later he removed to Cincinnati where he finished his legal studies under the Hon. Vachel Worthington.

Having been admitted to the bar he formed a partnership with Mr. George E. Pugh, who afterwards represented Ohio in the United States Senate. For two years he practiced law and made good headway in his profession. One testifies that "the thoroughness of his knowledge and his readiness as a speaker gave him great strength before juries."

The story of his first case in court is told as follows by Captain John Duble, an officer in the fleet of river gunboats that assisted in repulsing the Confederate forces when they laid siege to Cincinnati during the War of the Rebellion:—

"A neighbor and I had a difference, which involved perhaps $25, and we mutually agreed to employ counsel and settle it in Court. I didn't care much for the amount involved, and as little Sam Cox, as we called him, was a sturdy youngster, studying law, in a spirit of fun, and to see what was in him, I retained him. Little Sam sat up late at nights and worked like a Trojan to master the points of the case. He had some assistance from Stanley Matthews, later Justice of the United States Supreme Court.

"Young Cox had his legal guns well shotted at the convening of court. He was ambitious to win his first case, and this nerved him on in the struggle. Witnesses were examined, but when it came to making the plea he was a trifle timid and nervous. But as he warmed up he forgot the crowd, and when he reached his spread-eagle peroration he held them spell-bound. When he concluded, cheer after cheer rang through the old Justice Hall, such as had never been heard there before, and Little Sam was the hero of the hour."

The peroration of this maiden speech was about as follows:—

"Your Honor, I demand for my client only simple justice. If you refuse him this you will violate every rule of jurisprudence—rules as old as jurisprudence itself—which have been left undisturbed by the storms of fate since the day when Julius

Caesar planted his foot upon English soil, after the conquest of Gaul; since the first Indian explored the Western wilds of Ohio. Why, sir, refuse justice to my client, and you will shake the tabernacle of his soul and cause him to tremble for the destinies of his country. Your Honor, the case to me is as clear as the sun at noonday, when its beams penetrate, like shafts of living light, down to the bottom of the slumbering sea. The effulgence of that heavenly orb can fathom the profoundest depths of the human heart and open wide its portals that we may read its secret workings.

"Clear as that crystal sun the mind of man penetrates the deep recesses of the brain, where are opened wide to his prophetic vision thoughts which enable him to look into the book of fate, and as he turns over the leaves of that musty volume—mildewed by the breath of Time—leaves which have been sealed to the gaze of man since creation's earliest dawn, he half expects to hear the voices of oracles of the departed ages. Casting his mind's eye still backward he beholds the trillions passed away, and prophetic vision sees the untold billions of billions yet to come—all of whom had, and all will have, brightest hopes and aspirations fully equal to our own, and all uttering the universal cry of 'Justice!'

"Justice, Your Honor, blended with mercy, should be set in diadem high as the midnight heavens, and surrounded by a halo of the brightest planets, there, in letters of living light, to shine perpetually, that the moon and stars, in their regular rounds, may pay obeisance and bow in devotion to those talismanic words, 'Justice and Mercy.'

"Sir, the heathen Hottentot and the American savage have those heavenly attributes engrafted upon every principle of life and action. They behold it in the sun, moon and stars; they hear it in every wind that blows. It will be the Magna Charta of all generations of men. Why, sir, inspiration and poetry spring from thoughts of justice and mercy. For, blended with these is the poetry of heaven, when, in the gorgeousness of light, the sun proclaims, voiced as with a golden lyre, the powers of the eternal; or at night, when the moon and stars give forth, in silvery accents, the same adoring hymn. In these we find the poetry of the sea, when it speaks in rippled measure or thunders in the voice of its own rebounding billows; or in the storm, or in the green fields, in waving woods and delightful gardens.

"Your Honor, justice is what I demand from you, that justice with which Armand de Richelieu ruled France for 15 years, when he held her to his bosom in the dreadful strifes which desolated her —held her there, pillowed upon justice. Why, sir, thoughts fly through my brain in numbers like as blades of grass upon our boundless Western prairies, thickly as the hosts of Lucifer when he marshaled his forces upon the seashore to attack the angels—in numbers as many as the autumnal leaves that strew the rippled brooks on my own classic Muskingum."

It is needless to add that Cox won the case, and as Captain Duble puts it "with hands down." He adds: "The opposing counsel simply stated to the Court that Cox had fairly covered the ground, and that he had nothing to say, except that he knew

His Honor would decide the case by the strict rule
of justice. Immediately the Magistrate decided in
our favor, throwing costs upon the defendant."

In regard to the fee Captain Duble says:—

"I asked Cox what his fee was. With blushing
modesty and timidity he asked: 'Is $5 too much?'
I felt like pounding the young rascal, and concluded that he would never make a lawyer if his
charges were like that. 'Young man,' said I, 'you
do not know the first principles of your profession.
You don't know how to charge. Here, take the
whole amount awarded by the Court.' That first
case had a great deal to do with the subsequent
career of the great Sunset Cox."

BUCKINGHAM MANSION, ZANESVILLE, OHIO,

Where S. S. Cox wed Julia A. Buckingham.

CHAPTER V.

On one of his trips from Zanesville to Brown he was fortunate in securing the only vacant seat in a stage coach that had been chartered for New York by a party, among whom was Miss Julia A. Buckingham, who with her brother was about to spend the summer in New Hampshire. There is no record of what happened on that journey, but it is stated that whenever the young lady alighted from the stage to walk up the hills, the custom of the day, the student remained inside the stage; and when she remained he alighted.

When questioned about it the young lady, with an amused smile, remarked, "Oh! I only noticed that when I alighted from the stage for a short and restful promenade, the youth always remained inside the stage, and vice versa."

On his return to Zanesville, however, the acquaintance was renewed, and when he had completed his legal studies he sought her hand in marriage. The consent of the young lady was soon obtained, and the marriage ceremony took place in Zanesville, on October 11, 1849.

The Honorable Proctor Knott in his eulogy of Mr. Cox beautifully and truthfully describes the relations of this most devoted husband and wife. Said Mr. Knott:—

"Fortunate as he was in many respects, infinitely beyond the average of his race, Mr. Cox found the crowning blessing of his beautiful life in the affectionate devotion and genial companionship of his gifted and loving wife. Pure in spirit as thrice sifted snow, sweet in disposition as the breath of new blown roses, gentle in manner as the evening zephyr dallying with the violet's eye, faithful to every obligation, and cheerful in the discharge of every duty that affection, humanity, or religion impose, she was, as she is to-night, the perfection of the highest, holiest type of noble womanhood. To her devoted husband she was indeed the pearl beyond all price. His constant companion, his truest friend, his trusted adviser in all things, she was to him a crown of glory and a song of rejoicing throughout all the days of their married life. She shared all his high ambitions and gloried in his successes. Her gentle hand supported him in the dark hours of sorrow, and her loving smile gave a lovelier glow to the bright rays of returning joy. Hand in hand they trod life's journey together, strewing its pathway with the rich jewels of gentleness and charity, until in the full flush of his fame, with his blushing honors thick upon him he was beckoned to a brighter clime, to the real 'Wonderland,' whither he is wooing her in the soft, sweet music of an angel's whisper."

A few months after their marriage Mr. and Mrs. Cox sailed for Europe—a rare trip in those days. It was the year of the World's Exposition in London—the first of its kind in the world's history. They reached Liverpool on the night of May 17,

1851. They returned in the September following. Meanwhile they had made a tour through France, Italy, Germany, Belgium, Scotland, England and Ireland, with "delightful sojournings at Rome, Naples, Malta, Venice, Athens, Smyrna, Constantinople, Geneva and amid the Alps, and observations along the Mediterranean, amidst the Isles of Greece." Under the title "A Buckeye Abroad," Mr. Cox, on his return, published a delightful volume of reminiscence of his journey—a volume that met with such favor that it went into the eighth edition.

In an introduction to the seventh edition he wrote:—

"Since it was issued, in 1852, there have been six editions published; and although frequent applications have been made for it, especially in the West, it has been impossible for me to supply the demand."

Some one wrote: "His Buckeye Abroad is an excellent book for dyspeptics."

CHAPTER VI.

In his preface to the first edition of "A Buckeye Abroad," Mr. Cox says: "The pleasure of traveling was enhanced by companionship. We numbered four in our company, two ladies and a gentleman, Mr. Philo Buckingham, and myself—just the number for convenience and unity of movement, as well as for pleasure. The time, too, was propitious. The year 1851 may be truly called annus mirabilis, at least so far as travelers were concerned. The Great Exhibition—that novel phase of our civilization—was enough to entitle the year to the honor, as a special wonder." The favor with which this fascinating story of travel was received by the public, led the friends of its gifted author to urge him to abandon the law for the more congenial field of journalism. Acting on their advice Mr. Cox purchased, in 1853, a controlling interest in the Columbus "Statesman," the organ, at the State capital, of the Democracy, assuming in person its editorial conduct. As an editorial writer he proved, as was to have been expected, vigorous, original and brilliant. He was no novice with his pen. During his course at Brown University he had contributed both prose and verse to newspapers and periodicals. His first effort at magazine writing was for the old "Knickerbocker"

while he was yet at college.   It was an article descriptive of the river on whose banks he was born
—the Muskingum—with an account of the Mo-
ravian massacre at Gnadenhutten which took
place at the time of the War of the Revolution.
While at Brown, too, he had carried off prizes in
classics, in history, in poetic criticism, and in political economy; his theme on this last subject being "The Repeal of the Corn Laws."   In this essay
he took ground, which he ever afterward maintained, in support of the liberalities of commerce
against the "American system" of bounties for a
few from the many.

As editor of the "Statesman," Mr. Cox, then under thirty years of age, became at once an acknowledged power in the politics of his State.   In
the treatment of the issues of the day he was
strong and vigorous and, withal, refreshingly
original.

It was while he was in the editorial chair at Columbus that the sobriquet "Sunset" was conferred
upon him, a sobriquet fitting his initials and clinging to him thereafter all his days.   It came as a
sequel to an exceedingly picturesque description
from the editor's pen, of a glorious sunset.   This
description, under the caption "A Great Old Sunset," appeared in the Statesman May 19, 1853, and
read as follows:

> "What a stormful sunset was that
> of last night!   How glorious the
> storm and how splendid the setting
> of the sun!   We do not remember
> ever to have seen the like on our
> round globe.   The scene opened in

the west, with a whole horizon full of
golden impenetrating lustre, which
colored the foliage and brightened
every object in its own rich dyes.
The colors grew deeper and richer,
until the golden luster was trans-
formed into a storm-cloud, full of
finest lightning, which leaped in
dazzling zigzags all around and over
the city. The wind arose with fury,
the slender shrubs and quaint trees
made obeisance to its majesty. Some
even snapped before its force. The
strawberry beds and grass plots
'turned up their whites' to see Zephy-
rus march by. As the rain came,
and the pools formed, and the gut-
ters hurried away, thunder roared
grandly, and the fire-bells caught the
excitement and rung with hearty
chorus. The south and east received
the copious showers, and the west all
at once brightened up in a long, polished belt of azure, worthy of a Sici-
lian sky. Presently a cloud appeared
in the azure belt, in the form of a
castellated city. It became more
vivid, revealing strange forms of
peerless fanes and alabaster temples, and glories rare and grand in
this mundane sphere. It reminds
us of Wordsworth's splendid verse in
his Excursion:—

The appearance instantaneously disclosed
Was of a mighty city, boldly say
A wilderness of buildings, sinking far
And self-withdrawn into a wondrous depth.
Far sinking into splendor without end.

"But the city vanished only to
give place to another isle, where the
most beautiful forms of foliage
appeared, imaging a paradise in
the distant and purified air. The
sun, wearied of the elemental com-
motion, sank behind the green plains
of the west. The 'great eye in heav-
en,' however, went not down without a dark brow hanging over its de-
parting light. The rich flush of the
unearthly light had passed and the
rain had ceased; when the solemn
church bells pealed; the laughter of
children, out in the air and joyous
after the storm, is heard with the
carol of birds; while the forked and
purple weapon of the skies still
darted illuminations around the
Starling College, trying to rival its
angles and leap into its dark windows. Candles are lighted. The
piano strikes up. We feel that it is
good to have a home—good to be on
the earth where such revelations
of beauty and power may be made.
And as we cannot refrain from re-
minding our readers of everything
wonderful in our city, we have begun
and ended our feeble etching of a

sunset which comes so rarely, that
its glory should be committed to immortal type."

This vivid description has been criticised as being too florid, but critics are not always just. Sir
John McDonald, the eminent Canadian statesman,
when describing a sunset of phenomenal beauty,
in a letter to the Toronto Globe, quotes the entire
article by Mr. Cox, and refers to it as follows:—

"This has been thought to be highly imagina-
tive. Doubtless it is. None but a man of fertile
and poetic imagination could write it. It has been
thought to be greatly exaggerated, if not unreal.
I did not see it, and of it I cannot speak, but, having read the description over most carefully several times, it contains nothing which I cannot conceive as being perfectly possible; for had the castellated city, of which he speaks, appeared in the
azure belt, and had this in vanishing given place
to 'another isle, where the most beautiful forms of
foliage appeared, imaging a paradise in the distant
and purified air,' even these forms wondrous as
they must have appeared to one of his poetic imagination, would not have equalled the glory and
the grandeur of the sight which we were privileged to behold. For to us it appeared that the
very portals of heaven were opened, which led not
to the castellated city which presented itself to the
imagination of Congressman Cox, but to that
'great city, the Holy Jerusalem, descending out of
heaven from God, and her light was like unto a
stone most precious, even like a jasper stone, clear
as crystal.' I was better able to understand what

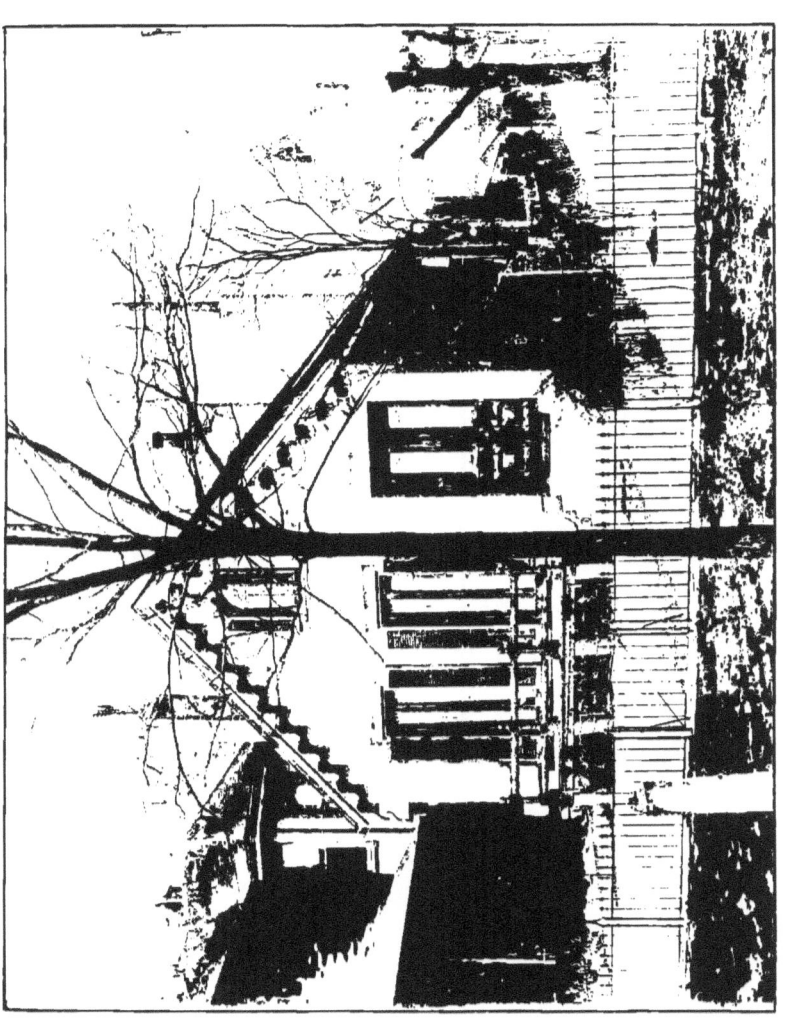

COX'S FIRST RESIDENCE, COLUMBUS, OHIO, 1853,

Where the Famous "Sunset" Editorial was Written.

others had written on the same subject by reason
of what I had seen.   When Humbolt was pursuing
his investigations in Camana he thus wrote: 'There
the sun does not only shed light upon a landscape,'
as with us, 'but it gives a coloring to the different
objects; it enfolds them, without destroying their
transparency, with a light which makes their coloring more harmonious, and spreads a repose over
nature.'

"But chiefly am I glad that it is in my power, by
my own humble testimony, to rescue the description of Congressman Cox from the charge of exaggeration and unnaturalness put forth by some, and
to express my own thanks that the description of
'A Great Old Sunset' was ever penned by one so
gifted—a description which will be perfectly in-
telligible to all who may be permitted to look upon
the glory of the setting sun under conditions similar to those witnessed by us at Labouchere Bay."

CHAPTER VII

With the mantle of editor of the leading Demo·
cratic organ of the State, came the mantle also of
party leadership. The chairman of the Ohio Democratic State Committee, in 1853, was Washington
McLean, the proprietor of the Cincinnati Enquirer,
one of Mr. Cox's earliest and staunchest friends.
Chairman McLean, anxious to be relieved of the
responsibilities incident to the conduct of the campaign, resigned the chairmanship upon the condition that Mr. Cox accept the place and direct the
canvass. William Medill was the Democratic
candidate for Governor. The opposing candidates
were Barrere, Whig, and Lewis, Free Soiler. Mr.
Cox threw himself into the campaign with all his
characteristic vigor and energy. Never, it is said,
were his tireless industry and his marvelous versatility better displayed. Besides doing the executive work of the committee of which he was the
head, he took the stump, electrifying the masses
by his eloquent reasoning, or convulsing them
with his keen wit, and, withal, not neglecting to
enforce the Democratic doctrine through the editorial page of his newspaper. His resources
seemed to be inexhaustible. Overwhelming victory crowned his efforts—Medill being elected

Governor by a majority over all of 11,497, and a plurality over the Whig candidate of 61,843.

By the prestige thus gained the young editor and stump orator was, in spite of himself, fairly launched upon the tempestuous sea of politics. In the words of another, young, quick-witted, ready, energetic, ardent, earnest, talented, graceful, and accomplished, no man was more fitted to win the plaudits of the people. He was the rising young statesman of the Buckeye State. His fame spread to Washington, and thither he was summoned by President Pierce. It was Mr. Cox's first visit to the National capital. President Pierce took a great liking to the brilliant Buckeye, and, in 1855, tendered him the post of Secretary of Legation at the Court of St. James. This honor was declined, Mr. Cox preferring, for reasons of his own, the less exalted post of Secretary to the Peruvian legation. The President freely acquiesced, and Mr. Cox sailed for Peru. Overtaken, however, by alarming illness at Aspinwall, enroute to his post, it was not deemed prudent for him to proceed further. Accordingly, as soon as able, he returned to the United States and resigned his commission. Thirty years—three decades big with the fate of the nation—were destined to pass before his re-entry into his country's diplomatic service, as Minister to Turkey.

CHAPTER VIII.

The turning point in Mr. Cox's life had come. A new career was opening before him, one in which he was to achieve a memorable and a unique success—one which was to link his name with the most eventful chapters of American history, and emblazon his fame on its brightest pages. Samuel Sullivan Cox was about to enter the national House of Representatives. It was the year 1856. The Republican party, as if having sprung, like Minerva, full-armed from the brain of Jove, although less than a year old, had already developed a strength which struck consternation into the heart of the ancient democracy. John C. Fremont, the "Pathfinder," was the Republican standard bearer, and to his standard the young men of the country in particular were flocking in serried hosts. The venerable James Buchanan, an old public functionary whose services to his country dated back for decades, was the democracy's candidate for President. The spirit of sectionalism was deeply stirred. The Democratic leaders plainly saw that if they were to retain the citadel of power, which they had captured four years before, no stone was to be left unturned. Everywhere they were putting the best foot forward. In the capital district of Ohio they in-

stinctively turned to the young and briliant leader, the eloquent orator and able editor, Samuel
Sullivan Cox.   Him they asked to be their candidate for Congress; and he accepted.   Samuel Galloway was his Republican opponent, while Mr.
Stanberry was the candidate of what was left of
the old "American" party, now mainly merged
into the new Republican body.   The campaign
was both exciting and bitter.   Mr. Cox was
elected by a plurality over Galloway of 355 votes.
He was now thirty-two years old, but he had an
equipment for the duties before him in education,
in experience of public affairs, and in general
adaptation, possessed by few young men of his
era.

Among Mr. Cox's papers is an autograph letter
from Franklin Pierce, written to the youthful Congressman from his New Hampshire home a few
months after his retirement from the Presidency.
Incidentallly the letter reveals the "high hope"
entertained of the national career upon which he
was about to enter, by the veterans of the Democratic party.   Writes ex-President Pierce:—

"Rockingham House, Portland, N. H.,
"September 15, 1857.
"My Dear Sir:—Accept my thanks for your kind
note of the 3d inst., and also for your admirable
address at Providence.   I was deeply touched by
your noble tribute to Governor Marcy.   It was
well earned by a long, useful, eventful life.

"I shall probably go to Cuba for the winter with
the anticipation of improvement to Mrs. Pierce's
health—but you must let me hear from you frequently after you enter upon your Congressional
career, to which I shall look with interest and
high hope.   Very truly your friend,
"Franklin Pierce."
"Hon. Samuel S. Cox. Columbus, Ohio."

CHAPTER IX.

March 4, 1857, the day that witnessed the inauguration of James Buchanan as President of the United States, the last of the ante-bellum line of chief magistrates, also ushered into national public life Samuel Sullivan Cox. It was midway of his career. Then thirty-two years old he had before him other thirty-two years which were to be spent mainly before the footlights of that great national theatre, the House of Representatives. It was the Thirty-fifth Congress. The new wings of the Capitol were nearing their completion, and to the Thirty-fifth Congress was to fall the honor of first occupying the new quarters.

With a Democratic President the country had returned a Democratic House of Representatives. The choice of Speaker fell upon James L. Orr, of South Carolina. In the distribution of committee chairmanships Mr. Cox, although a new member was not forgotten. He was placed at the head of Revolutionary Claims. Events contributed to bring the representative of the Capital district of Ohio into early and unexpected prominence, and, moreover, to signal to the world his independence of character and his moral courage. Environment added to the dramatic interest of the occasion.

The first session of the new Congress opened December 7, 1857, in the old hall of Representatives.

On the 16th of that month the House bade adieu
to the old hall, with all its historic associations.
and took possession of its new chamber in the
south wing of the Capitol, the same it occupies to-
day. To "Sunset" Cox, as it chanced, fell the
honor of making the maiden speech in the new
chamber. And to the consternation of the veteran leaders of his party who listened, that speech
was a gauntlet thrown to the new administration,
which he himself had zealously helped to place in
power! The issue on which this young member
had the temerity to lock horns with the party's
President, at the very threshold of his term, was
the Lecompton constitution. To the admission of
Kansas into the union under that pro-slavery constitution President Buchanan was committed.
The opposition thereto was led by the "little
giant" of the senate, Stephen A. Douglas, with
"popular sovereignty" for his shibboleth. In the
memorable conflict then just beginning, a conflict
that resulted in the rupture of the party and its
defeat at the polls three years later, Samuel S
Cox was an able lieutenant of Judge Douglas.
His was the first speech made in the House of Representatives against the Lecompton Constitution.
It was the keynote. By it the line was closely
drawn, on the one or the other side of which the
Democrats the country over ere long arrayed
themselves in frowning attitude.

Of that speech and the scene attending its delivery, the author in his "Three Decades of Federal Legislation," says:

"The 16th of December, 1857, is memorable in
the annals of the United States. Looking back to

that day, the writer can see the members of the
House of Representatives take up the line of
march out of the old shadowy and murmurous
Chamber into the new Hall, with its ornate and
gilded interior. The scene is intense in a rare
dramatic quality. Around sit the members upon
richly carved oaken chairs. Already arrayed upon
either side are the sections in mutual animosity.
The Republicans take the left of the Speaker, the
Democrats the right. James L. Orr, of South Carolina, a full, roseate-faced gentleman, of large
build and ringing metallic voice, is in the chair.
James C. Allen, of Illinois, sits below him in the
Clerk's chair. The Rev. Mr. Carothers offers an
appropriate and inspiring prayer. A solemn hush
succeeds the invocation. After some legislative
routine the members retire to the open space in the
rear to await the drawing of seats. A page with
bandaged eyes makes the award, and one by one
the members are seated. Then by the courtesy of
the chairman of the Printing Committee (Mr.
Smith, of Tennessee), a young member from Ohio
is allowed to take the floor. He addresses the
Speaker with timidity and modesty amid many in-
terruptions by Humphrey Marshall, Thomas S.
Bocock, Judge Hughes, George W. Jones, and
General Quitman, each of whom bristles with
points of order against the points of the speaker.
But that young member is soon observed by a
quiet House. Many listen to him, perhaps to
judge of the acoustic qualities of the Hall, some
because of the nature of the debate. And then
after a few minutes all become excited. Again
and again the shrill tones of Mr. Speaker Orr are

heard above the uproar. He exclaims: 'This is a motion to print extra copies of the President's message. Debate on the subject is therefore in order, upon which the gentleman from Ohio has the floor.' That gentleman is now the writer. His theme was the Lecompton constitution. As the questions discussed involved the great issues leading to war or peace his interest in the mis-en-scene became less. But his maiden speech—the maiden speech in the new chamber—began under circumstances anything but composing."

Judge Holman, of Indiana, said of this speech, on the floor of Congress: "It was one of the ablest and, under all the circumstances, the most courageous speech ever delivered in Congress . In words of burning eloquence he denounced the proposed Constitution as not expressing the will of the people of Kansas, and therefore as violative of their right to form and control their local government. That speech, placing him at the very outset of his Congressional career in antagonism to the administration as well as many of his political friends, opened up one of the greatest debates in the records of Congress." It resulted in the Lecompton constitution being referred to the people of Kansas, who promptly rejected it. At a later day Mr. Cox had the satisfaction of voting for the admission of Kansas into the family of States under a Free-state Constitution adopted by the people. This was one of the most signal triumphs of Mr. Cox's long public life. The President took his small revenge on Mr. Cox, by removing from the Postmastership of Columbus the friend whose appointment Mr. Cox had secured. He had, however,

in co-operation with Judge Douglas, saved the
Democratic party from the ineffable disgrace of
foisting upon the people of Kansas, in spite of
their protests, a constitution upholding the institution of slavery in that territory. In his Three
Decades Mr. Cox, referring to the far reaching
consequences of this conflict, says: "Had the Democratic party which came into power with Mr.
Buchanan and the Thirty-fifth Congress united in
wisdom to thrust aside the Lecompton constitution, there would have been no distraction in its
ranks as early as 1860. But it is not so sure that
the slavery question would not have come in some
form to have kept up the irrepressible conflict.
Had they thus united, perhaps the Charleston convention of 1860 would have agreed."

He was re-elected, to the Thirty-sixth Congress,
by a majority of 647 over Mr. Case, Republican. It
was an emphatic endorsement of his position on
theKansas question, an endorsement given after
"a campaign," to use Mr. Cox's words,
"unexampled for its unprovoked fierceness,
its base and baseless charges of personal corruption, its conceit, its ignorance, its impudence, its
poltroonery, its billingsgate, its brutality, its
monied corruption, its fanatical folly, its unflag-
ging slang, its drunken saturnalia, and its unblush-
ing libels and pious hypocrisy. In spite of all
this," he added, "the people doubled my majority
of 1856." The prestige gained by Mr. Cox in his
first Congress, his reputation for fearlessness and
independence, as well as ability and eloquence,
easily made him a leader in his second term. He
was still, however, at war with the administration, co-operating with Stephen A. Douglas, the

great leader of the Northern Democracy in the
Senate. The Democrats saw the first fruits of
their dissensions in the loss of the House of Representatives. After a protracted struggle for the
Speakership, in which John Sherman of Ohio was
side-tracked because he had unwittingly endorsed
Hilton Rowan Helper's book, "The Impending
Crisis," the mantle fell upon William Pennington,
a Conservative Republican from New Jersey.
During this Congress, which came into being
March 4, 1859, and expired March 4, 1861,
the lines of sectionalism grew more and
more distinct. The rumblings of the awakened
volcano came louder and louder, and it was evident, at the last of this Congress, that the eruption
was at hand. In the fierce passions of the hour
personal conflict was often narrowly avoided, and
once at least there was actual personal collision
on the floor of the House. The parties thereto were
Keith of South Carolina and Grow of Pennsylvania. Mr. Cox, who was a witness of the encounter, thus describes it:—

"It is after the hour of midnight. The passions
of the time are incarnate in that Congress and at
that hour. See the fierce clutch and glaring eye,
and the struggle between these heady champions!
Now, after nearly three decades I see, trooping
down the aisles of memory, as then there came
trooping down the aisles of the House, the belligerents, with Washburn, of Illinois, and Potter, of
Wisconsin, leading one extreme, and Barksdale
and Lamar, of Mississippi, the other. Then came
the melee, the struggle; the pale face of the
Speaker calling for order; the Sergeant-at-Arms

rushing into the area before the Speaker's desk with the mace as his symbol of authority. Its silver eagle moves up and down on the wave of passion and conflict. Then there is a dead hush of the hot heart and the glare of defiance across the Hall. As this scene is revivified, looking at it through the red storm of the war, there is epitomized all that has made that war bloody and desperate."

Of this Congress, which met for its first session December 5, 1859, Mr. Cox says: "Considered by results it was, perhaps, the most important congregation of men that ever assembled upon our continent. It held the destinies of our institutions and races in the hollow of its hand." It was during the life of this Congress, in 1860, that the Charleston convention, in the spring of that year, witnessed the formal disruption of the Democratic party, followed by the presentation of two candidates for the Presidency, and the consequent triumph of Republicanism in the election of Abraham Lincoln. "On a gloomy day in March, 1861," testifies Mr. Cox, "the Thirty-sixth Congress adjourns sine die. There are many sad and last farewells—for the pall of impending wrath hangs over all the land. Black clouds of war loom up all around, surcharged with the elements of death and devastation."

Mr. Cox had again been re-elected to Congress. His opponent in 1860 was his opponent of 1856, Samuel Galloway. Despite the flood-tide of Northern sentiment for Lincoln's election to the Presidency, and despite Democratic divisions, Mr. Cox defeated Galloway by a majority of 883. It was more than a political triumph: it was a personal tribute of a pronounced type.

The Thirty-seventh was the first war Congress. It was ushered in with the inauguration of Lincoln. Within fifty days the war clouds which had been so long gathering, burst; Sumpter fell; and the President had called the new Congress in extraordinary session to provide ways and means for saving the Union from threatened destruction. The extra session opened on July 4, 1861, a date whose associations were doubtless intended to add any needed stimulus to the patriotic uprising which followed the attack on Fort Sumpter. The great Southern leaders of previous Congresses were conspicuous by their absence. They had, as a rule, followed their States into the vortex of secession. Mr. Cox, in the previous congress, had clearly seen the drift of events, and warned his countrymen of the South in impassioned eloquence, to desist. "In Washington's sacred name," he had pleaded in the winter before, while State after State was joining the procession out of the Union, "and on behalf of a people who have ever heeded his warning and never wavered in the just defense of the South or of the North, I appeal to Southern men who contemplate a step so fraught with hazard and strife, to pause. Clouds are about us! There is lightning in their frown! Cannot we direct it harmlessly to the earth? The morning and evening prayer of the people I speak for in such weakness, rises in strength to that Supreme Ruler who, in noticing the fall of a sparrow, cannot disregard the fall of a nation, that our States may continue to be—as they have been— one; one in the essence of a national being ;one as the thought of God is One!

"These emblems above us, in their canopy of

beauty, each displaying the symbol of State interest, State pride, and State sovereignty, let not one
of them be dimmed by the rude breath of passion,
or effaced by the ruder stroke of enmity. They all
shine, like stars, differing in glory, in their many-
hued splendors, by the light of the same orb, even
as our States receive their lustre from the Union,
which irradiates and glorifies each and all." Having fruitlessly labored to avert secession in the
Thirty-sixth Congress, Mr. Cox came to the extra
session of the Thirty-seventh Congress prepared to
sustain the administration of Lincoln in every constitutional endeavor to put down the rebellion.

Judge Holman of Indiana, the intimate friend
and associate for so many years of Mr. Cox, bears
this testimony:—

"When the Thirty-sixth Congress adjourned, on
the 4th day of March, 1861, Mr. Cox and I started
homeward. We were detained a day at Wheel-
ing, Va. We spent the day together, talking over
the impending conflict. We both knew, as all men
did, that war was inevitable. What position we
should take as Democrats in Congress in relation
to the coming war, when it came, was considered
from every standpoint. There was no hesitation
on the part of either of us. The Union must be
maintained at every hazard. No vicissitude of fortune in the conflict of arms should justify ever the
consideration of the question of the dissolution of
the Union. The administration of President Lincoln in every measure deemed necessary or proper
to uphold the Federal authority in all the States
of the Union should be cordially sustained. The
records of Congress during the war attest how

faithfully Mr. Cox adhered to that determination."

Between the dates of Lincoln's inauguration and the opening of the extra session the country had been shocked by the sudden death of Stephen A. Douglas. On no one fell the loss more heavily than on Samuel S. Cox. The eulogy of the departed statesman by his long-time faithful friend in the House, was affectingly eloquent, drawing tears from those who listened to it.

Mr. Douglas' death at so critical a juncture of affairs, when his counsel and influence were especially needed, was deemed a great public loss. "Who," asked his eulogist, "is left to take his place? Alas! he has no successor. His eclipse is painfully palpable, since it makes more obscure the path by which our alienated brethren may return."

Mr. Cox was now serving his third term, as Representative of a district normally Republican. In each contest, desperate efforts had been made to effect his defeat, but all to no purpose. The happy thought occurred to the legislature to apply the gerrymander to the capital district of Ohio, and see how that would work as a political agency. In the new district Samuel Shellabarger, credited with exceptional strength as a candidate, entered the lists against the young but, in point of service, already veteran member. Again, however, Mr. Cox was elected, although his majority was, through the process referred to, cut down to 272.

A glimpse of "war times" on the border between the contending armies is afforded by the following private note from the venerable Kentucky statesman, Hon. J. J. Crittenden, acknowledging

an invitation from Mr. Cox to make his home at
Columbus his refuge during the rebel raids of Kentucky. Under date Louisville, September 26, 1862,
he wrote:—

"Soon after I was compelled to leave my home
and come to this place to avoid falling into the
hands of the Rebels, I received from the Hon. S.
S. Cox a very kind letter of invitation for myself
and wife to come to his house and remain with him
during the present hostile and formidable invasion
of Kentucky. Please to present him my best acknowledgments for that hospitable invitation and
say to him I could not leave Kentucky at such a
time. I must remain with her, if it be only to
share in her troubles and her dangers. * * *
Be pleased also to give to Mr. Cox my heartiest and
best wishes for his re-election to Congress. I have
had my prejudices against him, but he overcame
them entirely by his conduct and course in the
present Congress,—his course in my opinion ju-
dicious, intelligent and patriotic, opposing stead-
ily that abolition policy which sought to convert
this holy war for the defence of the government
and the union into a mere anti-slavery party war—
a policy calculated to prolong and embitter the
bloody war, without doing any good to the white
or to the black man. It is for the country to decide
whether such a policy should prevail. It is for his
opposition to it that I feel a solicitude for the
election of Mr. Cox."

Besides his magnetic hold on the affections of
the people, Mr. Cox, by his support of every Constitutional measure for a vigorous prosecution of the
war, drew to himself a large Republican vote.

The Thirty-eighth Congress, the fourth to which Mr. Cox had been elected, met December 5, 1863. The battle of Gettysburg had been fought in the previous July, and although the advancing legions of the Confederacy had been turned back, some of the most desperate fighting of the war remained. Mr. Cox had, from his second term, served on the Committee of Foreign Affairs, and had enjoyed in an eminent degree the confidence of the Secretary of State, William H. Seward. This Congress it was that submitted to the States the Thirteenth Amendment to the Constitution abolishing slavery. That institution had already been abolished in fact—abolished by the Proclamation of Emancipation issued by President Lincoln in 1862. It was desired, however, to place the work of the Proclamation beyond any possible question by incorporating it in the Supreme law of the land. Mr. Cox did not vote for this amendment, although he was disposed to favor it. In his Three Decades he explains this seeming contradiction. He had, he says, left himself free to vote for it, in case its passage would not interfere with attempts at peace negotiations. He fully intended, when he went to the House at noon of the last day of January, 1865 —the day fixed for taking the vote—to cast his vote for the amendment. But on arriving at the House he learned that commissioners to conclude peace were actually waiting to be conducted across the lines. Fearing that action on the amendment at that critical juncture might prove a serious obstacle to peace negotiations, Mr. Cox cast his vote against the amendment—a vote to be construed rather against the expediency of its

adoption at that particular time than against the
abstract principle the amendment involved.

In connection with this vote, Mr. Cox relates the
following interesting incident:—

"In striving to stay hostilities and prevent
butchery, the author (of the Three Decades) uncon-
sciously saved his personal probity from unde-
served reproach. This is the incident. He was
boarding at the house of an active radical Republican who had been on General Fremont's staff.
The writer had spoken, in confidence, about the
table and under the roof of this landlord of his intention to vote for the amendment. One vote was
then most momentous to make the requisite two-
thirds. This ex-soldier of fortune counted, in a
mercenary way, on improving his purse by his con-
fidential information. When the writer returned
to his Tuesday dinner, having given under the circumstances an adverse vote, the irascible radical
broke forth into such a torrent of abuse against
the writer, that the latter left the table in disgust
and bewilderment. The abuser in his wrath
averred—what he afterwards, when stricken with
blindness and repentant, directed his good wife to
asseverate in writing—that he was to get ten thousand dollars from New York parties for influenc-
ing the writer's vote favorably to the amendment.
The writer discovered the party who raised the
fund which was said to be ready and freely used
for corrupting members. Can anything be con-
ceived more monstrous than this attempt to amend
the Constitution upon such a humane and glorious theme, by the aid of the lucre of officeholders?
This statement was made in Congress after the

war, and with much detail. It was never challenged. It is true." This would have been by no means the first instance of a legislator's vote being sold with no knowledge of the transaction on the part of the man who cast the vote.

Mr. Cox was about to suffer his first defeat at the hands of the people. It was the fall of 1864, Lincoln was a candidate for re-election, and Gen. McClellan was his Democratic opponent. Mr. Cox was, for the fifth time, his party's nominee to represent the Columbus district in Congress. Again his opponent was Samuel S. Shellabarger. The tide set in strongly in favor of Republicanism, and Shellabarger was swept into Congress by the enormous majority of 3,169. The soldier vote, which was forwarded from field and camp, contributed largely to this result. With the completion of Mr. Cox's term, on March 4, 1865, the curtain was rung down on the last scene of a drama which had been eight years on the boards. After long wandering in the wilderness, the Canaan of peace was just ahead. Mr. Cox, as Congressman, was permitted to see its dawn, but not its noonday. Within six weeks after his retirement from Congress, Richmond had fallen. Lee had turned over his sword to Grant in the shade of the Appomattox apple tree, and, in the midst of the country's hallelujahs, had come the shock of Lincoln's assassination. Events of mighty import to the nation trod on one another's heels thick and fast in those six weeks. Mr.Cox, from his retirement looked back upon eight years of honorable service in the most momentous era of the nation's history—the era which led up to, and paralleled, the civil war.

Throughout the long struggle Mr. Cox consistently supported every constitutional measure for
the suppression of the rebellion, but was unspar-
ing in his criticism of measures which seemed to
him to be unnecessarily arbitrary and to infringe
upon personal liberty. Between himself and
President Lincoln the friendliest relations existed.
Among Mr. Cox's private papers appears
the following autograph letter, written by President Lincoln, a few weeks before his assassination:

> Executive Mansion Washington,
> January 31, 1865.
>
> Hon. S. S. Cox,
> My Dear Sir—Thank you for the speech. I
> sought it for the humor said to be in it; but while
> it meets expectation in that respect, it has a far
> higher merit, so far as I can judge by the hasty
> glance I have only found time to give it.
> Yours truly,
> A. Lincoln.

Prefacing his volume "Eight Years in Congress," Mr. Cox recalled with pardonable pride the
part he had taken in those stirring scenes. Addressing his old constituents he says: "I represented you truly, when I warned and worked from
1856 to 1860 against the passionate zealotry of
North and South; when I denounced, in and out
of Congress, the bad fallacy and worse conduct of
the secessionists; when I voted to avert the impending war by every measure of adjustment; and
when, after the war came, by my votes for money
and men, I aided the administration in maintain-
ing the Federal authority over the insurgent

states. Sustained by you, I supported every measure which was constitutional and expedient, to
crush the rebellion.   In the perusal of these
pages," he added, "no one will find any aid, by
speech or vote, given to those who raised the standard of revolt."

Valued testimony to Mr. Cox's services in support of war measures and notably of the amendment to abolish slavery, was borne by no less a
personage than William H. Seward, the illustrious
premier of the Lincoln administration.   In a public speech, delivered at Auburn, his home, in October, 1868, Secretary Seward said:

"I entertain no ill will towards the democratic
party or its leaders, and certainly have no unchar-
itable feelings toward that great constituency.
On the other hand, I cherish a grateful appreciation of the patriotism, the magnanimity, the heroism of many of my fellow citizens, with whom I
have cheerfully labored and co-operated while
they still retained their adhesion to the Democratic party.   How could I distrust the loyalty or the
virtue of Andrew Johnson, of General Hancock,
of General McClellan, of Senator Hendricks, of
Indiana, Mr. Niblack, or of Mr. Cox, formerly of
Ohio, to whom personally, more than any other
member, is due the passage of the constitutional
amendment in Congress abolishing African slavery."

CHAPTER X.

At the close of his eight years' service in Congress, Mr. Cox, tired of public life, and in the belief that he was through with it, decided to remove to the city of New York, and take up again the practice of the law. In this he had a partner, Mr. Charlton T. Lewis. In dedicating his volume, "Eight Years in Congress," to his constituents, referring to the conflicts illustrated therein, he had said: "I have had my share of such conflicts. No ambition now actuates me save that I may be instrumental, through these pages, in mirroring the past eight years, with the clearness and fidelity of truth." Few men at forty could boast a public service so long and distinguished, coupled with accumulation of so rich a store and such marvelous versatilities of general culture.

Although settled down to the routine of a New York lawyer, Mr. Cox was not to be permitted a long respite from public service. He relates an interesting incident respecting the attempted impeachment of President Andrew Johnson, in the winter of 1868. During the trial Mr. Cox received a dispatch summoning him to Washington. The success of the impeachers, it was understood, hinged on one vote—that of Senator Henderson, of Missouri. With this Senator, Mr. Cox was known to be on terms of close intimacy. It was thought that Mr. Cox's influence might resolve the doubts in the Senator's mind, and persuade him to cast his vote against impeachment.

Mr. Cox obeyed the summons, and was soon in Washington, closeted with the Missouri Senator. The sequel is thus told by Mr. Cox: "A public meeting had just been held at St. Louis, to instruct the Senator to vote 'guilty.' His sense of justice had been affronted by this. In this mood the writer found him. He seemed to want advice and counsel. It was not long before the writer was requested by the Senator to pen and send a telegram to the president and officers of that impudent St. Louis meeting. It substantially read: 'I am a judge in the impeachment case. You have no right to instruct me in such affairs. As I am an honest man I will obey my conscience, and not your will. I shall vote 'not guilty.' " And he did so vote. A copy of that telegram the writer took to the White House at midnight. He found the President gloomy. His fate depended on one vote —nay, on this one Missouri vote. Grimes and Ross were sure, but Henderson was not. The telegram was read to the President. A festivity was improvised on the good news; and the morning dawned with roseate hues for all interested in the righteousness of the President's acquittal, and the certainty of the vindication of a President, than whom no man was ever more vilipended without justifiable cause."

The object of Mr. Cox's mission to Washington was accomplished; the impeachers were foiled; and the President was saved.

CHAPTER XI.

In leaving Congress four years before Mr. Cox had said "adieu;" but fate turned it into an "au revoir." In the fall of 1868 he was nominated for Congress by his party representatives in the Sixth district, and was elected over George Starr, a popular Republican, by 2,680. Then began a Congressional service of twenty years, scarcely interrupted till his death. In fact he was a member, at one stage or another, of every Congress that sat thereafter, so long as he lived—from the Forty-first to the Fifty-first inclusive.

Heretofore he had represented the Capital district of Ohio. Henceforth he was to represent in part the great city of New York.

Shortly after his election Mr. Cox, accompanied by his wife, as ever on his travels, prompted by impaired health, set sail for Europe, returning the following autumn in time for the opening of Congress.

"Mr. Cox," writes the companion of his travels, "was worn out with the campaign of '67 or '68 and the doctor ordered him abroad. He had then symptoms of lung trouble—slight hemorrhages, &c., so we started for Jerusalem. Bought a trunk full of maps and books, to study up Palestine and the Orient. Arrived at Mentone, Dr. Bennett

DR. HENRY BENNETT,
Cox's Physician in Europe (1869), in his Garden at Mentone.

nearly took my breath away in his consultation.
"Mrs. Cox I will not answer for the life of your
husband, if he travels in this condition!" "What
shall I do, Doctor?" "Stay the winter here or in Algiers. Stay here or at Nice and I will invite you (a
thing I rarely do), to go as my patients in the
spring to Algiers. If Mr. Cox wearies, take him a
short trip to Corsica. It is unbeaten track."

"So ended our 'second grand campaign!' For
we had given it almost as much thought as the political campaign! Mr. Cox convinced by physician
and wife, remained and we had a very delightful
winter on the Riviera—extending to Vallembrosa
in Cannes and during the mild winter accomplished our trip to Corsica—perhaps the most
unique of any of our foreign sojournings.

"In the spring Dr. Bennett and an uncle, an old
India campaigner, with Mr. Cox and myself took
the steamer for Algiers and finished the African
and Spanish trip which he pictures in his 'Search
for Winter Sunbeams.' "

In this charming volume, which he dedicated to
his constituents of the Sixth Congressional district of New York, he has told the story of his
travels during that year. "My circle," in a resume
of his journeys he writes, "began at the Riviera
under the Alps; it includes Corsica; thence enters
into Africa, and passes through Spain and Southern France, until, again in the Alps of Italy, it
ends, with a view so eminent, that it seems to comprehend the whole sweep of nearly a year's tour of
travel."

The day that witnessed the return of Samuel
Sullivan Cox to Congress signaled the election of

Gen. Ulysses S. Grant, over Horatio Seymour, to the Presidency. The country was still struggling with the problem of reconstruction. The passions of the war were still far from being burned out. Mr. Cox believed that the greatest bar to a complete restoration of the union was the political ostracism of the men who had borne arms against the United States. Accordingly one of his first acts, on returning to the familiar scenes of Congress, was the introduction of a general amnesty bill. That was in 1869. He explains that his object in Congressional service was, since war could not be alleviated of its cruelties, to mitigate, in so far as it could be done, the proscriptive tendency which kept our people separated by a great chasm. Mr. Cox's bill came within two votes of passing the House, James G. Blaine being the Speaker, although under the fourteenth amendment a two-thirds vote was required. Mr. Cox urged the measure with all the force and eloquence he could command. The emphatic endorsement of his proposition by so large a majority—although falling just short of the requisite two-thirds—in a House politically hostile, was a decided personal triumph. But he did not give up the fight. In Congress after Congress he sought the passage of a bill bestowing general amnesty upon the South, as the shortest and quickest road to complete reconciliation. Speaker Blaine had, according to Mr. Cox, authorized the Committee on Rules, of which both were members, to report such a measure, only to retreat precipitately from the high ground he occupied in Committe, so soon as the bill reached the House. However that was,

it is certain that such progress towards amnesty
as was made in Mr. Cox's day, was due in large
degree to his untiring efforts and indomitable per-
severance.

Mr. Cox's antagonist in the Congressional election of 1870 was the famous editor of the New
York Tribune, Horace Greeley. Mr. Cox's majority was 1,025. Two years later the two were
running on the same ticket, the one for President,
the other for Congressman-at-large. The Forty-
second Congress, which came into being March 4,
1871, and died March 4, 1873, was the first to have
on its roll the names of representatives of the
lately enslaved race. In this Congress Mr. Cox
made a persistent but ineffectual fight against the
test oath system—seeking to abolish the entire
system in its application alike to jurors, and all
officers, including Congressmen. In its place, however, a modified measure was passed applying to
the oath to be administered to members of Congress, but not to jurors. But complete triumph
came to Mr. Cox two decades after the war, when
President Arthur, on May 13, 1884, signed the bill
repealing both the iron-clad oath and the jury-
test oath.

CHAPTER XII.

Mr. Cox's next race for congress, made in the fall of 1872, was under new conditions and in strange company. The revolt in the Republican party against Grant, had resulted in the nomination at Cincinnati of Horace Greeley for President, and his adoption as Presidential candidate by the Democratic National Convention at Baltimore. This action was followed by a practical fusion, a modus vivendi, of the Democrats and Liberal (anti-Grant) Republicans in several of the States, including New York. The Democratic State Convention at Syracuse, meeting concurrently with the Liberal Republican State Convention held in another hall in the same city, made a fusion ticket headed by Francis Kernan for Governor, with Chauncey M. Depew for Lieutenant Governor, and Samuel S. Cox for representative in Congress at large. A new apportionment had given New York an additional representative, who, for this time—the Legislature not yet having redistricted the State—was to be elected from the State at large. Mr. Cox's acknowledged strength with the masses of voters over the entire State led naturally to his selection, when strength for the mongrel ticket was the one thing needed and sought. It was a curious combination, Horace Greeley, the

high priest of protection, and life-long foe of Democracy, at its head; Francis Kernan, a Democrat
of Democrats, yoked with Chauncey M. Depew,
who never had been aught but a Republican
throughout; and Samuel S. Cox, an avowed advocate of free trade, and the antipode in general of
the editor of the Tribune. Mr. Cox was carried
down with the rest of the strange company in
which he had been placed. It was his second and
last defeat before the people—his defeat in his
Ohio district having been his first. Although he
ran ahead of his ticket, Mr. Cox was defeated by
Lyman Tremain, ex-attorney general of New York,
by a majority of 37,699.

Mr. Cox was on the stump for Greeley and the
rest of the Democratic ticket throughout the campaign. Greeley's nomination had been accepted
by the Democrats for the promise it gave that his
election meant amnesty and reconciliation, and a
return of peace and good-will between the lately
warring sctions. "The Democracy," said Mr. Cox
from the stump, in justification of the seemingly
inconsistent policy of the party in adopting a life-
long antagonist as its candidate for President,
"should remember that, while in the heat and dust
of other strifes Horace Greeley has not spared
them, yet, in generous rivalry, he has endeavored
with them to pursue the paths of peace. If elected,
he will, under God, impress his administration
with sentiments mellowed by new associations,
with charities silvered over by advancing years,
and with a reverence for the hallowed traditions
of our early national career, made glorious by that
Democracy which has, in the vicissitudes of par-

ties, become his ally in that progress, and a sharer in the common blessings and glories which his administration would bestow. The fulness of those blessings will come to our country, because they will be inspired by the spirit of reconciliation."

But the country was not yet ready, nor was the time ripe, for the proposed change. As Mr. Cox himself, years after, expressed it: "Civil governments South were still disorganized; lawlessness South begat timidity North; the military spirit was still rife and rampant; and the issues of the war were still uppermost in men's minds." Reconciliation came, but years later.

During that memorable campaign an epidemic of the epizootic seized upon the equines of the country, almost completely paralyzing industries dependent upon the use of horses. Writing from the stump to a friend Mr. Cox made playful reference to this epidemic and the general tendency of campaign orators to charge all existing ills to the party in power. "I lay the horse distemper," wrote Mr. Cox, "to Grant. Run me as the anti-epizootic candidate-at-large!" On the heels of the disaster, with his habit of looking for the silver lining to every cloud, he again wrote: "One of my chief joys, not a 'crumb' but a whole festivity of delights was the friendships I had formed in my campaign over the State. My heart goes out 'at large' to them. I am thoroughly dazed," he added, "with the result in the country."

On the result of the election being known, Mr. Cox at once wrote to his successful competitor congratulating him on his victory. This letter brought from Mr. Tremain the following reply:

"Albany, Nov. 11th, 1872.

Hon. S. S. Cox.

My Dear Sir—Accept my thanks for the friendly
sentiments expressed in your valued favor of the
9th inst., which, I assure you, are heartily reciprocated on my part. When I went to Hart's studio
in   Florence   with   our   mutual   friend
and   your   warm   admirer,   Captain   Boyd,
to   view   your   excellent   bust,   little   did   I
dream that we should be opposing candidates for
the office of member of congress. But, as Mr. Lincoln truly observed, we are controlled by events
and circumstances. The recent canvass, earnest
and exciting as it has been, has left no rankling
wounds in my breast, nor any other than the kind-
liest personal feelings towards a gentleman so universally esteemed for his genial qualities as my
distinguished opponent. Rejoicing in the convic-
tion that our political antagonism has in no manner disturbed our personal relations, I have the
honor to be   Yours very truly,
                    Lyman Tremain."

Again Mr. Cox supposed his Congressional career to be forever closed. Again he awoke to find
his mistake—his services were too important to be
dispensed with.

CHAPTER XIII.

The second session of the Forty-second Congress, expiring March 4, 1873, to attend which Mr. Cox returned to the National Capital the month folowing the "Greeley fiasco," and his own defeat, short as it was, proved long enough to earn for that Congress unenviable notoriety. At this session the "back pay grab," as the law increasing the salary of a Congressman was popularly known, was placed upon the Federal statute book. Its most obnoxious feature, in the popular estimation, was its retro-active provision, dating the increase of salary two years back, to the beginning of the life of that Congress. The bill found in Mr. Cox a vigorous opponent. When, despite his efforts to compass its defeat, the bill became a law, Mr. Cox, refusing to profit therefrom, turned his share of the "steal" back into the public treasury. Mr. Cox felt keenly the infamy the "back pay" law had brought upon Congress. In a private letter written a few days after the adjournment he said: "I did all I knew in the last Congress, but it seems as if even the decent people in Congress are embalmed in a common infamy with the worst. This is discouraging. I spoke and voted against every phase of the 'Back Pay.'" Stating that he had returned his own portion to the United States treasury, "where it belonged," he added: "I didn't expect it when I served; I did not contract for it; I am happy in being rid of it. I am foolish enough to take a pride in having my old constituents, and my last fall's supporters, 400,000 good fellows, think I am not a mean person, nor a selfish legislator."

The Treasury receipt of the "grab" which he had spurned reads as follows:

"Treasury of the United States,
Washington, April 30, 1873.

Sir:—For $4,812, received as per yours of the 20th instant, I enclose duplicates of my certificate of deposit No. 7,960, on account of miscellaneous receipts received from John A. Hardenbergh, New York, as a deposit from Hon. S. S. Cox, being amount retroactive salary due him as member Forty-second Congress by act approved March 3, 1873.

Forty-eight hundred and twelve dollars original certificate of deposit sent to the Secretary of the Treasury. Very respectfully,

F. E. SPINNER,
Treasurer United States.

John A. Hardenbergh,
No. 112 Broadway, New York."

Many a member of that Congress returned home with the "back pay" in his pocket only to meet a frowning and unforgiving constituency. Many a member of that Congress, having pocketed the "back pay," dated his retirement to private life from that untoward event.

CHAPTER XIV.

Relieved, as he supposed, from public cares, possibly permanently, Mr. Cox had planned another trip abroad, when intelligence was brought him of the critical illness of his venerable father. Between father and son the bond of affection was exceedingly strong. He hurried to his father's bedside in Ohio and awaited the end. Writing of his father's death (which occurred May 18, 1873, at Zanesville), Mr. Cox says: "We buried my father on Tuesday. I can hardly realize the loss. It seems as if my life, private and public, had been mostly to please him." Owing to this affliction the projected tour abroad was abandoned. "I must," he wrote, "give up my foreign trip for the present. My mother cannot bear the idea of my being out of the country. So I am to be here for a time at least, if not for the year."

Events other than domestic affliction, as it proved, contributed to the postponement of the trip he had planned, for the summer, in the old world. The death of James Brooks, a distinguished Representative in Congress from the new Sixth District in New York, had created a vacancy in the new Congress, which Mr. Cox was asked to fill. Consenting to the use of his name, he was, in

the fall of 1873, elected by the large majority of
6,932. He took his seat at the opening of Congress, in December. Thus it happened that there
was no actual gap in his Congressional service
caused by his defeat in 1872. Mr. Blaine was
again, for the third consecutive Congress, in the
Speaker's chair, and General Butler, of Massachusetts, was the acknowledged leader on the floor of
the House. Two prominent political measures
before that Congress pushed by General Butler
with all his characteristic energy and determination were the Force Bill and the Civil Rights Bill.
The opposition to these measures was marshaled
by Samuel J. Randall and Samuel S. Cox. The Civil
Rights Bill was finally passed, but the dilatory
tactics of the minority, under the leadership of
Messrs. Cox and Randall, were fatal to the Force
Bill. Referring in after years to the struggle over
the Force Bill, Congressman Bland, of Missouri,
said: "Justice requires me to say that the strict
impartiality shown by Mr. Blaine, the Speaker,
during this memorable contest extorted the highest warmth of admiration from his political opponents. In that fight there were two great men
and great characters brought more prominently
than before into public notice. These were Samuel
J. Randall and Sullivan Cox. Mr. Cox," in Mr.
Bland's opinion, "was truly our Parnell , while
Mr. Randall in many characteristics was to us a
Gladstone."

To the next Congress, the Forty-fourth, Mr. Cox
was elected by a majority of 10,334. The opposition had long before abandoned all attempts to
secure his defeat. For the first time since his entry into Congress eighteen years before, when

James L. Orr was chosen speaker, he found himself in a House controlled by his party friends. The "tidal wave" of 1874 which had swept over the land, had overwhelmed the Republicans in the House and given the majority to the Democrats. Mr. Cox was prominently mentioned for Speaker. He had beeen named for that position by his party associates when a nomination was but an empty honor. Now that it meant an election, why should the nomination not be conferred upon him? He had enthusiastic supporters, particularly among Southern and Western members. It was a triangular contest. His rivals were Samuel J. Randall of Pennsylvania, and Michael C. Kerr of Indiana. The choice ultimately fell upon Mr. Kerr. By him Mr. Cox was appointed chairman of the Committee on Banking and Currency. The rooms of this committee were historic. They were the old "Speaker's rooms" attached to the former hall of Representatives, and so used during the first nine days of Mr. Cox's service in Congress before the removal to the present Representative Chamber. Here it was John Quincy Adams, stricken while in his seat as a representative from Massachusetts, was carried, and saw the "last of earth." A bust of the famous ex-President and champion of the right of petition, placed in the main room, commemorates the melancholy event. Before the Forty-fourth Congress had ended its existence, Mr. Cox's committee rooms became additionally historic; for here, by his courtesy, met the House special committee, charged with the duty of devising some peaceable way out of the controversy which then threatened to embroil the country in another civil war, far worse than the one from which it had but recently emerged—a controversy arising from an election for the Presidency. The first steps towards the formation of the electoral commission were here taken. Mr. Cox, although not a member of this special committee, gave the bill it presented his passive support. When it became evident that the outcome would be the seating of Mr. Hayes, whom he had opposed, instead of Mr. Tilden, whom he had supported, Mr. Cox, in a speech in the House on the Louisiana case, washed his hands of all responsibility for the consequences.

Mr. Cox refused, however, to join in factious opposition to a result he felt bound in good faith to accept. His voice and vote were given consistently for loyal acquiescence in what he believed to be a reversal of the popular verdict, but still a result reached through the forms of law.

Early in the first session of this Congress, Speaker Kerr was seized with a critical, and as it proved, fatal illness. Speaker Kerr designated Mr. Cox from time to time to fill the chair during his brief absences, until the Speaker being compelled to leave the Capital in search of health, the House on the 19th of June formally elected Mr. Cox Speaker pro tem. It was a Congress embracing on the one side such men as Randall, Holman, Hewitt, Mills Lamar, Tucker, Morrison, Watterson, Hurd, Springer, Knott and Blackburn, and on the other such men as Blaine, Garfield, Gen. Banks, Kelley, Kasson and Hoar—an unusual aggregation of luminous intellects. "Samuel S. Cox," said one of his eulogists, "shone in this galaxy like a star of the first magnitude."

While acting as the temporary Speaker of the

House, Mr. Cox was chosen delegate to the Democratic National Convention at St. Louis, and left
the chair to attend the convention. Milton Sayler,
of Ohio, was chosen to fill the chair during Mr.
Cox's absence. The implied understanding was
that on Mr. Cox's return from St. Louis, his substitute would relinquish the chair to its former occu-
pant. That this was not done was one of the in-
scrutabilities of public life—one, too, which Mr.
Sayler never ventured to explain. Meanwhile Mr.
Kerr lay dying at Alum Springs, West Virginia.
Thither hastened Mr. Cox, on the adjournment of
Congress, to the bedside of his friend. In a letter
to a friend, dated August 23, 1876, Mr. Cox wrote:
"I have been weary enough from service in Congress and from waiting at the sad ending of Mr.
Kerr's life." Mr. Cox's eulogy on Speaker Kerr,
on the re-assembling of Congress, matched his eulogy, sixteen years before, of Senator Stephen A.
Douglas. It made a marked impression upon the
House. Alexander H. Stephens, of Georgia, who
was lying ill at his room in the National Hotel—
the room in which Henry Clay died—and who supposed his own end near, sent for Mr. Cox. As,
accompanied by his nephew, Wm. V. Cox, he entered the sick room, the distinguished Georgian
said: "I have heard read your eloquent eulogy upon Speaker Kerr, and have sent for you to make a
request—a last request. Will you promise to deliver my eulogy when I am gone?" Mr. Cox's
prompt reply was: "I would like you to promise to
make my eulogy. You will be the survivor." The
Georgian did indeed rally, and lived years of use-
fulness. He crossed, however, to the other shore,
long before his genial friend.

Mr. Cox's election to the 45th Congress was practically unanimous. Only 41 votes were cast against him. The House was again Democratic, and Samuel J. Randall, who had at the second session of the Forty-fourth congress been chosen to succeed the lamented Kerr, was again the Speaker. Mr. Cox was placed at the head of the committee on the Tenth Census. It involved a work in which he took a peculiar pride. He was the author of the bill, which became a law March 3, 1879, providing for the census. In its perfectness no census the country had witnessed could compare with it. Except his legislative achievements in the Life Saving Service and for the Letter Carriers, nothing accomplished by Mr. Cox during his long service in Congress gave him greater pleasure, or was a source to him of greater pride than the Tenth Census. It stands to-day a monument to his painstaking, and his wonderful grasp of details.

He was re-elected in 1878 to the Forty-sixth Congress, and in 1880 to the Forty-seventh Congress by pluralities of 4,581 and 9,863 respectively. In the latter year, James A. Garfield, who had been his colleague for nearly two decades, was elected President, and with him was returned, for the first time in eight years, a Republican majority in the House of Representatives.

CHAPTER XV.

In the spring of 1881, soon after Garfield's inauguration, Mr. Cox, accommpanied by his wife, sailed for an extended trip abroad. The story of their travels he has told in two volumes entitled "Arctic Sunbeams, or from Broadway to the Bosphorus, by way of the North Cape," and "Orient Sunbeams, or from the Porte to the Pyramids, by way of Palestine." Together these titles summarize their eight months' journey. They "comprehend a travel in which some twelve different nationalities are involved; and each and all of them in process of mutation, politically, socially, morally and religiously." Some of the scenes in the land of the Turk and in the far east were revisited after a lapse of thirty years

He halted for a brief rest in London, and while there attended a session of Parliament, and the funeral of Lord Beaconsfield. To a friend at home he writes of these events and the impressions they made as follows:

"London, Eng., April, 26, 1881.

"My Dear Friend: I am enjoined from doing any sort of work—my wife being the judex—so I do not, cannot give you a description, as I hoped, of the Parliament, whose sessions began last night after the Easter recess. Having been lucky in get-

NORTH CAPE GROUP.

S. S. Cox, Wife and Guide—1881.

ting a front seat, I had an opportunity of looking
down on the scene, and heard and saw the opening
of the performance in behalf of the Irish people.
The morning papers are full of the debate, and you
will doubtless have abstracts of it by telegraph.
When the House met, at half-past 3 o'clock, there
was but one of the Cabinet on the government
benches. Soon the hall filled, and some five hundred members were on hand.   Mr. Bright was
there, looking none the worse for the twelve years
since I last saw him. Mr. Gladstone did not come
in till the member from the University of Dublin
(Mr. Gibson) was nearly done his trenchant and
dashing speech for the landlords. The debate came
near falling through, owing to some weary and peculiar tactics. In fact, a motion to adjourn it was
made. This aroused Gladstone, and he and Northcote, the Tory leader, had a tussle ,and some others
of less note grappled. The debate went on until
Mr. Speaker Bland went out for tea, and I adjourned myself to look after the pictures in the corridors. There was not much interest manifested
until a young inchoate Duke of Portsmouth (Lord
Lymington) took the floor.   He spoke well, and
with sympathy for Ireland and her grievances. The
debate was kept up till after midnight, and was
resumed last night, when I was present again, Mrs.
Cox being in the box of Mrs. Speaker Bland, and
shut in from observation, though able to hear and
see all below.

"It is difficult for gentlemen to obtain access to
the Commons, and still more so for the ladies.
Thanks to the courtesy of the Speaker, we had
double advantages. My seat was in the Speaker's

gallery, front row, and facing the Speaker and looking down upon the seats.

"Thirty years ago I attended Parliament, but it was in the old St. Stephen's, full of Parliamentary traditions. The present chamber is in the New House. It will not hold one-fifth of the people who can assemble in our lower House. It is well lighted somewhat as our House is, from the ceiling with gaslights above colored glass squares. There are stained windows on either side, with diamond panes, colored red and green, and galleries all around and above the chamber. These galleries on either side are two seats deep, for embassadors and other privileged people, and at either end seats for the reporter over the Speakers' chair, and for those admitted by the Speaker's card. The seats are ample. They are of green leather, but, strange to say, only one seat for a half-dozen Peers. The reporters come and go every hour as the big bell in the tower near by dings out the time. The Speaker's seat is under an oaken canopy. In front of his chair are the seats and desks of the clerks (or clarks), and still in front of that desk is the "table," on which are some volumes, and on either side two reddish boxes, one holding the printed oath, and the other the affirmation, and still further, at the end of this table, is the mace, golden or gilt, as old as the Stuarts, and more potential now then the "bauble" of Cromwell's day. It is the emblem of the authority of the House, and, like our own mace, is in its place when the House is in session. It has a golden crown at one end—unlike our mace, which has a silver eagle at the end of a diminutive barber pole.

"On either side of the table sit the prominent members. To the right of the Speaker and in front is the Treasury Bench, on which sit, or repose on the small of their backs, and with hats on, generally, the members of the Cabinet when the House is in session. Behind this bench of notables are the immediate supporters of the government. Opposite are their opponents, led by Sir Stafford Northcote. There is an aisle crossing the house, and below, or remote from the table (below the "gangway" as it is called), sit the Independent, Radical, and Irish members. I have not time for a photograph of the scene presented when the house is in session, but I have had the privilege of hearing two grand debates—one on the Irish bill, and the other on the Bradlaugh case.

"In the latter affair there was a scene. The like has not happened in our Congress, certainly not since the war. A member-elect, well authenticated, appears and tenders himself to take the oath. It is objected that he is an atheist. He still insists that the oath will bind. His objectors contend that his swearing is profanation. He responds: 'I comply with the law. The conscience involved is not yours, but my own.' He is rejected on a division. Gladstone, Bright, et al., are discomfited. Cheers resound; so that you might hear them across the Thames. Still Bradlaugh insists on his seat. He is removed by a pretense of force. He escapes to the table; is again removed by an old sergeant-at-arms dressed in tights, shoe-buckles, sword and wig, but again returns from the bar to the table. In the melee the House adjourns. He appears next day and goes through

the same performance. The Ministry are to pon-
der the problem. The result will be, as I prophesy,
that a general law, exempting all who cannot take
the oath required by the existing law, will be
passed.

"It is not for an American to laugh at this proceeding. England was slow to remove Catholic
and Jewish disabilities, so that these religionists
should sit in Parliament without tests. England
has removed from her statutes dozens of oaths required in custom house and courts. She has sub-
stituted declarations or affirmations instead; but
in the United States Congress the anomaly
remains that Garfield, Bragg, Ewing, and all who
sustained the Government during the rebellion
must take the "ironclad" oath, while the rebel is
exempt, and only swears to the Constitution! Time
and again I have, with others, tried to remove this
absurdity, but in vain. The time will come, however, when oath-taking will become such a profanation, by its levity, familiarity and frequency,
that it will be discarded altogether. Then we shall
all be Quakers, on that point at least.

"The debate on the Irish Land bill went on last
night. Many ordinary speakers spoke. The Attorney General of Ireland closed the debate. Mr.
Parnell will speak next week, and I hope to hear
him.

"The debate, thus far, leaves upon my mind this
impression, that while the government means to
redress Irish tenant grievances, and has, by cun-
ning and just devices, endeavored to ameliorate
the hardships of rents and the trouble of insecure
tenure, that no absolute and lasting cure can be
realized for the unhappy isle until self-government

is accorded to the Irish people. Call it separation, or Home Rule, or what you please, the remedies proposed, even by the best friends of Ireland, seem to me like attempting to cure the pimples upon the cuticle when the disorder is so chronic and deep-seated as to require heroic remedy.

"But one more allusion to Ireland. Scarcely five days ago, in a smooth sea and on a sunny day, we passed around Cape Clear and inside of Fastnet rock and lighthouse. The mountains arose upon our vision, and the rocky shore left its impression —a sad one. Since then we have seen the old town of Chester, and the residence of the Duke of West-minster near by—Eton Hall—his paddocks and horses, mares and colts, including Doncaster, the chestnut winner of the Derby and the splendor of horses! Since then we have re-visited St. Paul's, Westminster Hall and the Abbey, the great mu-seum, the Courts of Queen's Bench, Exchequer and Common Pleas, and traveled over and under ground throughout this vast metropolis. How much we have seen in five days!

"But had any one said to me, before I left the dock at the foot of West Houston street, and even after the faint impression came of the rolling and rocking "cradle of the deep," that within a fort-night I should attend the funeral of Benjamin Disraeli, Earl of Beaconsfield, I should have thought him or her crazy! But it is accomplished.

"A passenger came aboard our vessel at Queens-town, and informed us upon Thursday of Disraeli's decease the preceding Thursday. On the succeed-ing Tuesday we were at Hughenden, a sweet, beautiful manor of hill and dale in Buckingham-shire, to observe the obsequies to the political wizard of the century. This marvel of statesman and author, this strange genius of a proscribed race, was generously and nobly entombed in a rural spot by the loving hands of a tenantry who seemed to admire and respect him. He was entombed within the same vault, under a Christian church, where his Christian wife had been buried, and amid a throng of authors, statesmen, and nobles, who filled the manorial grounds on that pleasant April day, to do the dead statesman homage.

"One incident happened to us—a lucky one. Our tickets being first-class—as sovereigns should ever be—led us to the carriage in the train to High Wycombe (the depot for Hughenden), next to that of the princes of the realm! The Prince, and heir apparent, and his two brothers, were the recipients of great attention. At every stop of the train scores of good people, being advised by the wire, were awaiting the royal advent, so that we saw the loyal demonstrations en route, made in honor of the three nice young men—handsome and well behaved—whom it is the pleasure of England to keep as the figures at the head of affairs, which they do not in any wise control.

"But more of this hereafter. The jaunt was truly a relief after a long voyage. The blossoms and hedges, fields and trees, the greenery and the sunshine, were all enchanting, so that our first week's experience on this island has been one of recreation tempered with novelty and instruction.

"Sincerely yours,
"S. S. Cox."

In a letter to an American friend dated Beirut,

Syria, October 4, 1881, en route to Jerusalem, Mr. Cox wrote, of Broussa:

"We began by an inroad upon Broussa. It is South of Constantinople and across the Sea of Marmora. Our experience there, with its silks and caravans, its fruits and fountains, its baths for health and its sepulchres of the founders of the Ottoman Empire—of which it was the first capital—would form a chapter of romance. One thing our trip to Broussa did; it inducted us into the mysteries of Asian land travel. In Constantinople we had met many peculiar types of men and many muffled forms of women, as well as of society. They were hard to understand. In our vexation we exclaimed:

> " 'There are spirts, clad in veils,
>   Woman by man is never seen!
> All our deep conniving fails
>   To remove this shadowy screen!'

"But when we broke into the unreserve of the interior and its mixed travel—by steamer and en route—the muffler dropped. In this trip we were associated with an Irish solicitor from Dublin, and his amiable daughter. You may well believe that there was a richer indigo in the azure of the sea, a new sparkle to the lively waters of Broussa, and fresh glows to Mount Olympus, at morning and evening, as we talked, and smoked beneath its roseate hues and cool shadows, rare fun when we stopped in our Druidical groves of oaks, half way, amidst camels and donkeys, turkeys and chickens; other wonders in the capacities and oddities of the animals which carried the cocoons and other burdens to the city from the sea; rare attraction

in the strange, brown faces of the turbaned beg-
gars we met, and alluring beauties in the broad
vales made fruitful by streams from Olympus, and
which spread beneath us, from our hotel balcony,
like the vega of Grenada, as seen from the walls
of the Alhambra! Good company does so much
in travel. This was our first really hot day, and its
discomforts need the mitigation of society. Since
we began, at the North Cape in the Arctics, we
have had no such calorific experience. I began to
long for a little one-story thermometer with nothing but zeroes all ranged in a row. But the ranges
of Olympus soon became refreshing—for had we
not, along with them, the pleasant society of our
witty Irish lawyer and his fair daughter?"

This will interest the ladies:

"After my wife had made the promenade of the
silk bazaars—with much cost and instruction—we
called on a merchant at his house to see some 'por-
tieres' ordered by a friend in Constantinople. He,
with his wife and mother, received us. The latter
sat at her embroidery frame; and when my wife
exp ressed a desire to see how the work was accomplished so beautifully, she smilingly resumed her
labor. A fine steel crochet needle is held in the
right hand close to the face of the velvet, while
the bobbin of silk or gold thread is held in the left
hand under the frame on which the velvet is
stretched. The needle is pushed through the material and catches up the thread underneath, with
great regularity and rapidity, in the hands of a
skillful worker. This is the way the Damasucs
fabrics are adorned."

In the same letter he describes the view from

Mount Olympus: "Looking off from the highest of its heights—5,500 feet to the snowy crest—how small the donkeys seem, even when loaded! The Lombardy poplars and cypresses not as big as thistle needles. The flat dark roofs of the city are leveled with the green in which they are embowered; and the domes of the mosques—and they count here by hundreds—look like little bulbous toys. The old plain trees, some of which measure 24 feet round, ever honored in the East, as well for their shade as for some genius of the past, look like little shrubs, even under a magnifying glass. From the height of the classic mount, the sea of Marmora and the Euxine, the minarets of Constantinople, the Bosphorus and Dardanelles, and the tall grandeur of Mt. Ida and its range, and the rivers, lakes, green belts and broad savannas of the valleys, appear in splendid array. It is a grand observatory for a superb panorama!"

Continuing his picture of Oriental life, Mr. Cox writes: "Our trip to Broussa was a relief, after our long stay on the Bosphorus. One drawback to our return was the early rising. At three A. M. we are in our carriage, and passing market people coming to the city, with their beasts laden with grapes and other product of the happy valley. Long lines of camels, dressed in red ornaments, pass us in the gloaming. They seems monsters of the prehistoric epoch. We find them at daylight, under the oak trees of the half-way grove, resting after their nightly journey from the seaside. Did you ever notice how strangely the camel is built, and how oddly he moves? Like a pompous ante-diluvian he treads over the roughest stones, and in the softest sands. The legs on one side move at

and with the same time; and then with a gawky
swing of the shoulder and haunch of the other side
so as to keep up the odd locomotion.   He seems to
be put together on springs or loose hinges; but as
with the elephant, you may get accustomed to his
ungainly gait." Mr. Cox was becoming acquainted
with the beasts concerning which he wrote so
learnedly in a school-boy composition!

"As we start afresh," the letter continues, "the
clouds which hung half-way over Olympus and its
range floated down into the valley. From the
sea hills we look back upon a roseate lake. It is
no mirage but an illumination of the clouds below,
out of which the brown mountain tops rise, like
enchanted isles. At noon, we reach out seaport,
whence we sail, in five hours over the blue Marmora, and have a richly colored picture never to be
seen too frequently, of the beauteous mosques and
mirarets, the walls and towers of Stamboul. What
we saw and heard on our route and on the boat—
full of all the oddest costumes and people— it
would take a volume to tell. We are now but one
day's sail of Jaffa. Thence we go to the main ob-
jective point since we left the setless sun in the
Arctic ocean, Jerusalem!"

A   private not penned hurriedly at Ephesus, September 9, 1891, says: "I send you
a note for Samuel—as it were, an epistle
from Ephesus.   It is an odd place, and
we are safe from brigands, having returned from
our wonderful ride and walk amidst those stupen-
dous ruins.   Ruins! magnificent in their beauty,
and giving at every turn the glimpses of the ta
kala you and I used to read of. Mrs. Cox is

finishing her lunch on mountain grapes; and she got an appetite, for her mule never failed to use his heels at every fly—until Mrs. C., seated astride, ran canals of sweat. But she is safe. This," he adds, "is a picture of the mule"—accompanying the words with a graphic pen and ink sketch of the oriental beast of burden.

They were near Tarsus, the birthplace of Paul, Mr. Cox says, when a few days later they were shocked by the news, in a telegram from the consul at Smyrna, of the assassination of President Garfield.

CHAPTER XVI.

By the middle of November they were back in London, preparing for their return homeward. "I am halted in London for a time—say a day—" he wrote, "and so I look about a little before we leave. What a look-about it is, since we left here in May! What a circle of felicity! What a round of pleasant observation and experience! How much have we done, written, and seen!" The first of December found him back in New York, ready for his duties in the new congress, about to assemble. That body came together under the shadow of the crime of the assassin which had plunged the nation in mourning. President Garfield had been succeeded by President Arthur. The House, again Republican, chose J. W. Keifer of Ohio as its speaker. Mr. Cox returned to his native land to find that still other changes in the political kaleidescope had occurred during his absence. Senators Conkling and Platt, of his adopted state, had thrown up their commissions, and, after a contest that threatened the disruption of their party, had been succeeded by others. Those were troublous times in American politics. They gave a stimulus, however, to the civil service reform movement throughout the country, and that movement, designed to soften the asperities of politics, found in Mr. Cox a cordial supporter. "The assassination of General Garfield," according to Mr. Cox, "gave impulse to the civil service reform bill. The evils which its provisions were intended to remedy are acknowledged by most men of judgment and experience in public affairs."

In the election of 1882 Mr. Cox's majority for Representative in the forty-eighth congress was 11,317. The same election swept Grover Cleveland and David B. Hill into the chairs of Governor and Lieutenant-Governor of New York by pluralities close upon 200,000. It was the answer of the people to "Federal interference" in the politics of the state. The return swing of the pendulum restored the Democracy to control of the House of Representatives. A Kentuckian, John G. Carlisle, was chosen speaker and for three successive congresses held the gavel. Mr. Cox, who had already succeeded in placing upon the statute books important and beneficent laws relating to the life saving service and the letter carriers, in this congress rendered a hardly less valuable service in urging the passage of a bill restricting the importation of foreign contract labor.

Mr. Cox's next election to congress, in 1884, was synchronous with the election of a Democrat to the Presidency. It was the first coincidence of the kind since his first election to congress, twenty-eight years before. "Thank God,' 'he wrote to an old friend, soon after Cleveland's inauguration, "we have lived to see, in measureless content, the old party of our love in the ascendant."

CHAPTER XVII

President Cleveland tendered to Mr. Cox the mission to Turkey. It was accepted. The Senate, on the nomination reaching that body, at once confirmed it, without the usual reference to a committee—a compliment rarely extended any nominee who is not or has not been a Senator.

ᐧ Soon afterward, to an old personal friend, Mr. Cox wrote:

"You and others wonder why I leave a prominent place in Congress for a mission to Turkey. Well, first, many things tended to make me feel that I lagged somewhat superfluous on that stage. My faculties and qualities, such as they are, never were in better condition; and the equipment of a quarter of a century for the work of debate, of committee, and legislation was as nearly rounded on every theme as a sturdy and stern sense of duty could make it.

"But the advent of new men, as is natural, has pushed me to the rear, so that while abreast if not ahead of my party on most themes, I was not even able to command my old and favorite foreign committeeship, or my former Smithsonian regentship, always accorded to me even by Republicans. Beside so much work in Congress and no result—the rolling, rolling, rolling up of the stones which rolled down 'with a resulting bound,' the foolish modes and rules, which few in control cared to correct—all this and more made me think it was high time to seek the land of sleep and rest on the banks of the Bosphorus. Besides, without the intervention of any one, save a kind word from a Missouri and Tennessee member, this oriental compliment came to me directly, gracefully, and spontaneously from the President alone. The Senate gave me confirmation quite complimentary without referring it; and these facts, together with my pleasant reminiscences of the happy days spent in the olden capital of the Greek Empire (upon two visits to the Orient), were predominating reasons why I propose to have a respite in the land of the Ottoman."

It was not, however, without some hesitation that Mr. Cox reached his decision. "I am half inclined at times to give it up," he wrote from Washington shortly after his appointment, "but for this 'demnition grind' in Congress." And again: "It seems pretty hard to go away from this country, but you do not know what a relief it is to be removed from this everlasting grind of Congress, that produces so little." Nearly thirty years of this "grind" had not been without its effect—the brain was weary and called for rest.

In the midst of his preparations for embarking for his new field of duty, he was summoned to the bedside of his dying mother. From his old home, Zanesville, Ohio, on April 4, the day following her death, he writes: "I was not unaware of my mother's illness and its probable termination. I was summoned just in time to receive her conscious

blessing, and it was a great comfort to her and to
her son. We bury her body to-morrow. If I go
abroad I do not have the 'lengthening chain' of
filial fear ever dragging me homeward—that is
one of the sad compensations." In a later letter,
again referring to his mother's death: "It is a hard
blow for me, as I was attached to my mother beyond all thought or words to tell."

Meanwhile he was engrossed in the preparation
for the printers of his volume, "Three Decades of
Federal Legislation," an elaborate review of the
times of which he had been a conspicuous part.
Anxiety to complete this work before sailing postponed for a time his departure for Turkey. Meanwhile, too, reluctance to part with a Representative who had served them so faithfully and so long
had led to a powerful pressure on the part of Mr.
Cox's constituents to induce him to decline the
mission and remain in Congress. His longing for
the rest, so much needed, decided him. Under
date of May 15, in a letter to an old friend, he
wrote:

"My opinion is that I have got to go. Not as a
galley slave to his work, but I ought to go, for
there is nothing worth being in Congress for now
except a scramble, and worry, and wrangle, and
jangle, and tangle. Tell your friend that if he
had only served twenty-five years in Congress, as
I have, he would know what it is to be among the
heathen, and seek even a fresh, beautiful, anno-
tated edition of heathen. * * * It is a curious,
strange experience for me that after I had reached
my acme, and the ladder was all golden and beautiful like that of Jacob's, somebody jerks it from

under me, and I have got to float away serenely
into an Oriental haven for Democratic virtue."

On the evening of the 8th of June the new Minister to Turkey was tendered at the Hoffman
House in New York, a farewell banquet. Gathered around the table were the representative
men of the metropolis, including ex-Mayors Cooper
and Ely, Roswell P. Flower, Congressmen Dors-
heimer and Hewitt, Everett P. Wheeler, Edward
Kearney, Herman Oelrichs, Judges Lawrence, In-
graham, Van Brunt, Barrett, Gildersleeve and
Truax, Joseph J. O'Donohue and others. Abram
S. Hewitt, afterwards Mayor of New York, presided and made the opening speech. Also present
was the Turkish Minister, Tewfik Pasha. In the
course of his brilliant speech, in reply to the toast,
"Our Guest," Mr. Cox said:

"Adequately to acknowledge this climax of personal honor, one should have thoughts impearled
upon vestments of Oriental light and imagery
sweeter than the roses of Cashmere. The charm,
the mis-en-scene, and the company give to this
night's entertainment something of that bewilder-
ing enchantment which one might enjoy for a
thousand and one nights and never surfeit. Could
I have the melody of the Persian nightingale who
sang his love to the rose, in the tender idyls of
Hafiz; could I draw from the depths of the Brah-
minical philosophy, whose generalizations are the
fountain of our Emersonian transcendentalism;
could I evoke from nature her hidden poetry and
primal meaning, I could perhaps answer for this
banquet of affectionate regard given to one whose
life has been a life of labor, not untinged with
some romance.

"Coleridge has said that, in pursuing his muse, he had his own exceeding great reward. It is not always so in pursuing politics. But to me, politics as I have endeavored to follow them in their fickleness, have been for a quarter of a century a great source of enjoyment and a great incentive to practical exertion.

"Upon an occasion like this, surely I may be allowed to improve it by referring to some points—even points of the compass—which are somewhat personal. I am of the west—of Ohio—not the greater, but still the great west. For some reasons, mostly domestic, a reflux wave brought me to the east. After two generations from some tall tower or Trinity steeple, I can overlook the ancestral congressional district along the shores of east Jersey. Perhaps this will account for my tender relations to the life-saving service, and my inherited tendencies toward congressional pursuits.

"Although from the west, and having a pseudonym which indicates only a descending orb, I am here to-night as the recipient of an oriental ovation, whose oriental magnificence is equaled only by its oriental significance.

*   *   *   *   *

"There is something still more attractive than diplomacy or commerce in the Orient. It is the land of a deep blue sky whose concave is set thick with stars. The eastern sky, with its marvelous purity and beauty, early developed the spirtualities of human nature. If it also called out sensualism there was a compensation beyond all expression, in the purity of its thought and in the elevation and unity of its worship. When the

Koran prohibited men from drinking wine, but gave full privileges of water and coffee, the Paynim voluptuary was not altogether enshrined among the beatitudes of the demi-gods. Epicurus may now and then sit with his Chibouk cross-legged on the banks of the Bosphorus as dreamful as any German metaphysician. But beyond and above all, from the land of India, Arabia, Egypt, and even from the desert places, came the religions which have made mankind gaze hopefully and earnestly into the unseen world. Whether Hebrew, Christian, Brahmin, Mohammedan, the worshipper bowed only to the one Invisible Supreme being. Faith in each lifted man by a higher code of ethics into a higher plane of thought. The religions which drew from the Holy of Holies and from the infinite deeps which environ the eastern sky had and have an inspiration that gives solace to the suffering and dying of every land, and enlightens our last moments with the hope that takes from the grave its sting and from death its victory.

"It is a difficult thing to give up old associations and to form new habitudes. Since I have resigned my place at the capitol I have wandered about through its corridors and halls like the ghost of my departed self. Almost every image seemed to wave "adieu." Even the old hall in which I first served to the new chamber wherein I made the first speech, echoed with personal thoughts and pleasant associations. But there must be an end of all occupations, and, for a wholesome, thorough living, there must be more or less of change. We must sometimes fold our tents like the Arabs. No longer for me the speaker's gavel, with its "rap," "rap," "rap," no longer the fierce debate and the loud applause "which made ambition virtue." No longer the five minutes debate upon a sixpenny appropriation. No longer the previous question, that dynamite which destroys so much of parliamentary power. "Othello's occupation's gone"—gone to the Hellespont."

Accompanied by his wife, he sailed, in June, on the Gallia, but they were several days delayed in their voyage by a misadventure—their ship having broken her shaft in mid-ocean. The first of August found him at his post, in the Turkish capital. Under date Constantinople, August 9, 1885, he wrote to a friend he had left behind: "For fear that you are anxious about us—know that we are, and that we are here! at our post. In vain the Gallia broke her shaft—it fell hurtless and we moved on to our goal. Ten days ago we saluted the Bosphorus, and were met by our flag and our friends. It was a renewal of old times; and yet it is a sort of exile. But still what a rest is here! The laps of the waters almost at the foundation of our house and home at Therapia—an hour above the city—makes music for us, and its breezes blow health from Caucasus. I am already improving. My health was below par; now it is, say, 65 per cent. above, and going up. Is this caused by freedom in Turkey— from all political worry?"

"Twice before my appointment as Envoy to Turkey," he wrote, in introducing the story of his official life at the Turkish capital, "I had been to Constantinople. On the first occasion in 1851, in life's

U. S. LEGATION, THERAPIA, ON THE BOSPHORUS.

(U. S. Minister Cox seen on balcony).

morning, we sailed thither in a French steamer up the Mediterranean. On the second occasion, thirty years afterward, we traveled to Turkey from the Land of the Midnight Sun. Unlike our first voyage, the difficulty in reaching Constantinople in 1885 was at the start. There were strong bonds which attached us to our home and city, and myself to long-accustomed Congressional life. It was as difficult to leave the harbor as it was to obtain the consent of constituents. Then, in mid-ocean, among the icebergs of Newfoundland, the steamer of the Cunard Line—the Gallia—broke her shaft as if reluctant to bear us away. Our ocean voyage was nearly a score of days when it should have been but half of that time. Between Washington and Constantinople forty days are allowed the Minister. Every one of these days was occupied, partly by the misadventure to the Gallia, and partly by reason of the earthly rest at London, Paris, Munich, Vienna and Buda-Pesth." At last they found themselves on the wharf of the Turkish capital.

As they landed they were met by the Sultan's Foreign Minister, Assim Pasha, and bidden a cordial welcome. The residence assigned to the United States minister was beautifully situated at Therapia, on the banks of the Bosphorus, a few miles above Constantinople. "The home in which we are esconced (at Therapia) for the summer," he wrote, "has one window looking out upon terraces upward three hundred feet. This garden is leafy and green in the moist warmth from the waves below. Its roses, magnolias, heliotropes, jessamine, Virginia and other creepers make an exquisite picture.   Out of another window there is a prospect of the hills of Buyukdere—one of the beautiful villages of the upper Bosphorus, where my colleagues of many Legations reside.   The clappotage of the waves against the stone quay almost under our window lulls one into a poetic swoon." The contrast between this and the life in Congress, with all its whirl of excitement and worry, was doubtless most refreshing to a man who had had almost three decades of the latter.

The sad news of the death of Gen. Grant was nearly a month traveling to Constantinople.   It was made the occasion of a meeting of the American colony to do honor to the hero's memory. "As General Grant," wrote Mr. Cox, in his account thereof, "was from my native state of Ohio—the home of the Shermans, Sheridans, McPhersons and McCooks of our conflict—it was my special pride to be known in Congress as his devoted friend, perhaps next in that body to Mr. Washburn of Illinois.   It was my privilege, just before the close of the war, when Grant's army was before Petersburg and Richmond, to be the General's guest; and just before leaving Congress I had the honor to introduce the first bill to reinstate him in the army.   This relation gave me the privilege to speak with emphasis of the eventful life which had just closed, and in which cloud and sunshine so strangely alternated."   No sublimer eulogy of the immortal Grant came from any lips than that which Mr. Cox gave to the American colony on the far off shores of the Bosphorus.

In a letter to an American friend under date Constantinople, September 10, 1885, Mr. Cox thus

pleasantly refers to his new book and his life at
Therapia:

"The book ('Three Decades') is out (1 Sept.).   It
pleases me.   It was close, hard, overtasking work.
I wonder how I survived it; and yet I look now
calmly in the mid-September at the white pinions
of the bluest blue sea, ever God-closed, the Euxine, as it rolls its murmurs to our very door or
quai, under tunical breezes that have made roseate our Caucasian ancestral cheek! For the winds
blow over the blue from the Caucasian peaks. Yet
there is quarantine here—four days—why? Because poor Spain suffers—and therefore the
mouth of the Black Sea is shut by a previous
question raised in Hidalgo-land."

Musing, in the same letter, on a situation in
home politics, it occurs to him that "after a man
passes twenty-five years in Congress unscathed;
and goes over the ocean on a broken shaft in sev-
enteen days; and meets the Sultan with a Sublime
Porte; and can sail in the United States yacht
launch to the Cyaraean rocks, and go through like
one Jason of the Argo; and never lose a 'fo' top
sail,' or bilge a marlingspike—he is fit to give
advice discreetly to a new Administration.   But,"
he asks," will they take it?" The diplomat's divorce
from American politics was not yet absolute. The
dolce far niente influence of Eastern life had not
yet its perfect work.   "Here I am," he writes a
few days later, "from the arena of politics ever so
aloof!   It is a sensation."   In the following he
describes to an American friend a street spectacle
on the occasion of the Sultan's appearance in public:

"Constantinople, Sept. 21, '85.

I went down to see the Sultan yesterday by special invitation to all the Ministers. He "received" or would, at the opening of "Bairum," a festal occasion of five days. Business suspended and things Sabbath-like among the pious people. The truth is, the Turks are a religious people, more so than the Armenians or Greeks or —us! Well, half way down (got up at 5 A. M.) met a despatch boat with letter from Munio Pasha. (You know Munio? No? Why, he's head chamberlain!) to say that the business of State so pressing that reception postponed. There is a threatened war between Bulgaria and Turkey, and the palace was in a pother. Nevertheless, Mrs. Cox being in full dress, and myself also, concluded to land and see the Sultan come out of the mosque and palace en route to his kiosk at Yildiz. Directly, say an hour, while we waited at a guard house, about one hundred and fifty Beys, Agas, Effendis and Pachas came along, all gilt, in their private carriages; then came soldiers and soldiers; at last a four-horse gilded coach, with two pachas in front —Osman and another I couldn't recognize—and the Sultan behind in the back seat. Then along pell-mell, higglety-pigglety, on horseback, the gayest circus riders you ever saw, full jump, mostly grey barbs and splendid riders. Some of the head Pachas colored as ebony. Well, we saw it all, and came home happy to listen to the music of the murmurous Bos!"

His partiality for the solar orb manifested itself on every occasion. His sobriquet "Sunset" was conferred upon him, as has been shown, because

MEHEMET - COX'S FAITHFUL KAVASS (GUARD).
While U. S. Minister in Turkey.

of his enthusiastic description of a sunset, while an Ohio editor, and because the initials of his name corresponded to it. The titles chosen for his books of travel, "Winter Sunbeams," "Arctic "Sunbeams," "Orient Sunbeams," as well as the genial glow of his own nature, further illustrated this characteristic. On the shores of the Bos-phorus he found sweet content. For, in a letter dated October 7, he exclaims: "I have had sun-beams, and beams and beams, until heaven is dark with glory here. This is the land of light and romance."

The new Minister's first formal reception by his Sultanic Majesty was set down for a certain day by the First Chamberlain, and then   postponed. The reasons for the postponement are curious and interesting.   The United States Minister was re-quired to furnish the Turkish Minister of Foreign Affairs with a copy, in both French and English, of the speech he was to make to the Sultan on the occasion of his presentation to that august per-sonage. "I had more difficulty," confessed   Mr. Cox, "about the French than the English portion." It was the French translation that created the mare's nest.   One sentence in our tongue read in part: "The United States would not, if they could, **depart** from the invariable policy which   forbids all entanglements in foreign affairs."   Although the speech caused our Minister, as he confesses, "barrels of perspiration," yet one word   in   the translation became almost a casus belli.   It was the word "entanglements." Mr. Cox's   amusing account follows:

"I had in my mind Washington's Farewell Ad-dress as to all foreign entangling alliances. There is no synonym in French except the word which, after much research, I had selected. When my French speech was scanned by the leading linguist in the Foreign Office in Stamboul, assisted by a cohort of polyglots, they lit upon the word 'enchevetrement.' What could it mean? Was it an American torpedo, or polysyllabic dynamite for the overthrow of the dynasty? Whatever might have been their opinion of the explosive and perilous composition, I was satisfied, from intimations, that the delay of my reception for some days was occasioned by the confusion incident to this terrible six-footed word. The speech was finally accepted in the sense in which it was intended, and thenceforth the respective countries never ceased to dwell together in diplomatic unity."

The eagerly awaited reception by this Oriental monarch, Abdul Hamid II., came at last, and was on a scale of splendor and ceremony to which occidental nations are entire strangers. "As we are ushered into the presence," says Mr. Cox in describing the scene, "we make three bows—one at the door on entering, the second half way, and the last when we stop a few feet from his person. We do not bow as low as the Turkish Ministers, but we do our best!"He had seen the Sultan twice before—first in 1851, when His Majesty was a boy of eleven, in company with his father; next in 1881, when Mr. Cox was presented to His Majesty by General Wallace, then our Minister to Turkey. "I confess," he writes, "before I had an idea of being here in any but a tourist's capacity, to an enthusiasm for this monarch. He is a king every inch, and without any dramatic ostentation. He

deserves great regard for his rare ability. He is
his own adviser. Amid his troubles and cares,
and with the populations of the divers religions
and races, which he must reconcile to rule, he is
not unworthy of the fame of Abdul Medjid, whose
memory is to me a part of my earliest association
with the city of Constantinople."

The coming to Constantinople of a new American Minister to a neighboring kingdom, en route
to his post, during the November following is thus
duly chronicled: "Our Minister to Greece has just
arrived, and I owe him a devoir. He is ahead of
me, at first sight, in the diplomatic game. He is
Minister to Roumania, Servia, and Greece.   He
holds three kings and three queens. That is his
pot—or flush, or what is it? But I hold one king
(Abdul Hamid II.) and all the rest of the pack
queens!"

In a New Year's greeting "from the Salt Seas
of Marmora and Euxine to the salt—the 'old salts'
—of Onondaga," he confesses that he "felt a little
funny when Congress met and I not there. But,"
he added, "it is a good time here to observe impartially the doings and sayings." Evidently the
"sunbeams" were not oppressive on New Year's,
for he writes: "The winter here is damp bad—
worse than Washington. Summers superb.   I
have been indoors for a week with rheumatix; but
about well. Am writing despatches and reading
up. Such a reader you never saw."

With improved weather the barometer of the
American Minister's humor went up also, as is
evident from the following sunburst:

"Constantinople, Jan'y 18, '86.
"Mrs. Cox is enchanted with the magic of this

realm. I guess and persuade myself I am the magic!! When the magic goes to N. Y., expect the 'Excellenzia'—as they call her—also. It nearly kills me to be 'called' at all; but little Samuel was! But now here all call me—'Excellency,' 'Son' 'Excellency!' etc., and it is too much!! Overdose! It hurts me in'nerds. However, it is polite; and I reciprocate, and believe all to be excellent, prima facie, which is a violent presumption. The weather is getting better, and so am I. It was horrible and wet; but Egypt is not quite such a cynosure, or Greece, as it was for delight and refuge. * * * The papers say I play the flute. Laws! How the journals lie!"

That Minister Cox had fully recovered from his "rheumatix" before January had gone by, is evident from the following private note in which, among other things, he describes his experience in teaching a Turk what he knew about farming:

"U. S. Legation,
"Constantinople, Jan. 26, '86.
"I am here at work and again on my pedal extremities, using them more than the other extremity. The weather has come like ethereal mildness, gentle spring. Now the festive peasant, etc., etc. which reminds me of my magnificent agricultural experiment the other day. Mrs. Cox drove me out —I mean a coachman did—upon the grand hills and unto the superb valleys that suburb this city. There are, be it known, fine farms, and gardens plenty upon these hills. From them one may overlook Asia, and almost Africa. Well, we saw a man, a full breasted, well turbaned Turk, with a

THE NILE PARTY.—A COSMOPOLITAN GROUP, 1886.

1. Russian Cavass.
2. Russian Consul General.
3. A French Gentleman.
4. German Consul General.
5. S. S. Cox, U. S. Minister.
6. Count De Fleury.
7. Mme. D'Ehrenthall.
8. A Russian Judge.
9. Swedish Consul General.
10. Dutch Bridegroom.
11. Arab Cavass.
12. A Swedish Child.
13. Dutch Bride.
14. Countess De Fleury.
15. Emma D'Ehrenthal.
16. Mrs. S. S. Cox.
17. Sec'y to Russian Consul.

goad, and a sash of endless length, driving two noble oxen, descendants of the ox which forded here
with Europa many dim centuries ago, worthy to be
sacrificed to Jove, who had retired behind Olympus, 70 miles away—when I took the plough handle! There was only one handle. Ceres smiled
sere-ously! I "hawed" and 'gee'd" the oxen, but
they did not understand the lingo of Ohio cat-
tle. Box and Cox is an old farce; but Ox and Cox
—well, I brought out of that field more mud than
Cincinnatus did when he left the only "share" he
took stock in, and made Rome howl for him as a
patriot and a "Cult." My shoe black charged me
five piasters extra for the soil I did not turn up
except on my boots! And this from the farmer's
friend, just from the Sciatic Court; and in view of
an Asciatic who regarded my effort with earthly
gravity."

Whether the American minister made due report to the State Department at Washington of
his progress in inculcating the principles of agri-
culture, a la Americaine, in the Turkish brain, he
has not informed us!

Among the diversions of the diplomat during
the winter of 1886 was a revisit of Greece and
Egypt. At Athens he heard of the deaths of two
eminent Americans whom he had supported for
the Presidency, Horatio Seymour and General
Hancock. "Yes," he wrote, "our great and good
leaders are going to their long home. I am about
the only one of the ante-bellum men of public life
left." By April first the tourists were back in
Constantinople. A letter of that date thus refers
to the interesting journey:

"We have been in Egypt. Need I say our trip

up the Nile had all the charm of novelty, as well
as of unusual social and festive displays, occasioned by the four nationalities officially represented on our boat—three of Europe, Russia, Germany, and Sweden, and the one from America.
The four flags floated from our little steamer, and
naturally the Arabic race were curious as to the
occasion of so much display.   But the old temples
and ruins are all that has ever been claimed for
them; massive and unique beyond idea."

The American Minister and his wife shortly
after   their   return   to   Constantinople   were
entertained at a State dinner by the Sultan.   In
a private letter penned the next day, he thus referred to the event: "I have just gone through a
royal scene! The long-promised dinner from the
Sultan came off last night, 29th May. Mrs. Cox
was toiletted until she beat me to death in my
little 'swallow'—but when it came to the swallow
of the menu I was there! I had been reading up
in Ottoman history, and knew the 29th May was a
'Big Day' for Constantinople and the Ottoman;
for Mahomet II. came in and took things from
Constantine Palaeogus on that day, 433 years
before! Observe the sequel. Well, we went up to
the palace of Yildiz and through the labyrinth of
rare gardens and pleasure houses until we were
received by His Majesty. But I must send you a
paper for the particulars." An interesting incident at the conclusion of the royal dinner was the
decoration of Mrs. Cox with the Grand Cordon of
the Benevolences, the Chefekat. The ceremony is
thus described by Mr. Cox: "After being seated the
dragoman surprises my wife and the company.

He approaches her with a box. 'I have something to show you, Madam,' he says. 'Yes,' she responds. 'It is lovely outside. What is it?' He opens it, remarking, 'Shall I put it on you?' 'What do you mean?' she inquires. 'I have the pleasure of decorating you, at the Sultan's wish, with the Grand Order of the Chefekat.' Thereupon he throws the cordon over her head, and, with the aid of the German Ambassadress, who is familiar with the decoration, it is decorously arranged. It is a surprise as well as an honor, coming as it does almost within one year of our service with the American Legation. It is a star in brown, gold and green enamel, with diamond brilliants. It has five points and twenty-six diamonds on each point. Surely no woman of good training would refuse such a gift! It is fastened upon the front of the corsage, and, with the cordon, it serves as an ornament to the dress. The Pashas, the aides and the officers make their felicitations upon the happy event. My wife told me confidentially afterward that she thought for a brief, ineffable moment that she was a bride again. This decoration originated with the present Sultan, or his father, in order to honor Lady Layard for her services in the hospitals during the Crimean War. It is called the Order of Good Works." Mr. Cox afterward confidentially informed the writer that the sight of this Chefekat caused an almost irresistible feline impulse to meouwing!

The Sultan's clever way of dismissing his guests is worth telling here: "The Sultan now arises. He will detain us no longer. It is etiquette at the palace to remain until the Sultan gives the signal to leave. This he generally does by a glance at his watch, saying: 'I fear you will be late;' or, 'Perhaps I am detaining you.' He shakes hands with the ladies first, and then the gentlemen, with their best grace, back out. The bouquets are distributed to the ladies." Apparently there was one part of the palace our American Minister was not allowed to inspect. "As we retire, after many kindly greetings," he writes, "we look in vain for lattice and curtain to indicate the harem. Every window opens into a beautiful garden, and every garden is filled with flowers and sparkling fountains. It is a fairy scene; but no houri."

The summer of 1886 was spent among the Isles of the Princes, mainly on the Isle of Prinkipo, in the Propontis. "There were nine muses. The Princes Isles are the same in number as those sisters. Their beauty and allurements are as varied as the hues of the waters around them." From Prinkipo, soon after taking up his summer residence there, he writes: "Such is life here that I am getting better, on a lovely isle, with only 5,000 Greeks and lots of good breeze and piney woods." Here, at last, he seems to have realized that dream of complete rest for which he had left his country. One of his letters breezily describes a visit to a neighboring island: "Tempus—early in the morning, by the sunrise. Strange noises in the isle. Roosters and jackasses. Both make music in harmony with **various venders of** verdant vegetables! Crowd of hamals, gamins, fishermen, etc., on the scala (quai), looking at the mystery of the screw-going vessel. These were the circumadjacent circumstances of our condition as we moved out of

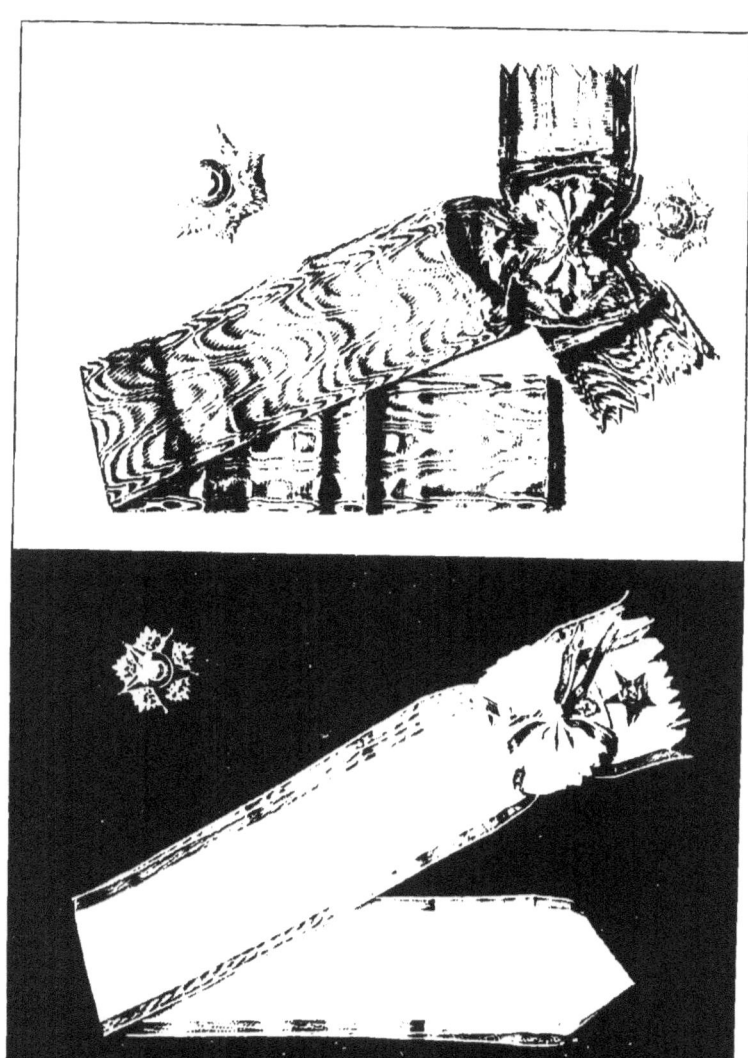

DECORATIONS CONFERRED BY THE SULTAN OF TURKEY

No. 1 and Mrs. Cox, "Order of Chefakat." No. 2 and Mr. Cox, "Order of Medjidie."

our harbor of Prinkipo this morning to visit our
neighbor isle of Halki (Grec. Chalki, or copper).
This is the isle the copper came from that made
the Colossus of Rhodes. Here, too, are the theo-
logical seminaries of the Orthodox Greek Church,
as old as Justinian, too; and some of their old
churches and monasteries look it. To this isle,
whose profile is that of a Spanish saddle, and
whose tops are crowned with colleges, and whose
valley and coast line is a pretty Greek town,—we
direct our prow, Ulysses like, toward the Isles of
Syrens—for the isle is full of beauteous females,
who almost rival those of Prinkipo! These Isles
of the Blest, nine of them, lie (all but two) close
to each other. We have the finest in all in the
neat lay of the land—rock and mountain and inter-
vale."

At Prinkipo the Minister was not distant from
the sphere of active diplomacy, which, he tells us,
"had no surcease during the summer and fall."
In the story of his enchanted life among the classic scenes of the Princess Isles, he writes in closing:

"The story of our summer is told. The wreaths
begin to wither on the tomb. A thousand
thoughts and studies hang over them. But these
are not dead garlands. The angels of memory
will resume their places at the gate of this paradise. The flaming sword drives us into the old
and busy world, under the glaring sun and the
uncloistered heat and dust of our earnest and
active American life; but amidst all the turmoil
and worry of that life, we shall turn to the 'Pleasures of Prinkipo.' "

"In the shadow of thy pines, by the shores of thy
          sea,
On the hills of thy beauty, our heart is with thee."

CHAPTER XVIII.

As the summer wore away, with the accumulation of a new store of health, came the desire to be once more amid the activities of American politics. "Circumstances," to adopt his own words, "partly domestic and partly political," led him to resign his office as Minister and to return home to resume his former position as a Member of Congress from the city of New York.

As to his reason for the change, we have his own statement: "It was not because of any dissatisfaction with the service, nor from any derogative treatment by the officers of the Porte or the Sultan, nor because of any disenchantment of the Orient. The heart has no reason; or, rather, it has reasons of its own. Call it homesickness, or patriotism, or an inclination after old and fixed parliamentary habits, or the ineradicable desire to be near one's own—and you have the best explanation that can be made for my premeditated and unprecipitated return. I had done all that a Minister of my ability could do to place the Legation and the American interests in excellent condition." From Constantinople, September 11, he wrote to a friend: "Your letter found me packing for home. We sail from Havre 2d Oct. for N. Y. Hurrah! I already feel the sweet lager-bier breezes from the Isle of Coney!"

Shortly after his resignation and return home he received the decoration of the "Order of the Mejidieh" from his Imperial Majesty, the Sultan Abdul Hamid, the decoration of the "Order of the Chefakat" having, as we have seen, already been bestowed on the Minister's wife in Turkey. Both these decorations are at present in the care of the National museum in Washington.

An enthusiastic welcome awaited Mr. Cox on his arrival home.

He returned to find himself twice a candidate at the same election—a candidate for the seat in the Forty-ninth Congress vacated by the resignation of Joseph Pulitzer, as well as a candidate for the full term of the Fiftieth Congress. To both seats he was elected by his old-time majorities. "So far as I have been able to ascertain," said Representative Cummings, "Mr. Cox is the only man who has ever been twice elected to the same Congress"—alluding to his second election to the Forty-ninth Congress. His reappearance in the House of Representatives, which had sadly missed his familiar figure and the genial warmth of his presence, was gladly welcomed by colleagues of all parties. On that camp-ground Richard was indeed himself again—once more on his native heath.

In the autumn of 1888 a strong pressure was brought to bear upon Mr. Cox to resign from congress and accept the Democratic nomination for Mayor of New York. He firmly refused such use of his name, although his nomination would have been equivalent to an election. He felt that his

proper sphere was the Hall of Representatives. He
accepted a renomination to congress and his re-
election followed as of course. It was his last. He
died before the fifty-first congress, of which he
was a member-elect, met.

In the fiftieth congress, which began its existence March 4, 1887, and expired March 4, 1889, Mr.
Cox chose the chairmanship of the Census committee, and was assigned to that position by Speaker
Carlisle. Preparations were making for the eleventh census, a work in which he took a leading interest. The bill under which the enumeration of
inhabitants and statistics of the industries of the
country were taken, in 1890, was reported by him.
In its fulness and elaboration he took a pardonable pride. He was proud of the increase in both
wealth and numbers, of the component parts of
the union, and rejoiced in all signs of public prosperity. To measures before that congress having
for their object the irrigation of the arid plains of
the far west, and their restoration through a supply of water, to fertility, Mr. Cox gave earnest support. As object lessons he pointed to Syria and
Asia Minor, where, by the destruction of mountain forests and neglect of irrigation works that
once existed, water supplies had been lost, and
sterility had ensued where once were fertile lands
sustaining great populations and prosperous
states. Another proposition that enlisted his active sympathy and earnest support related to the
admission of four new states. Considerations of
party expediency, which arrayed many of his party associates against giving the far west additional
votes in the electoral college, had not weight with
Mr. Cox, who disavowed such considerations as of

too narrow a guage for broad statesmanship. He looked upon the rise of the free commonwealths in the northwest with only a patriot's eye. That his efforts were fully appreciated was made manifest by the popular ovation which greeted him on his flying trip through those new states in the summer of 1889, a few weeks before his untimely death. "On the 4th of July," says one account, "Mr. Cox stood in the midst of assembled thousands of his fellow citizens at Huron, in the then territory of Dakota. No more imposing or grander ovation was ever given to an American citizen than was given him on that occasion. The prairies, the towns, and the villages for miles around were deserted, for their inhabitants would look upon their great deliverer. These people would hear the voice of the eminent statesman who, in the House of Representatives, had raised his voice for fair play. They were not drawn to the place so much to hear the great orator as to look upon the man whose great heart had borne him beyond the line which his party had set for him. He was their hero. They pressed upon him, for they deemed him something nobler than a mere orator or statesman. They felt him to be a fellow citizen, kind, generous and full of good will."

It was the middle of August when Mr. Cox, with his wife, arrived home from the trip above described. He hurried to Manhattan Beach, as many times before when wearied by overwork or overtravel, to regain needed rest. In a hasty note to a friend he said: "Hither I have hied to the salt sea beach where I correct my abnormal condition of health and my printer's proofs. To-night the waves dash high over the walks where yesterday

we gallanted each other. It's fine!   Here come
those thoughts which make one sedate; for here
we walk

"Thoughtful, silent, on the solemn shore
Of that vast ocean we must sail so soon."

Little he thought how soon! A note dated August 25 from the Manhattan Beach hotel, "this gorgeous marine hospital," as he styled it, the note
written while the ears were "dimmed with the
music of the band," said: "We leave in the morning for home."

Prophetic words!   It was "home" indeed to
which he was going, and so soon!

The last occasion on which he went out of the
house was Friday evening, August 30, to attend
the "grand annual summer night's festival of the
New York Letter Carriers' Association," at the
Empire City Coloseum and Washington Park. He
had been ill two weeks.   That one evening, feeling
better, he was urged and consented to ride up in
a close carriarge for the purpose of receiving from
the letter carriers a large and beautiful album,
which they had been waiting six months to present him.   He professed not to be much wearied;
he made a brave effort to keep up.   It was, however, his last effort to leave his room. Eleven
days later the end came.

CHAPTER XIX.

Samuel Sullivan Cox was just thirty-two years of age when he was first elected to a seat in Congress. His last election to membership in that body was when he had doubled those years, and was just sixty-four. His congressional service was cotemporaneous with the incumbency of every president, save one, from Buchanan to McKinley. That exception was President Andrew Johnson. While Mr. Cox was in the public service at one end of Pennsylvania avenue there sat in the White House, at the other end of that historic avenue, in their order, eight presidents: James Buchanan, Abraham Lincoln, Ulysses S. Grant, Rutherford B. Hayes, James A. Garfield, Chester A. Arthur, Grover Cleveland and Benjamin Harrison. Of these he was in political sympathy with only two —Buchanan and Cleveland—and with the former the bonds were broken almost at the very threshhold of their association in public life, and never altogether re-cemented.

His Democracy was of the Jeffersonian order. He was a firm believer not only in the right, but as well in the capacity of the people to rule. Throughout his long public career he strenuously opposed any and every proposition to abridge or abbreviate this right. His democracy was inherited from his ancestors on both sides. His break

with the Buchanan administration was because he
saw that administration attempting to throttle
the will of the people of Kansas by foisting upon
the new State the Lecompton constitution. His
first speech in the House—the first ever made in
the present Hall of Representatives—was a gauntlet thrown to that administration which, he believed, was attempting to strangle popular sovereignty. Whenever his party refused to follow
the teachings of Thomas Jefferson and to remain
true to the people, Mr. Cox broke loose from party
ties, and obeyed the dictates of his own conscience.
In obedience to these dictates, in his last
session in Congress he separated from most of his
party associates in advocating the admission of
four new States, believing that such questions
should be decided on broad grounds of public policy, without consideration of their probable effect
on this party or that. The scope of his horizon
was too broad for a party-at-any-price follower.

In the album of a classmate at Brown University, just as he was leaving that institution, he
made this entry, in which he refers to his inherited
love of the party he served so well:

"Samuel Sullivan Cox, Zanesville, O. Born
about midnight. 30 Sept., 1824. Expect to study
law if I don't get better. Shall live in Ohio till I
die, provided I live till I get there. The friend
who reads this will, I hope, forget the many faults
and recollect the few (very few) good characteristics of the writer. That he has anything to recommend him to recollection he modestly doubts,
yet he would be remembered by a classmate as he
himself expects to remember. One failing he re-
joices in—his 'unterrified Democracy.' He drank

in with his mother's milk the spirit of liberty, and
tradition says that at his birth a scroll of fire
danced around the bedposts with the words written thereon: 'Salus populi suprema lex.' "

He was ever true to the spirit of the tradition.
His was too genial a nature to brood long over
wrong done him, or permanently to treasure the
spirit of revenge. Years after the Lecompton
controversy had passed into history, Mr. Cox, still
in Congress, received one day from the venerable
Buchanan, then in retirement and nearing the end
of his eventful life, a letter almost pathetic, asking
of him a personal favor. "Only to you," said the
letter, "can I lok now for such kindly favors." He
looked not in vain. The recollection of decapi-
tated postmasters in his district did not deter Mr.
Cox from gladly seeking to oblige Buchanan, the
ex-president, with a zeal not a whit behind that
with which he opposed him as President when he
believed him in the wrong. So kindly a nature
could not long carry a spirit of resentment.

At one time or another, during his long Congressional service, he was a member of almost
every important committee of the House. He
served on Revolutionary Claims, the Ways and
Means, always standing for the free trade principle, Appropriations, Foreign Affairs, Naval Affairs,
Banking and Currency, the Census, and others.
Of several of these he was, when his party was in
the ascendancy, chairman. Although the drudg-
ery of committee work was hardly to his taste, he
was a faithful and conscientious worker in committee, and no member's services were prized more
highly than his. Capacity for details was especially shown by him in the preparation for the

tenth and eleventh census, by the committee over
which he presided. It was a revelation to the
census-makers. He was regent of the Smithsonian institution for many years, and took a warm
and active interest in its welfare. As a member
of the Library Committee he was largely instrumental in bringing about the erection of the present magnificent structure for housing the Congressional library. But it was on the floor of the
House that he shone resplendent. Here he wielded a free lance. By the splendor of his equipment,
by his breadth and depth of knowledge of whatever subject came before the House, he was a constant wonder to his associates. When had he
gathered such resources, and where had he stored
them with such method as never to be at a loss
whence to draw them? No orator in Congress,
when he rose, more quickly hushed his audience.
The confusion at once ceased, members gathered
around him the better to hear his words, and the
galleries listened intently to catch each syllable.
They watched, generally not in vain, for the sal-
lies and flashes of wit, with which his speech was
illumined. But these were merely accessories,
side lights, as it were. He spoke ably on every
question of national interest that came before
Congress in his day. Many of his speeches, aside
from their other merits, were gems of literature.

He was an untiring worker. He was not content to deal with the surface of things, but must
needs go to the very bottom. He knew no idle
moments. In the arrangement of his papers and
in the outline of his work he was method itself.
He learned it, he said, from the same source from

FROM PHOTOGRAPHS OF S. S. COX AT DIFFERENT PERIODS.

which he imbibed his political economy, from
Francis Wayland, his president at Brown.

His oratory was as polished as the Damascus
blade. History, mythology, science, philosophy,
literature, sacred and secular, were resources ever
at hand from which to illustrate or adorn. He
was a great student of the Bible, and few men in
public life showed an equal familiarity with its
pages. For religion he had naught but respect,
and never was heard to indulge a sneer at things
sacred. He was true to his religious training.

Of his vast number of "set" speeches, on about
every important subject before Congress in his
long career, none excelled in beauty of diction his
obituary addresses.

"These efforts," well said a contemporary publication, "full of delicacy, seriousness, appreciation,
grandeur of thought, and the poetry of pathos,
show how close the fountain of tears lies to the
fountain of laughter in the mysterious cham-
bers of the heart. The man who laughs most easily is almost always the one who weeps most easily and feelingly. The power to perceive what is
incongruous and comical in thought and act, and
touch the chords of humor, is akin to that other
power which sees and feels the grandeur of duty,
the heroism of action, and the solemnities of fate.
If Mr. Cox is capable of the former, he is a recognized master of the latter."

Sir Edwin Arnold, in an interview in London
with an American newspaper correspondent, after
his return from a visit to the United States, referred to Mr. Cox as "a statesman whose name
should be sacred to the heart of every true Ameri-

can—one who has done so much for his countrymen."

Gen. W. T. Sherman, in a conversation with a
friend a few days before his death, regarding the
statue, which it was then proposed to erect to the
memory of Mr. Cox, in which he manifested a
warm interest, on being told where it was likely to
be placed, made this comment: "But I should
think you boys would try and secure a site in the
Central Park for the statue, and as near to that of
Daniel Webster as possible—in that circle opposite; then you would have here two great common-
ers together, the one representing the Senate, and
the other representing the House of Representatives."

There was ever a warm place in his heart for
his Alma Mater, Brown University. Whatever
success in life he attained he attributed in no small
degree to the training he there received. On its
part the University was proud of the honors
heaped upon its brilliant son. Beside the degrees
of Bachelors of Arts, in course, in 1846, and Master of Arts in 1849, Brown University in 1885 conferred upon Mr. Cox the degree of Doctor of Laws.

CHAPTER XX.

In the exciting scenes that led up to the framing of the Electoral Commission bill, in the winter of 1876-7, and its adoption by Congress, Mr. Cox maintained rather a passive than an active role. With a majority of his party he accepted the proposed scheme for the solution of the ugly problem with which the country was confronted, but at no time was sanguine as to its outcome. He voted for the bill, but did not share in the enthusiasm over it indulged in by the majority of his party. His relations to the measure were forcibly stated in a speech made on the Commission's decision of the Louisiana contest, February 19, 1877, when no longer a doubt was felt anywhere as to the final outcome. "Mr. Speaker," said Mr. Cox on this occasion, "after many years of active service as a member of this House, recalling all the vicissitudes of our politics for twenty years, I cannot feel responsible to-day that after the verdict of the American people it should prove a fruitless verdict. In 1864, on the 16th of May, I presented a resolution to this House, which passed. It related to the regularity and authenticity of the returns of electoral votes and for a law to provide for a jurisdiction as well as the course of proceeding in case of a 'real controversy.' The Judiciary Comimttee took no action at that time. Allow me to quote the resolution. It is a compend of the situation:

'Resolved, That the Judiciary Committee be directed to take into consideration the propriety of reporting a bill providing for the decision of any question which may arise as to the regularity and authenticity of the returns of the electoral vote for President and Vice President of the United States, or the right of the persons who gave the votes or the manner in which they ought to be counted; and that such law provide for the jurisdiction, as well as the course of proceeding, in a case of real controversy.' "

Had the action contemplated been taken, and the legislation proposed been engrafted upon the Federal Statutes, the crisis of 1876-7, in which for months the country stood upon the brink of civil war as the fruit of a disputed election for the Presidency, might have been averted. "Peril," added Mr. Cox, after quoting his resolution of 1864, "gives the lessons of years in a day." The speech which was thus prefaced was, he subsequently explained, made for history—the judgment being foregone. In the course thereof he said:

"Peril gives the lessons of years in a day. * * * Whether the steps were wisely or unwisely taken in framing the Electoral bill is not to be now considered. That bill is the law. We know what it is, what its provisions are. We knew and felt that some virtue had gone out of this House when we passed it, but we did not exactly see where the virtue had alighted. We

knew the old privileges of the Commons had departed, but in the interest of peace we gave a
reluctant vote for the bill. It was voted for in a
spirit of confidence and in a moment of peril, and
under terror of force and revolution, which speaks
more for the caution than for the pluck of our people. Still it was enacted. We are bound by its
decisions, but not by its reasons. The faith of
those who voted for it was strong in the integrity
and purity of their case; and next in the fidelity
and independence of the tribunal. We placed our
faith in the ermine. * * * We are graciously
permitted under this bill to argue after the matter
is accomplished, and although we vote, and
although we carry our vote in the House, we are
'gone.' We gain nothing. We are permitted to
talk ten minutes after the counting and the conclusion. It is the old Virgilian line over again about
Rhadamanthus, judge of hell,—Castigatque audit-
que dolos—the old rule of hanging a man and trying him afterward. That is our condition to-day."

Then caustically reviewing the Commission's
decision, by a vote of 8 to 7, to refuse to go behind
the returns—treating all such testimony as aliunde—Mr. Cox (we copy from the Congressional
Record of that day) thus closed as the hammer
fell:

"Mr. Cox—With permission of the House I will
read from Psalms 94, verse 20: Shall the throne of
iniquity have fellowship with thee, which frameth
mischief by a law—

"Mr. Kelley—I object. (Laughter.)

"Mr. Southard—I hope the gentlemen on that
side will listen to those words, that they may have
time to repent.

"Several members objected.

"Mr. Cox—The Bible is aliunde with these gentlemen. (Great laughter.)"

Mr. Cox's record was in harmony with this speech: he refused to be a party to obstruction of the enforcement of the law, believing that, however subversive of justice as viewed from his standpoint, the result was to be accepted in good faith.

CHAPTER XXI.

So long ago as 1859 Mr. Cox flung boldly to the breeze the flag of Cuban annexation. President Buchanan, in his annual message, had recommended an appropriation—$30,000,000 were the figures fixed upon—for the purchase of Cuba. In a speech in the House on January 18, 1859, Mr. Cox took the ground that Cuban annexation was manifest destiny.

"There is" he said, "a logic in history which is as inexorable as fate. The disquieting aspect of cis-Atlantic politics signifies the consummation of territorial changes on this continent, long predicted, long delayed, but as certain as the logic of history! *   *   * The largest expression of this law of annexation is: That no nation has the right to hold soil, virgin and rich, yet unproducing; no nation has the right to hold great isthmian highways, or great defences, on this continent without the desire, will, or power to use them. They ought, and must, inure to the advancement of our commerce. They must become confiscate to the decrees of Providence.

"Had the Thirty-fourth Congress aided President Pierce in the Black Warrior matter, we should now have representatives from Cuba on this floor.

As to Cuba the reasons for its acquisition are well understood by the country. Its geographical position gives to the nation which holds it, unless that nation be very weak, a coign of vantage as to which self-preservation forbids us to be indifferent. While the island is of little use to Spain, save as a source of revenue, it is to us of incalculable advantage.

"Our unsettled claims, and many other difficulties, growing out of our relations to Spain, demand settlement, but receive none. How long shall we continue in this condition? During the pleasure of Spain? Is there no redress? Is our every attempt to be construed into usurpation? What impediments have we to meet? There is one which has, since Mr. Adam's time, proved insurmountable—Spanish pride.

"It is well said by an old poet that
"Spain gives in pride, which Spain, of all the
          earth,
May freely give, nor fear herself a dearth."

"Since then there has been no curtailment of that pride. True, Spain has now little to be proud of but her recollections. Poor, sensitive, corrupt, she holds to the punctilio of dignity without its substantial energy. If Spain will not sell Cuba to us, we must insist upon her changing its policy. We have tried in vain by diplomacy to unloosen these shackles (on commerce). * * * Nothing but the sword can cut them off. Such a system in this era of commercial freedom is a shame to civilization, and if international law were rightly written, it would itself be a cause of honorable war! * * * Call it by what name you will, I am ready to answer the call of the President, if for nothing else, for the benefit of the $250,000,000 of yearly trade which must pass under the range of Cuban cannon.

"I am ready to vote for the bill looking to the purchase of Cuba. In case of our failure to purchase by honorable negotiation I would favor its seizure in case of foreign war or of a European intervention. * * * We have become a Colossus on this continent with a strength and stride that will and must be heeded.

"With our domestic policy as to local governments established, we can go on and Americanize this continent and make it what Providence intended it should become, by a perpetual growth and an unsevered Union—the paragon in history for order, harmony, happiness and power!"

When, taking advantage of our civil war, Napoleon, Emperor of France, was seeking to erect a throne in Mexico and seat Maximilian thereon, Mr. Cox, with William Cullen Bryant and others, addressed a vast mass meeting at Cooper Institute demanding that the Monroe doctrine be enforced and the French driven out of Mexico. Some of his words read to-day prophetic. "There is," he said, "one fact in connection with the Monroe doctrine. At present it has only been regarded as a brutum fulmen; it has been simply an enunciation, not backed up by the power or force of the United States. But, sooner or later, the time will come when the force of the United States will be invoked in support of a doctrine which is, as it were, the first letter of the alphabet of the American people. That doctrine will ultimately become the only doctrine which can be followed out in the interest of the honor of this great country. * * * There is no room on our continent for the establishment of monarchies. United in the determination to preserve this continent to republicanism, we shall be able, should the duty of the hour require it, to put a million of men in the field; and with such a force, the American people, if the issue be put upon them will revindicate their policy."

Resolutions in favor of recognizing the Cubans as belligerents in their struggle to throw off the Spanish yoke, introduced by Mr. Cox into the Forty-second Congress, elicited, on January 10, 1872, from the New York Evening Mail (Rep.) this empahtic approval:

"We thank one of the ablest representatives in the House, the Hon. S. S. Cox, for the introduction of a series of resolutions in favor of granting belligerent rights to the struggling patriots of Cuba. It is as plain as noonday that the struggle in which one hundred thousand Spanish soldiers have, during the past three years, been engaged, is as much of a war as was waged by any one of half a dozen South American colonies for independence from Spanish tyranny." The same paper warned the (Grant) Administration and its Representatives in Congress that "they must not allow Mr. Cox and his party to appear before the country as the especial champions of recognition," as "on such an issue as this there should be no party lines." Had these resolutions been adopted, how different might have been the course of American history! But the country was not yet ripe for the course proposed.

It was on the eighth day of January, 1872, that Mr. Cox introduced a "joint resolution for the recognition of belligerent rights between the kingdom of Spain and the so-called Republic of Cuba," as follows:

"Whereas, the inhabitants of a portion of the kingdom of Spain, to wit, the island of Cuba, have been waging war against Spain for their independence for a period of now more than three years, the existence of which war has been and is acknowledged by Spain in sundry public acts and documents; and

"Whereas, During this war Spain has been allowed to supply her armies and navy from the factories, dockyards and arsenals of this country with every material requisite for warfare, while the Cubans, in direct opposition to a fair spirit of neutrality, have been denied similar advantages, and vessels freighted with arms and ammunition, destined for the Cubans, in accordance with the legal right of American citizens to trade in arms with peoples and powers who are at war, and in the exercise of what has been declared, both by the Executive and a Federal court, to be a legitimate voyage, have, in violation of law and equity, been detained and subjected to delays by an unfair perversion of justice, to the detriment of the interests of American citizens; and

"Whereas, Measures should be adopted to protect the rights and interests of American citizens engaged in legitimate commerce, and to prevent the recurrence of losses which may arise from the fact that this Government has not yet acknowledged the existence of the Republic of Cuba; and

"Whereas, The majority of the independent republics of this hemisphere have recognized the belligerency of Cuba, which acts have tacitly been admitted by Spain to be not incompatible with the spirit of amity toward herself; and

"Whereas, Spain has herself, by acknowledging

the independence of sundry republics on this continent, once her colonies, acknowledged the rights they had to wage war for their independence as Cuba is fighting to-day for hers; and

"Whereas, by the principles of international law an inherent right is vested in the sovereignty of every independent nation to declare, when convenient, the existence of belligerency between any other nations, or between the inhabitants of any integral portion of any such nation; and

"Whereas, The rendering assistance to all peoples struggling in this hemisphere for the rights of self-government, by all just means not in contravention to international law, is a thorough American policy, consonant with the principles on which our own independence is based; therefore,

"Resolved, By the Senate and House of Representatives of the United States of America, in Congress assembled, that it recognizes the existence of a state of war between the kingdom of Spain and the so-called republic of Cuba, and hereby declares both parties to the conflict entitled to all the rights conceded to belligerents by international law."

This resolution was referred to the Foreign Affairs Committee, in which it slept the sleep that knows no awakening. Mr. Cox, on the 17th of February, by leave of the House, submitted his views on the subject, which, he said, were not only "in the interest of commerce," but in the line he had "carefully marked out as a student of international law.' He added: "Loving the Island of Cuba as a rare and wonderful portion of our star, knowing the vicissitudes of its history, feeling the indignation as a man, almost, I might say, as a boy, 'who is father to the man,' against the horrible massacre

of American citizens and Cuban students by the
nation whose flag is a river of blood between banks
of gold; believing that the welfare of the present
and rising generation in Cuba depends on the action of this nation, I propose to vindicate by a con-
cise statement the resolution I offered. It is now
before the Foreign Affairs Committee, and it sleeps
there as serenely as if there were no crimes against
the law of nations committed in Cuba, as if there
were no outrages against childhood, humanity and
God, illustrated by the fiends, who, under the
name of volunteers, rule the rule of Spain to make
a hell of that paradise of islands." This was pre-
lude to a forcible argument from the standpoint
of international law in favor of the proposed recognition. More than a quarter of a century later the
country found itself on his platform. "Do you ask
me," asked he at a mass meeting at Steinway Hall
on the heels of the Virginius outrage, "do you ask
me for the remedy? I answer, the intervention of
civilized nations to stop such atrocities."

Again, in a speech in the House, December 12,
1879, in favor of strengthening our coast defenses,
he referred to Spain as a perpetual menace to our
peace. "It will not do," he said, "to rely on a divine
Providence altogether for our future defenses.
Ericssons, with their monitors, are not to be improvised every day against surprises of the Merri-
macs. The engineers may continue, mechanical
processes take time, but the nation that has both
is the victor. * * * If complications, at any
time possible, should arise between the United
States and any foreign naval power, great or
small, what would we do except to submit if we
were unable to resist an attack on the sea coast or
the sea?

"Am I told that there is no danger of a breaking
out of hostilities, and therefore no need of making
appropriations for the armament of our forts? The
time has not yet come for the lion and the lamb to
lie down together. The ploughshare and pruning
hook are liable at any time to be converted into
the bayonet and sword. Our increasing trade and
growing relations with other countries admonish
us to be ready at least for defence, if not for ag-
gression.

Think of our critical relations with Spain. How
often in late years have we been on the verge of a
conflict with Spain! Her present commercial relations with us are a perpetual menace. Her tariff so discriminates against this country that it is
almost robbery. When we consider our exports
and imports to Cuba alone, the discrimination
against us is so marked an evidence of selfishness
and enmity that it is almost a casus belli. *   *
We have been Spain's best customer. Yet how
shabbily and meanly we are treated by her. The
Spanish tariff favors her own vessels to such an
extent as to deny to us advantages given other
countries. Do you say that this kind of tariff will
be ameliorated? Never while we are at the mercy
of Spain's 800 rifled guns, her six first-class iron-
clads, and her armored ships; never while the city
of New York can be placed under these guns and
exactions made by the hundred millions. Is it not
therefore, wise and prudent to prepare for the
armament of our fortifications that we may back
our negotiations by proper force and make our
country respected for its position as a power on the
earth?" But the warning passed unheeded.

CHAPTER XXII

Mr. Cox ever refused to recognize any distinction between American citizenship that was native and the species that was adopted. Consequently he insisted, always, that, at whatever cost, the government should protect all alike who should rightfully claim its protection. He was a thorough believer in the doctrine that when a naturalized citizen of the United States returns to his native land he is still an American citizen, and as such is ever entitled to the aegis of American protection. No American statesman did as much to advocate, defend and protect, the rights of American citizens abroad. It was the pressure brought on the government by him that opened the doors of British prisons and let in the light to the victims there confined.

When in the winter of 1880 Charles Stewart Parnell visited the United States, it was a resolution offered by S. S. Cox that opened the Hall of Representatives to Ireland's eloquent champion, and brought that body to lisften to his plea for Ireland, delivered from the speaker's place. His resolution did more—it requested the participation of the House in the ceremonies, "because of the great interest which the people of the United States take

in the condition of Ireland, with which this country is so closely allied by many historic and kin-
dred ties."

The incarceration of Capt. Edward O'Meagher
Condon in a British dungeon received a prompt attention from Mr. Cox, at the time chairman of the
Committee on Foreign Affairs. For Condon, it
was claimed, and truthfully, that he was an American citizen. On the 13th of June, 1878, he reported from the committee a joint resolution request-
ing the President to take such action as would secure Condon a speedy and impartial trial. In a
forcible speech in support of his resolution, Mr.
Cox cited the Revised Statutes to prove that the
law was ample in its provisions for an executive
demand on the British government, and for intervention in such a case. The House was so impressed with his argument that the resolution was
promptly adopted. The next day it passed the
Senate and was signed by the President on the
next.

In a speech made July 15, 1876, he said:"When
our nation began its first century it had but a population of 2,750,000. Its area has been extended
from 800,000 miles to 3,603,844 square miles. Annexation has quadrupled our area since the Revolution. But with all our purchases of Florida,
Louisiana, New Mexico, California and Alaska we
gained fewer than 150,000 inhabitants, while the
acquisition of Texas and Oregon merely restored
to citizenship those who had emigrated from the
United States. In more senses than one, therefore, should we rely upon immigration to develop
the vast resources, mineral, agricultural, and manufacturing, which tend to make a country great

and prosperous.   What a commentary, therefore, in this view is the false platform and narrow policy of the anti-naturalization and anti-immigration party."

"It is not a new thing for the American Government to take an interest in Irish prisoners. Every generous heart will recognize the fact that Ireland and her destiny cannot be dissociated from her warm-hearted sons in this country.   From the time of Cromwell and his attempt to root out the Celtic-Irish with his penalties, down to the present time, millions of Irishmen have had their property confiscated, their families scattered, and their bodies killed to gratify some unreasoning and bigoted vengeance on the part of her Anglo-Saxon enemies and rulers.   But her spirit has never been conquered.   It is impossible for a true Irishman, unless you rend his heart and paralyze his brain, not to love Ireland.

"The people of my district, Mr. Speaker, a large portion of whom are descended of those who emigrated thence, would find me derelict in my duty did I not sympathize with their sympathy.   By cable and steamship and by the thousands of letters and messages of affection, by whole clans and counties, they are interweaving the island of Manhattan with the island of Ireland.   This sympathy is quicker than the sub-ocean lightning.   It is the instinct of son and daughter for mother and father. It has been enlarged, warmed, and fused into a heavenly radiance.   Again and again, are the wrongs of Ireland spoken of most significantly in public meetings and at the domestic hearth.

"The history of Ireland is not alone the history of her religious faith, but the history of political independence and civil freedom. Before the time of the Tudors, before the time when the King's writ ran beyond the pale about Dublin, down through harsh penal laws and ecclesiastical establishments, foreign to her best emotions about the seen and unseen world, through evictions, land laws, and trade exactions, she has been galled without cowardly wincing, but galled at times into courageous revolt.

"Our sympathies belong to Ireland, for our revolution was hers.

"Ireland, too, had her revolution; but unsuccessful revolutions are called rebellions; but did she not contend, and does she not, through Isaac Butts, O'Connor Power, and others, to-day contend for the principle of her early day when Grattan thundered and Emmett died? Did she not contend, not alone in her own land, but here, and wherever the sword of Erin flashed, for the banner above all battle-flags: representation, and no taxation without it. Concord, Monmouth, Saratoga, Valley Forge, Yorktown, all testify of deeds done in liberty's name, but deeds done for man's capacity for home-rule. Jefferson taught the truth, which Irishmen loved to champion, that feudality in form or substance was tyranny; that absenteeism was robbery; that vassalage was cowardice, and independence courage; and that the fire and smoke of war are simple butchery unless beneath there is the pure molten white heat of patriotic devotion. Jealous of power, confiding in the people, and instinct with a love of country, he gave his theory and conduct to the illustration of that heaven-imaged scroll of stars, moving in harmony about the central sun, the type of our stately cluster about the Union and its splendid ensign.

"To Ireland, America is indebted as well for her prosperity in a great degree as for her early settlement. After the English revolution of 1688, when the barbarous Orange policy inaugurated by England drove men from their island home, a tide of emigration set in toward the American colonies. Irish trade and manufactures were destroyed and wars and penal laws drove Irishmen across the ocean. They filled our colonies with their emigrants. At least a million of the three million who inhabited the thirteen colonies at the beginning of the Revolution were Irish by birth or descent. They spread and multiplied in our land from the Potomac to the Ohio, from the Saco to the Juniata. They enlivened the land with their humorous spirit, their cheerful industry, and their alacrious belligerency. When independence came to be our only prospect, the first undaunted rebel was John Sullivan, who with his Celtic band marched upon the fortress of William and Mary, in New Hampshire, and captured it. This was the first blow of the Revolution. In May, 1775, the O'Briens, six in number, fought the first naval battle of the war, and won it. The names of gallant Irishmen shine like stars all through the murk of the Revolution. To recount them is to recount the stories of Monmouth, Saratoga, Bennington, Valley Forge, Stony Point, and Yorktown. Why, one of the charges against the Irish in England was that 16,000 of them fought on the side of America. This was one of the pretexts for refusing redress to the Catholics of Ireland. A steady influx of immigration since has filled our confines

with 14,000,000 of Celtic blood. The names of
Barry, Montgomery, Jasper, Warren, Clinton, Rut-
ledge, Wayne, and Jackson but feebly portray the
gorgeous galaxy of Irish patriots who gave to
America their fervor and their fighting, their
bravery and their blood.

"Mr. Speaker, it is in this mosaic, made up of all
races and nations, in which we find our growth,
happiness, and unity. The streams of thought
and feeling from the Old World have made us
something more than a congeries of British colonies or a unity of selfish States. Our very motto,
"From many, one," indicates the cause of our
greatness as well as of our growth; it speaks of
our varied vitality fused with united patriotism.

"It is not possible, Mr. Speaker, to roll back the
shadow on the dial-plate of time. The sun will
not stand still at human voice. This immigration from the Old World, with its thousand elevat-
ing and assimilating qualities, will go on. No
sectarian bitterness or bigoted hate can turn away
the people of this country from the belief in the
principles of religious freedom fixed and eternized
down in their organic laws."

CHAPTER XXIII.

Closing a speech on the persecution of the Jews in Russia, made in the House May 21, 1880, he paid that ancient race this tribute:

"Whether it shall ever come to pass that this remarkable race shall repossess the land of their ancestors; whether the temple shall again arise within the walls of Zion; whether the teachings of their religion and all the elevated thoughts of their poets, prophets and priests shall be sung even 'within thy gates, O Jerusalem,' one thing is to be conceded, that in America, under our free institutions, they are permitted, unmolested, to worship the Jehovah of their fathers! Here at least they have a highway out of Egypt into the promised land! Wherever may be their local habitation, from the summit of Mount Sinai still radiates the eternal lesson cut in stone; from the calcined soil and the sacred mountains of Judea goes forth an effluence to civilize, cheer and bless.

"No one can be so darkened in his understanding as not to see the wonderful power of that little land through which the Jordan flows, with a population not larger than one of our own countries, which for two thousand years and more has held the world in thrall by its teachings and by its worship of the invisible Jehovah. Its people have carried the ark of their covenant into many lands and climes; and though bigotry may still be pleased to think that their dispersion as a people is a curse, still from their migrations humanity has been beautified, justice purified, and liberty glorified! Out of their rigid and austere code there springs and flows forever an influence as gentle as the dews that fell upon Hermon and as potential as the quaking of Sinai, out of whose throes came the moral law of mankind!"

A resolution having been introduced into the House which looked like an apology to Chancellor Bismarck for resolutions previously passed by the House, expressing sympathy for the death of Edward Lasker, a member of the German Reichstag, Mr. Cox opposed the implied apology with fiery eloquence. Incidentally his speech was a splendid tribute to the Jewish race. Among other things he said:

"This manly man, Herr Lasker, was a type of a great class. He was a friend of labor. He was its interpreter and prophet, its friend and adviser in a realm where the word of the Kaiser was law, and liberty was suppressed by penalty and force. He was the representative of democracy in the larger sense of that term. He was an orator and a splendid type of the great race that has come down to us from the 'chosen people,' in earlier times. The tribute paid to his memory was also a tribute to the race from which he sprung—a race whose history runs back into the dawn of time. To that race we owe our entire system of ethics and the preservation of the foundations of religion. Amid centuries of glorious nationality and through long ages of intolerance and most cruel persecution, Hebrew virtue, pride, and courage remain untarnished by the hand of time. In everything that broadens civilization, Hebrew genius, intellect, research, and learning stand forth pre-eminent.

"What a race has been stricken by the death of this distinguished German and Hebrew! I say it is only a part of the history of persecutions which in this day of the nineteenth century are a humiliation and not to be tolerated in this country. In the Middle Ages one nation alone sacrificed six hundred thousand Jews. They were the flower of science, the devotees of literature, skilled in art, and enthusiastic in poetry. They were men of industry, enterprise, and commerce— honest, social and hospitable. I would not suffer for a moment that we should give even a possible shadow of excuse for bowing before the terrible specter of persecution.

"Twice have I called the attention of the House to the persecutions of the Jews in Russia. We have become used to the persecutions in that country. It is a part of its barbarism. But it is only within the past few years that the same ruthless system of persecution has obtained in Germany. The time of Hebraic liberty will come, and I trust soon, as it has come in this and some countries in Europe, notably in Spain, which has invited the Hebrew exiles of Germany to her shores. To the Hebrew race it is proclaimed by God himself in Holy Writ: 'I will shake all the nations, and the desire of all the nations shall come, and I will fill this house with glory, saith Jehovah the Lord of Hosts.'

"It becomes us especially who have offered an asylum to these stricken people, and in view of their remarkable attainments in all that civilizes and blesses, that the indirect insult to their race, through one of their distinguished sons, shall receive no mitigation by tenders of semi-sympathy to the organ of autocratic power, even where that power is concealed in the silken glove of an accomplished statesman."

CHAPTER XXIV.

The upbuilding of American commerce was ever a pet object with Mr. Cox. To this end he constantly advocated every measure before Congress which promised to remove the burdens imposed on American merchant marine, and to encourage the American foreign-carrying trade. One of his many speeches on this subject was delivered in the House April 26, 1884. "Free Ships and Free Materials" was its watchword. In the course of that speech he said:

"When the causes of our commercial ruin have been brought home to the understanding of our toilers in the ship-yards and the merchants in their counting rooms, the system of prohibition is doomed. Is American industry to be forever like an imaginary cripple, afraid to lay aside its crutches though he be able to walk better without them? Repeal our restrictive laws and five years will not roll away before we will, by free labor, hold our own market and contend with the foreigner successfully in the markets of the world.

"In my despair at the dilatory, not to say unwise legislation here for the revival of our navigation, I turn as a believer in our material advancement to the Baconic inductions of physics and the

probable results of our utilitarian methods of research.   Invention is not a newborn muse which
descants upon a new order to usher in a new era;
for the ancients reckoned the inventor as among
the heroes and demi-gods along with the founders
of empire. What may not come in the form of material development to relieve us and bring back our
olden and golden glory upon the sea!   Our age is
one of natural forces with wondrous practical applications. These forces, including the vapor of
water and the spark of electricity along with other
elements not yet known, are the subtle agents har-
nessed by man, powers we know not what or
whence, but powers in league with the reason and
genius of man, to do his work on land and ocean
for the amelioration and civilization of our kind.
By these forces we are day by day bringing nations
closer and closer to each other.   Oceans no longer
divide.   That mysterious realm is no longer an
abyss. It is bridged. The elements harmonize
and unite. Where once there was a flaming
sword, now there are well known paths over the
bosom of the deep, traced by the genius of Maury
and traveled by the steamer which mates the ocean
in its wildest saturnalia. This House, elected on
principles of reciprocity and liberality, may in harmony with material advancement, at least do what
was done by the last Republican House, which,
professing no special creed on these topics, and although it repented of its generous vote the next
day and reversed its action, did adopt the two
propositions I have here urged—one for free materials, to help the ship-builder, and the other for
free ships, to help the ship owner. I trust that
these may clasp hands and go as one and together,

for the enhancement of our mercantile marine and for the glory of our starry flag." (Applause.)

One of his last efforts, and for which the City of New York thanked him, was the passing of a law effectually preserving New York harbor and its tributaries from destruction. Although he abhorred war and regarded it as the resort of barbarism, Mr. Cox was not unmindful of the necessity of defense and the needs of national honor, as his speech in the Forty-Eighth Congress as chairman on naval affairs will show. In his speech, which was delivered on June 30, 1884, he illustrates in a remarkable degree the conscientious legislative labor and foresight of the man.

"For my part," said he, "I would prefer to expend four millions of dollars for one first-class war vessel that would be able to overhaul the Oregon or Alaska, and merchant steamers of that type when armed as cruisers, than have a dozen such cruisers as the Chicago, Boston, Atlanta or Dolphin for the same money. I have no confidence in the slow speed policy of the Advisory Board in this age of high speed and scientific advancements. The steel cruisers which we are now building are already behind the requirements of the day. I risk nothing in saying this when I can point to such British merchant steamers as the Oregon and Alaska. These are types of all large British merchant steamers that are hereafter to be built. None are to be inferior to these. Most of those yet to be built will surpass them. We who have no technical naval knowledge can easily see that our steel cruisers, the Chicago and the others, are a mistake. They are not capable of effective cruising service in war time."

Has not the war with Spain, in showing the superiority of fast-atiling cruisers abundantly demonstrated the wisdom of the policy Mr. Cox advocated many years ago?

CHAPTER XXV.

THE "LETTER CARRIERS' FRIEND."

Mr. Cox was the earliest and most steadfast of champions of the interests of the employes in the postal service, especially the Letter Carriers, and every important measure standing on the statute books for their benefit was placed there through his efforts. Chief among these measures were those affecting the Letter Carriers. The first, gives the Letter Carriers an annual vacation of fifteen days without loss of pay—authorizing the employment meanwhile of substitutes. The second gives them a fixed salary, which the Postmaster General himself is unable to disturb. The third limits a day's work to eight hours, and provides that for any additional hour or hours the carrier may be employed, he shall "be paid extra for the same in proportion to the salary now fixed by law." The gratitude of this class of public servants to Mr. Cox was manifest on many notable occasions during his life, and is no less manifest now that he wots not of it.

When Mr. Cox took up in Congress the cause of the Letter Carriers, his first efforts were directed to the securing of legislation which should give them stated salaries. He saw that the compensation of a Letter Carrier was governed largely, if not altogether, by the caprice of the Postmaster under whom he was serving. A lump sum was given a Postmaster to be distributed among his employes, according to his own sweet will and pleasure. Naturally, he had his favorites, and naturally, too, these were taken better care of than those on whom he smiled not.

It was to preclude all favoritism, to put every Letter Carrier beyond the power of suffering from this caprice of his employer, and to equalize as well as fix salaries, that Mr. Cox entered upon an undertaking beset by many obstacles, and which took years to fully accomplish.

More or less the carrier was a foot ball of politics. Sometimes he was sent for by the party boss and threatened with a reduction of pay if he hesitated to grind the ax of that boss. He knew not, at the beginning of a campaign what would be his fate at its close. It was emancipation from this state of servitude that Mr. Cox sought and obtained for the letter carriers.

In an address before the Letter Carriers of Boston and the workmen at the navy yard, in historic Faneuil Hall, Mr. Cox briefly referred to his labors in Congress in behalf of the Letter Carriers. "I tender my acknowledgments," said he, "to the Letter Carriers of Boston for recognizing my humble efforts, through many years, to raise their wages to an adequate sum. At last, on February 21, 1879, my bill passed both houses. It was signed. It was left unexecuted under various pretenses. 'Oh!' it was said, 'the carriers are not yet classified and would not be until July 1.' A mere show and not at all creditable to any concerned. The committees in both houses endeavored on that their

LITTLE ETHEL VAN ZANT SULLIVAN.

(Grandniece of S. S. Cox, who unveiled Letter Carriers' Statue.)

pretext to cut down the salaries of that bill below the sums allowed, and to begin the lower pay on the first of July. When the bill went to the Senate it was not only thus curtailed but was loaded down with riders as to swamp lands, Osage interest money, railroad mail transportation pay, and what not. I had to fight these in detail. Some were throttled, some not, to save the bill. Happily the Carriers have their tasks requited with a larger salary."

Another measure in the interests of the Letter Carriers, obtained through Mr. Cox's efforts, is known as the "Carriers' Vacation Law." Under its provisions every letter carrier in the United States is entitled to an annual vacation of fifteen days, with full pay during that time, his duties, meanwhile, performed by a substitute, who is also paid by the government. Before the passage of this act a vacation to a letter carrier came only through the grace of his Postmaster. It comes to him now through the law of the land, and no thanks to either Postmaster or Postmaster General.

In recognition of this important service at a special meeting of the letter carriers of the branches of the New York postoffice held on July 20, 1884, the following preamble and resolutions were unanimously adopted:

"The letter carriers of the branches of the New York Postoffice feel deeply indebted to Honorable Samuel S. Cox for the valuable service he has rendered them and the letter carriers generally in the United States by his advocacy before the United States Congress of just and proper legislation in their behalf.

"And whereas they desire to place on record some suitable expression of their warm esteem for him personally and their very high appreciation of the valuable services rendered them, therefore be it

"Resolved, That the most earnest thanks of the letter carriers of the branches of the New York Postoffice be and are hereby unanimously tendered to the Hon. Samuel S. Cox for his efficient and indefatigable efforts to secure by act of Congress to the letter carriers a much needed annual vacation of two weeks.

"Resolved, That we recognize in the Hon. S. S. Cox, not only a true friend, but an eminent statesman and legislator whose official power has been wisely exercised for the best interests of the public service.

"Resolved, That this preamble and resolutions be suitably engrossed, framed and presented to the Honorable Samuel S. Cox as an expression of our warm personal esteem and of our united wishes that he may long continue to do honor as an able and upright public servant."

The presentation of an elaborately engrossed copy of these resolutions to Mr. Cox at his residence by the committee was accompanied with the further presentation of a magnificent gold watch, which was prized by him to the day of his death as one of his choicest possessions.

This was followed, after Mr. Cox's return to Congress succeeding his mission in Turkey, by the eight hour law being applied to Letter Carriers. Mr. Cox's part in passing these three measures of inestimable value to the Letter Carriers, was thus summed up by one of their numbers, George H.

Newson, in a speech presenting a statue of the
'Letter Carriers' Friend" to the City of New York,
July 4, 1891. "When," said Mr. Newson, "Mr.
Cox understood that the Letter Carriers were receiving less compensation than the driver of a
horse car and the laborers on the street, he did not
believe that the qualifications on the one side and
the compensation on the other were evenly bal-
anced. He saw a duty, and when Congress met,
he introduced a bill to increase the carriers' salaries. We well remember how patiently, hopefully, and yet fearfully, we waited and watched for
the result. We felt that our cause was in the
hands of a good friend, and would not suffer for
the want of devotion on his part. An illustration
of his earnestness might be told here. The bill
had passed the house and was pending in the Senate. The House was in continued session, it being
the last few days of Congress. Mr. Cox thought
his work was done, and returned home to New
York for a much needed rest. He left word with
the carriers' representative that if the bill was
amended in the Senate, he would be on the confer-
ence committee, and that if he was needed he
should be sent for, and he would return. One
night at about eleven o'clock we received a dispatch from Washington stating that Mr. Cox
would be needed next morning. A messenger
hurried to Mr. Cox's residence, found that he had
retired; but when he was made acquainted with
the nature of the message, he immediately arose,
and although the train to Washington left Jersey
City at 12:15 midnight, Mr. Cox was on that train,
and arrived at the Capitol at 8 o'clock next morning, and before the sun went down that day, the

salary bill had become a law as far as the Senate and House were concerned.

"It had been a custom of the Postmaster of New York to grant a ten days' leave of absence to all carriers in the New York postoffice. He was not required to do so by law, nor was the same privilege granted to the carriers of any other city. For some reason or other, a few years after the passage of the salary bill, the department at Washington instructed the Postmaster at New York to discontinue these vacations. When Mr. Cox became aware of that fact, he presented and had passed in both houses, before the next vacation season came around, a bill giving all of the carriers of the United States a fifteen days' leave of absence, with pay, and provided some one to do each carrier's work—so that, instead of the carrier receiving the vacation as a compliment, he received it as a matter of right."

Respecting the history of the act constituting eight hours a days' work for a carrier, and allowing him pro rata pay for all overtime, Mr. Newson said: "When the fight began, if we may call it a fight, Mr. Cox was in Turkey, representing the government. We felt that our leader was gone, and that we must go into the fight without him. We had already waited through one session of Congress without any action, and were willing to wait two, three, or four, whatever the case might be, or until we succeeded, when we received word that Mr. Cox was to return home again. We felt that with his presence we should surely win. We gave him a royal reception when he returned home and a few weeks after that he returned to Congress, and immediately espoused our cause. That we won you know full well."

Not at once, however, were the fruits of the victory gathered. The Postoffice Department, which had been unable to defeat the passage of the law, now sought means to nullify it. The Department set up the claim that eight hours a day meant fifty-six hours a week—that if a carrier was not employed beyond this number of hours per week there was no overtime. If not employed at all Sunday, the fifty-six hours might be divided through the other six days—an average of over nine hours a day—according to the postmaster's sweet will. In this contention, strange to say, the Postoffice Department was sustained by its legal adviser, the Assistant Attorney General for that department. The eight-hour law, drafted by Mr. Cox, was placed on the statute book May 24, 1888. For nearly three months the new law was ignored altogether. In August, in pursuance of a policy of general extension of the free delivery service, the Department, in place of putting on new carriers, undertook to increase the working hours of the carriers already employed beyond the legal eight. Overtime began then and there. The letter carriers, as usual when in perplexity, appealed to Mr. Cox. Their committeee called his attention to what had been represented to them as a flaw in the law and to the construction put upon it by the Department. Mr. Cox promptly replied that in his judgment the act was complete—that its language fully bore out his intent in framing it, which was that each day was to be considered by itself, and was not to be bunched with half a dozen others. And he advised them to fight it out on that line.

For every hour of overtime on any day, regardless of any other, Mr. Cox maintained that the Government must pay pro rata.

Still, year after year the overtime went on under the department's construction of the law. Finally, three years after Mr. Cox's death, came the vindication of the law and its author. A test case, involving all the points at issue was made up, under Postmaster General Wanamaker, and submitted to the Court of Claims. That court decided in favor of the letter carriers. Postmaster General Wanamaker appealed the case to the Supreme Court of the United States, and the highest tribunal in the land affirmed the decision of the Court of Claims. That settled it for all time. What Mr. Cox intended the law should be, such it was. Mr. Cox had not been drafting laws thirty years for nothing.

What was the upshot? The letter carriers were bidden file their claims for overtime during the more than four years the department had, under bad advice, misconstrued a perfectly plain enactment. The claims were filed, established by legal proof, and for their payment the Government had, up to September, 1898, appropriated nearly $3,- 250,000.

The legal end of the carriers' claims for overtime was handled by the Washington attorneys, the brothers George A. and William B. King. In the face of many discouragements these attorneys bravely fought the case from its inception in the Court of Claims to its triumphant conclusion in the Supreme Court of the United States. And they have since successfully prosecuted the claims for overtime of many hundreds of carriers throughout the United States. It is no small tribute to Mr.

STATUE OF S. S. COX, ASTOR PLACE, NEW YORK.

(Erected by the Letter Carriers).

Cox's legal astuteness that the line on which they fought and won in the highest court of the land was precisely that laid down by the author of the law himself, without amendment or qualification.

The Supreme Court, in a decision delivered by Mr. Justice Samuel Blatchford, March 13, 1893, held in substance as follows:

1. That a carrier is entitled to count all work performed by him under proper authority, whether on the street in delivering or collecting mails, in making up mail in the postoffice for delivery, or in doing other postal service under direction of the postmaster.

2. That a carrier is entitled to extra pay for any time which he works in excess of eight hours upon any one day, even though he may work less than eight hours on some other day .

Said Justice Blatchford:

"The Court of Claims, in its opinion, arrived at the following conclusions: (1) That the letter car-riers were entitled to recover, not only for all work done by them on the street in delivering and col-lecting mail matter, but also for all work done in the postoffice, in receiving and arranging the let-ters of their routes. (2) That, as to the distribution of mail matter for the boxes and general delivery, during the times intervening between one trip and another in the same day, the regulations of the De-partment could properly be construed as permit-ting such services; and (3) that, as to the services of the same character rendered after the termina-tion of the last trip for the day of the carrier in delivering and collecting mail matter, they were services fairly within the power of the postmaster to prescribe.

"We are of opinion that, in respect of all such services, the letter carrier, if employed therein a greater number of hours than eight per day, was entitled to be paid extra. To hold otherwise would be to say that the carrier was employed contrary to the regulations of the Department, when it clearly appears that he was employed in accordance with such regulations. The statute manifestly was one for the benefit of the letter carriers and it does not lie in the mouth of the Government to contend that the employment in question was not extra service, and to be paid for as such, when it appears that the United States, in accordance with the regulations of the Postoffice Department, actually employed the letter carriers the extra number of hours per day, and it is not found that they were so employed as clerks. The postmaster was the agent of the United States to direct the employment, and if the letter carriers had not obeyed the orders of the postmaster they could have been dismissed. They did not lose their legal rights under the statute by obeying such orders.

"Judgment affirmed."

Mr. Cox did not live to witness the crowning triumph of his labors in behalf of the letter carriers, but the gratitude of the men he so zealously and effectually served is undying.

It is worthy of note that the last public appearance of Mr. Cox was at a festival held by the Letter Carriers, when he received a testimonal from their hands and made his last public speech. The passage of the eight-hour bill was celebrated with great enthusiasm by the Letter Carriers of the United States in the Academy of Music, New York, on the Fourth of July following. At this

OFFICERS OF NATIONAL LETTER CARRIERS' ASSOCIATION, 1898-9.

E. J. Cantwell, Sec'y,
Washington, D. C.
Jas. Arkison, Ch'n Leg. Com.,
Fall River, Mass.
J. F. McElroy, Ch'n Ex. Bd.,
Bridgeport, Conn.
A. K. Young, Ex. Bd.,
Cincinnati, O.

Conrad Trieber, Vice-Pres.,
San Francisco, Cal.
John N. Parsons, Pres.,
New York City.
W. J. Knott, Ex. Bd.,
Newark, N. J.

M. J. Conners, Treasurer,
Chicago, Ill.
Chas. R. Raedel, Ch'n Civ. Ser.,
Canton, O.
Francis J. Bourke, Ex. Board,
Syracuse, N. Y.
Chris Lougheed, Sec. Ex. Bd.,
Detroit, Mich.

meeting the following preamble and resolutions
were unanimously adopted:

"Whereas, the Letter Carriers of the United
States do feel deeply indebted to Hon. Samuel S.
Cox for the service so generously rendered by him
to secure the passage of the measure limiting the
hours of duty of Letter Carriers to eight per diem,
and

"Whereas, our efforts would have been futile
were it not for the encouragement given and labor
expended in his own sphere and field; and

"Whereas, we recognize in Hon. Samuel S. Cox
a true friend to the cause of labor and a gentleman
who, although employed in the more important
questions of State and Nation, saw the justice of
our cause and enlisted in it for justice's sake;
therefore be it

"Resolved, That the thanks of the Letter Carriers of the United States are due, and the same
are hereby extended to Hon. Samuel S. Cox for his
unselfish devotion to our cause and the many sacrifices made by him in our behalf, the result of
which has been to make our labor less a task and
more a pleasure.

"Resolved, That a copy be engrossed and presented to the Hon. Samuel S. Cox of New York."

When Mr. Cox died, by none was he mourned
more sincerely than by the Letter Carriers of the
United States. Resolutions expressive of their
sorrow were adopted by the carriers of all the principal cities of the United States. The letter carriers of Philadelphia resolved that with loving
hearts in grateful remembrance, we heartily pay
tribute to his sterling worth as our champion,
friend and protector. He was universally be-

loved, respected and admired, ever ready to give his time and efforts in our behalf. "Where," they asked, "will we look for another such true friend? Everywhere, only to be disappointed. With one accord we place upon record this slight token of our loving regard and devotion for our dear friend —the incorruptible statesman who has passed away, leaving an unstained career as a fitting memorial of a life well spent."

The branch at Jacksonville, Fla., resolved "that in the death of Samuel S. Cox the nation has lost a loved and honored statesman, humanity a friend, Christianity a devout follower, and the Letter Carriers of the United States a zealous champion, supporter, benefactor and advocate. That, excelling in all the walks of life, we have known him best as the honest statesman and the friend of the employes of the nation."

The San Francisco carriers unanimously passed this resolution: "That as employes of the free-delivery system of the United States postal service we shall ever hold in grateful remembrance the painstaking research, laborious compilations, eloquent pleadings for which on so many occasions during his long and honorable career in the halls of Congress Mr. Cox so ably assisted in securing for ourselves and our fellow employes of the service mentioned the just provisions which from time to time have been accorded to us by Congressional enactments." Besides these, the Golden Gate Carriers addressed a personal letter to the widow showing their appreciation of his "tireless advocacy" of their rights in Congress, and their sorrow at the loss of their "most zealous friend and advocate."

Memphis, Tennesee, joined in the procession of mourners, declaring in the resolutions of its Letter Carriers that "the council of the nation loses one of its brightest lights, America one of her noblest sons and grandest statesmen, and the laborers, and especially the Letter Carriers, a friend of inestimable worth," and that the letter carriers of Memphis "in mourning the loss of a friend so great and true do share in the bereavement of the nation and his family."

The Boston carriers put on record their deep sorrow at "the loss of one who had endeared himself to us by his kind, able, and willing assistance at all times," and one who "was ever the champion of our cause." Hardly a branch of the National Letter Carriers Association was too small or too remote to join in the acclaim of testimony to the services of the "Letter Carriers Friend." The annual decoration of his grave in Greenwood by these grateful servants of the public, attests that their gratitude is not evanescent or merely spasmodic, but is as enduring as the memory of his services in their behalf.

The crowning proof of the grateful appreciation of the Letter Carriers of the United States, towards their benefactor, stands in Astor Place, in the midst of the busy life of the metropolis. It is a bronze statue. The figure is of heroic proportions, and represents Mr. Cox in the attitude of addressing the House. His right hand is extended, while his left is at his side. The statue, eight feet high, rests on a pedestal of polished granite, twelve feet high. It cost $10,000, every dollar of which was the voluntary contribution of the Letter Carriers of the United States. The pedestal bears this inscription:

"Samuel Sullivan Cox,
The Letter Carriers' Friend.
Erected in grateful and loving memory of his ser·
vices in Congress by the Letter Carriers of
New York, his home, and of the United
States, his country, July 4th, 1891."

The movement for the erection of a suitable
monument to testify to the gratitude of the Letter
Carriers of the United States for Mr. Cox was
started the day following his death. A special
meeting of the New York Letter Carriers' association held September 11, 1889, after a preamble declaring that "the Letter Carriers of the United
States feel that they have lost a friend who devoted his greatest efforts in their interest and welfare and one who we feel will never be replaced,"
adopted this resolution:

"Resolved, That a committee of the New York
Letter Carriers' Association be authorized to con-
fer with the Letter Carriers of the United States,
for the purpose of raising a subscription for a suitable monument to be placed over the remains of
the devoted friend of the Letter Carriers of the
United States."

In the end the erection of a statue in Astor
Place was decided upon. The dedication of this
statue, on the anniversary of the nation's independence, was an imposing ceremony. Delega-
tions of Letter Carriers came for the purpose, from
far and near, even the Pacific Coast and the Gulf
States being represented. Two thousand carriers
turned out from New York and Brooklyn alone.
Charles P. Kelly, President of the Carriers' Association, New York, was grand marshal of the procession. George H. Newson, chairman of the

statue committee, made the speech of presentation
to the city, and President Arnold of the Board of
Aldermen, received it in the city's behalf.   The
orator of the occasion was Gen. Thomas Ewing,
formerly of Ohio, an associate of Mr. Cox in Congress and the friend of his earlier years.   In the
course of his eloquent tribute, Mr. Ewing said:

"Letter Carriers of the United States: Well may
you commemorate his public services.   The work
he did for you would not have been done by another.   When he espoused your cause in Congress
you had no national organization through which
to command public respect, and there were not
enough of you in any one constituency to give you
any other champion in Congress than him whose
support went out to you without a thought as to
your numbers or his own interest.   But for his
unselfish sympathy and zeal you would have no
redress of hardships and grievances, but would
have gone on to this day tramping your weary
rounds from daylight to dark, through winter's
cold and summer's heat, underpaid and over-
worked."

Recognition of Mr. Cox's effective aid to the Letter Carriers' has been freely and on every suitable
occasion made by them.   And in the House of
Representatives in June, 1898, graceful acknowl-
edgment thereof was made by Mr. Cox's successor
in these words:

"Mr. Bradley—Mr. Chairman—Representing as
I do a district which was formerly represented by
one of the ablest men that ever graced the halls of
Congress, a man to whom the Letter Carrier was
the darling of his heart, and who did more to build
up the postal service than any other one man in

the United States, the late Samuel S. Cox, I feel
that I would be an unworthy successor of his if I
failed in my humble way to do what I could to further the work which he did so much to forward."

Mr. Cox's last speech made in Congress, in February, 1889, was in behalf of the postoffice clerks,
to extend to them the benefits already enjoyed by
the carriers, as to classification and fixed salaries.

"Mr. Chairman," he said, "in opening his
speech, "I have the honor and the pleasure to take,
perhaps, an unusual interest in the postoffice department. That interest has been special, and on
certain lines it is somewhat limited. The delivery
system has long been associated with my duties
here, and, I may say, even my anxieties abroad.
But the Letter Carriers have had not an unreason-
able, on the contrary, quite a kindly, provision
made for them as to the increase of their pay, their
vacation, their recreation, and their hours of service. But how superbly have they recompensed
the government for its benfactions! As the facts
justify our pride over my previous efforts in their
behalf, may I be permitted to present now and
here the last results of this free delivery or letter
carrier service? Facts furnish the vindication of
this system. They simply astound the mind as
well as please the heart." The work which would
have placed the Postoffice Clerks on the same
plane of protection as the carriers, he did not live
to finish. Nor does the flight of years in anywise
lessen the Letter Carriers' grateful appreciation of
the valued services of their deceased benfactor.

CHAPTER XXVI.

Of no achievement to which he could look back at the close of his legislative service was Mr. Cox more proud than of the creation by Federal statute of the Life Saving Service. This measure was not only introduced into Congress by him, but it was pressed with tireless zeal, until he had the triumphant satisfaction of witnessing its passage and the service duly established.

A Chicago paper, after his death, characterized the Life Saving Service "a grand monument to his wisdom and humanity." In that very year, the same authority stated "over 3,950 persons were rescued and ships and cargoes valued at $7,966,660 saved" through this service. "Ages hence," it added "S. S. Cox will be remembered by those who go down to sea in shiips and are rescued from the treacherous waves by the crews of life boats." Mr. Cox, in a speech in 1878, in the House, attributed the inspiration of his efforts in this direction to a storm in the Scilly Isles, in the winter of 1868, when a great steamer barely escaped shipwreck. "It was," he said "the worst tempest in thirty years upon that coast. When we arrived in port, the day after the peril, the English journals were full of the glorious exploits, by rocket and signal

and coast guard and mortar and life boat. I won-
dered, if so much could be done in England, with
her forty-five hundred miles of coast line, why
should not our country, with double that number
of miles, have a similarly efficient service. It was
this that led me to propose what the superintendent of the service called the efficient beginning
of the patrol of the Jersey coast. Since that time
how much has been done for the well being and
rescue of imperiled lives! How much of comfort
and joy has been vouchsafed to families and
friends of the beneficiaries of that mercy which
droppeth as the gentle rains from heaven in this
warm-hearted legislation, blessing and blessed."

The close of his speech was as follows:

"Mr. Speaker: I have spent the best part of my
life in this public service. Most of it has been like
writing in water. The reminiscences of party
wrangling and political strife seem to me like neb-
ulae of the past, without form and almost void.
But what little I have accomplished in connection
with this Life Saving Service is compensation
sweeter than honey in the honeycomb. It is its own
exceeding great reward. It speaks to me in the
voices of the rescued; aye, in tears of speechless
feeling; speaks of resurrection from death—

In spite of wreck and tempest's roar,

In spite of false lights on the shore;
speaks of a faith triumphant over all fears in the
better elements of our human nature. It sounds
like the undulations of the Sabbath bell, ringing in
peace and felicity. It comes to me in the words of
Him who, regardless of His own life, gave it freely
that others might be saved.

"Humanity and civilization should walk white-

LIFE SAVING STATION, PORT HURON, MICH.

handed along with government. They strengthen
and save society. In the perils which environ our
country, from passion and prejudice, from old animosities and new irritations, let us do good deeds
—pray hopefully that our vessel of state be free
from leakage, collision, wreck and loss. Send out
the life-boat; fire the line over the imperiled vessel; free the hawser for the life-car, and then with
stout hearts and thankful souls lift up our prayer
to Him who holds the sea in the hollow of His
hand."

The effect of this eloquent appeal was electric.
Almost immediately the bill passed the House, and
without one dissenting vote.

The speech attracted wide attention and elicited
everywhere the highest encomiums. At a meeting
of the Board of Aldermen of the City of New York
held June 11, 1878, the following preamble and resolution offered by Alderman Morris were adopted:

"Whereas, Hon. Samuel S. Cox, one of the representatives in Congress from this city, has delivered
an effective and patriotic speech in the House of
Representatives in behalf of humanity and the suffering; and as he has given almost his whole life
to assist in perfecting the Life Saving System and
to establish its workings on our coast, from Maine
to California, by which thousands of lives and millions of dollars have been saved to all nationalities.
Therefore be it

"Resolved, That the Board of Aldermen of the
City of New York tender to the Hon. Samuel S.
Cox and to all members of Congress and other persons conected in any way with this life saving and
humane institution, their sincere and heartfelt

thanks, not unmindful of the assistance given to
it by the press of the country. And be it further

"Resolved, That the Clerk of this Board be authorized and directed to have this engrossed and
forwarded to the Hon. Samuel S. Cox.

Adopted by the Board of Aldermen, June 11th,
1878.

Approved by the Mayor, June 17th, 1878.

Francis J. Twoomey,
Clerk Common Council."

In Congress after Congress the onslaught upon
the Life Saving Service, assuming one guise or another, was renewed, and as often successfully met
by its sturdy champion. Some of the most eloquent
appeals ever heard on the floor of Congress were
made by Mr. Cox on these occasions. The following
extracts must suffice as examples:

[From a speech in the House, 1878]

"This service is, in a high sense, divinely beautiful. Although it is limited to this country of ours,
yet its benefaction knows no boundary, and its
example is an incentive to the benevolent of all
lands. It rescues the people of all nationalities.
No wonder that the nations are following our example.

"Denmark is seeking to introduce our system
amidst her belts, coasts, and isles. No wonder
that Holland—the child of the sea—is asking for
our instructions, signals, and paraphernalia for
life-saving. If I may be allowed to say it, the
Turkish and Russian maritime people are endeav-
oring to adapt our system to the increasing commerce of the Black Sea, at the mouth of the historic Bosphorus. Two thousand years ago—after
Jason had navigated to Colchis for the golden
fleece—temples were built to the gods of Greece

at the perilous mouth of these classic waters. At
their altars the votive offerings of sailors were
laid, because of the tempestuous character of that
inland sea. I have recently seen the ruins of
these temples that were dedicated to Jupiter,
Neptune and other heathen gods, to whom invoca-
tions were made to save the adventurous naviga-
tor from disaster and death.

"Whereas, Mr. Speaker—these ancient mariners
appealed to Jupiter and Neptune—we appeal to
practical mechanics. We invoke the genius of
chemistry, with its colored signals, its line, car,
buoy, powder and howitzer. We add to electricity and steam the dauntless heroism of the surfman. Odessa and Constantinople, by voluntary
effort are copying our example in thus rescuing
the imperiled.

"Yet, sir, in conclusion, there is a higher sanc-
tion than the Constitution or humanity. It is that
of Him who stilled the waves of Galilee to save
imperiled human life. It is said that in the beauty
of the lilies Christ was born across the sea, and
in the glory of his bosom he transfigured you and
me. He died to make men holy, and for the salva-
tion of human souls in desperate shipwrecks
through sins. We may not imitate his example,
here, sir, except afar off, but, by our voice and
vote, we may do something by this measure to
throw around our legislation a divine aureole
and save human life, so precious to Him who gave
His life to save the lives of others. (Applause.)

"Ah! sir; there is a pathetic poetry belonging to
the sea, which is all too sad for the ordinary prose
of human composition. The sea has been the
theme of praise by many writers; their vivid de-

scriptions remain in the memory. They have ap-
plauded its services as the great purveyor of the
world's commodities, for the diversity of food
which it yields, and, most of all, for the 'wonders
of the Lord in the deep.' But no pen has ever done
justice to the grandeur of its aspect, even in calm,
or to the might of its tempests in storm. It is
said that it entertains the sun with vapors, the
moon with obsequiousness, the stars with a mirror
the sky with clouds, the air with temperateness,
the soil with subtileness, the rivers with tides, the
hills with moisture, and the valleys with fertility.
It gives meditation to the mind, and the world to
the world, all parts thereof to each part, by the art
of arts—navigation. Still, above all is that restless, overwhelming power, in the wild tumult of
its wrath, when its crested waves make a compact
with the clouds and the winds, the thunder and the
thunderbolt, and sweep on in their dread alliance.
And yet, to sustain the art of navigation, there is
another art, called into being by the genius of man,
which dares contend against the wild, insatiable,
and reckless Saturnalia of the sea. Oliver Wendell Holmes compares the sea with the mountains,
to the great disadvantage of the sea. He loves—
as who does not—the mountains, where the least
of things seem infinite; but the sea is to him a huge
feline, licking your feet, purring at times pleasantly, but ready to crack your bones and eat you
for all that, and then wipe the crimsoned foam
from its jaws as if nothing had happened. The
sea had for him a fascinating, treacherous intelligence, stretching out its shining length, and by
and by lashing itself into rage, showing its white
teeth, and ready to spring at the bars while howl-

ing the cry of its mad fury! That furious wild animal, the arts of man has caged and bound! Before the genius of man the wildest waves become calm. Parent and child, wife and husband, brother and sister and lover, who are tempest-tossed and stranded, are rescued from the washing and wasting element, which is subdued and enchanted by human bravery. As Byron has sung, "Man has wantoned with its breakers, and that which was a terror becomes a pleasing fear." Our noble crews defying its billows, have laid their hands upon its mane and tamed it to their will. In the old days it was said that it was beautiful to die for one's country. Under the inspiration of martial music and other martial exercises patriotic men rush to the conflict and die. Nations vote pensions and decorations to the hero who first plants a flag on a parapet or rescues it from an enemy. How much nobler to decorate and pension the man who, seeing one of his own kind, though a stranger, in the struggle and despair of death, plunges into the very jaws of the unseen future amidst darkness and danger to reclaim his fellow-being from a watery grave. Who can measure the wonderful grace of that government which not only provides for the rescue of the victims and the stranded ships from the storm, but gives consolation to those who, as Jeremy Taylor well says, have not yet suffered shipwreck, but who amidst the dark night, an ill guide, and a boisterous sea, and broken cable, and hard rock, and a rough wind, may be dashed in pieces with the fortunes of a whole family, and they that shall weep loudest for the accident have not yet entered into the storm? We may construct upon our

shore the image of Liberty holding up its torch to
enlighten the world; we may allure the immigrant
to our country by this lustrous imagery at the harbor of our great metropolis; but no such light,
even though dazzling with its electric brilliancy,
will attract the attention of the good men of our
kind like the serene and blessed illumination that
radiates from our life-saving statute and proclaims to all the world—to men of every condition,
race and nationality—that when overcome by the
terrific disasters of the sea, they have at every perilous point upon our coast the heroic courage of
men who are equipped and ready to leap into the
surf, to launch their boats through its 'league-long
rollers,' to breast the tempest in its angry howling,
and to rescue those who are hanging upon the vast
abyss and about to be swallowed by the angry
waters. It is said in the New Testament that a
man will give his life for his friend. But these
men, almost without pay, with a lion-hearted courage far excelling that of the soldier under the impulse of patriotic devotion—are ready in the pursuit of their high duty to glorify our human nature
by laying down their lives, if need be, for those—
even those who are aliens and strangers."

[From a speech. 1888.]

"May I not, then, take pardonable pride in the
establishment and progress of this system, which
has no peer in the world for its effective work and
no paragon in the history of nations for its inspiration? I sometimes think, Mr. Speaker, that I
have, through the mercy of God, more than my
compensation for the little I have done in the pro-
motion of this service. When struggling for life
one year ago, in this city, when the little will

power which was remaining was ready to succumb before the ravages of disease and the agony of pain, and when friends had almost given up my surviving, I cast my eyes upon two pictures at either side of my sick bed.

"One was that of the life-boat going out through the storm to the rescue of a ship wrecked upon a rock-bound coast, while there on the shore the relatives of the surfmen stand speechless with anxiety as to the fate of the brave men who hazard all for the rescue. The other picture is that of the same life-boat coming in. It is laden with its precious freight. The howling storm, the chime of the breakers, and the dark clouds around the beetling cliffs; the cry goes up from thankful hearts, 'All safe; all well.'

"In my poor sick fancy I grasped the tiller of the life-boat. I clung to it with the tenacity that overcame the sinking heart of an emaciated body. The good doctor, when I related to him the incident and the source, and how it had inspired me with a fresh hope and a new life, gave me smiling assurance that I might still survive as a rescued man to plead for the Life-Saving Service in many Congresses.

"I have said, Mr. Speaker, that we have one beautiful statute which as a sacred halo around it. It makes a sunshine in the shadow of our selfish, sectional, and patriotic codes and laws. It is that which preserves human life. It is not merely a sentimental humanity, but a real benefaction. Like the orange tree, it bears fruit and flowers at the same time.   *   *

"It is no exaggeration to say, in view of its object, that it gives us a glimpse, though dim, of the

golden age. The world's heart clings to it as if
it were a memory of a past paradise or the home
of a paradise regained. The sea itself plays its
mighty minstrelsy in its honor.   *   *   *
Life is precious because its loss can not be repair-
ed.   Jeremy Taylor has told us that while   our
senses are double there is   but   one death,   but
once only to be acted, and that in an instant, and
upon that instant all   eternity depends.   Other
losses may be recompensed by gains, but loss   by
death never.   No one is so lordly or powerful as to
stay this irreparable loss.   Every day puts us   in
peril; while we think we die.   What care and esteem can equal the eternal weight of human life?
Can any legislation be too ample or adequate for
its production?"

In grateful recognition of his devotion to the upbuilding of the Life Saving Service, the members
of that service presented to his widow, a few
months after his death, a memorial vase. The pre-
sentationwas made with appropriate ceremony at
Mrs. Cox's home in Washington, in the presence of
a notable gathering of relatives and friends, the
General Superintendent, Sumner I. Kimball, representing the Service. "The vase," as described in
one of the publications of the day, "is two feet in
height, two feet one inch in circumference, and
weighs one hundred twenty-five ounces. On the
front of the vase is a scene representing the life-
savers engaged in rescuing people from a stranded
vessel by means of the breeches buoy. Some distance out, where the sea rises in mountains, is the
wrecked vessel, with torn sails and shattered spars.
At various points along the beach life-savers are

VASE PRESENTED TO MRS. COX BY LIFE-SAVING SERVICE.

seen lifting bodies from the heavy surf and carrying them ashore. In direct contrast with this
wild scene is the ornamentation that circles the
body of the vase. This consists of a cable net in
which are caught starfish, seaweed and odd-ap-
pearing plants and shells that are known to in-
habit the depths of the ocean. A ledge formed by
a ship's chain supports this net, while above is a
profile of Mr. Cox circled with laurel against a
background of sea coral. A life buoy crossed with
a boathook and oar rests at the top. The handles
at the sides are composed of two beautifully
formed mermaids, who, with bowed heads and
curved bodies, hold in their upraised hands sea
plants that grow from the side of the top. The inscription is as follows:

THIS MEMORIAL VASE

IS PRESENTED TO

MRS. SAMUEL S. COX.

BY THE MEMBERS OF

THE LIFE-SAVING SERVICE OF THE UNITED STATES

IN GRATEFUL REMEMBRANCE OF THE TIRELESS AND SUCCESSFUL
EFFORTS OF HER DISTINGUISHED HUSBAND,

THE HONORABLE SAMUEL SULLIVAN COX,

TO PROMOTE THE INTERESTS AND ADVANCE THE EFFICIENCY AND GLORY
OF THE LIFE-SAVING SERVICE.

———

He was its early and constant friend;
Its earnest and eloquent advocate;
Its fearless and faithful champion.

General Superintendent Kimball, in his presentation address recalled the history of the Life-Saving Service. "The system," he said, "was initiated in 1871, but the way was prepared in 1870 when an amendment to an appropriation bill to provide for the employment of crews of surfmen at the stations on the New Jersey coast for the winter months having been defeated, Mr. Cox, after a sharp and persistent contest, secured the passage of a substitute authorizing their employment at every alternate station. This was probably the first time his attention had been attracted to the idea of rescuing the shipwrecked by organized effort from the shore, and from that hour he became its devoted adherent and champion.

"It opened the door to the subsequent employment of crews at all the stations, and only through this door lay directly the way to the establishment of the present organization. As Mr. Cox anticipated, the very defects of the provision hastened and aided the advance. The next appropriation bill providing for sundry civil expenses of the government, approved April 20, 1871, appropriated a sufficient amount to permit the construction of several additional stations and to replenish the equipments of the old ones', and authorized the Secretary of the Treasury to employ crews at such stations as he might deem necessary. He caused their employment at all. This permitted, upon the limited stretch of coast to which the stations were confined, the initiation of a plan of organization which was the prototype of the system that to-day extends over the entire coast of the country. The result that followed was so immediate and striking as to arrest general attention. At the close of the season it was found that not a life had been lost within the field of this guardianship."

But the struggle was not over. The opposition to apropriations for the Life Saving Service was renewed Congress after Congress, originating generally with members representing districts far remote from the seacoast. It was seemingly a "battle once begun, never done." Mr. Cox was at the front of every battle and invariably saved the day for the life savers. In the Forty-fifth Congress he secured his most signal victory. It was proposed to transfer the service from the treasury to the naval control. A long and desperate contest ensued, Mr. Cox marshaling the forces of the opposition to the proposed change, which he believed to be fraught with infinite peril to the system. "The closing days of the session," said Superintendent Kimball," brought a signal victory for the service, and witnessed one of the most notable triumphs for Mr. Cox that has ever marked the annals of Congress. It was in the final encounter of this protracted struggle that he made that memorable speech that must always be accounted the ablest of all the great speeches that distinguished his long and brilliant career. Its effect upon the auditors was magical and a scene ensued that has rarely if ever been paralleled in Congress. " A member who was present thus describes the scene:

"A number of speeches had been made; his was the last. No especial interest was manifested in the subject; nothing to distinguish it from the ordinary discussions that daily take place in the House. It was in the morning after the routine business had been disposed of that Mr. Cox arose. The attention of members was gradually arrested.

The calling of pages by the clapping of hands grew less frequent as he proceeded. In a short time the members sat enchained by the eloquence of his address. Now and then there was applause, but when he stopped a profound silence pervaded the House.

"In a moment or two it was broken by a member near by extending his congratulations to him. He was quickly followed by another; then two or three pressed forward to take him by the hand; when almost simultaneously a score or more approached him, and in less time than I can describe it every member was on his way up the aisle towards him to extend his congratulations. No attempt was made to continue business. The speaker of the House acquiesced in the temporary interruption and only called the members to order when they had resumed their seats. I sat immediately oppo site to him during the delivery of the speech and was the last member to grasp him by the hand. As I did so I saw that he had been moved to tears and not a word passed between us. I doubt very much whether, in the whole history of this body, any speech had such an instantaneous effect. It was a high tribute to the orator. Aye, it was more. It was a homage paid to his subject. He struck the key-note of humanity, and all within its sound responded to its spell."

"Probably," said Superintendent Kimball, "no speech ever made in the House produced so conspicuous a change of sentiment upon a pending question. The bill passed without a dissenting voice. The chosen leader of the opposition, a member distinguished for his eloquence and ability, had entered the hall before the discussion began

SUMNER I. KIMBALL.
Superintendent of Life Saving Service.

with books and documents which he intended to use in closing the debate for his side. When he saw the whole House file up the aisle to congratulate his antagonist he joined the throng, and upon reaching him said: 'Mr. Cox, you have anticipated and answered every point I expected to make; you have left me nothing to say.'

"Is it any wonder," asked Superintendent Kimball, "that when the announcement of his death flashed over the land, and was repeated by telephone from station to station, a gloom fell upon the coast from Maine to Texas on the Atlantic, and from Washington to the southern boundary of California on the Pacific, and all around the shores of the great inland lakes, such as had never overshadowed it before?"

Senator William P. Frye, of Maine, chairman of the Senate committee on Commerce, followed Superintendent Kimball, in an eloquent tribute, of which the following is a part:

"I knew Mr. Cox well; served with him in the House ten years; was honored with his friendship, and admired him intensely. He was a remarkable man. Michael Angelo, for more than four hundred years, has stood out in bold relief—painter, sculptor, architect, poet, and engineer. Mr. Cox was as many sided as he, not standing, it may be, so far above his fellows, but neither ordinary nor commonplace in any of the elements of his greatness. He was an orator, capable of moving to laughter or to tears. He could subdue the stormy House to quietness and make its members listeners. His imagination occasionally inspired him to wonderful flights of eloquence skyward, but he could, too, when it served his purpose, keep close to the ground. He was a logician, strong in solid argument to convict and convert. Thoroughly equipped by hard study, ceaseless toil, extended travels, long experience, he was a ready disputant whom no man could afford to despise.

"But the crowning quality of his greatness—that which will keep his memory fresh when others, his peers intellectually, are forgotten—was his great loving heart, his humanity to man. The dying soldier and the cup of cold water alone immortalized Sir Philip Sidney. It was this trait of character that made all his colleagues in the House his warm personal friends, even through contests sharp and sometimes bitter. It was this that preserved a sweetness neither time nor age nor contest, nor disappointed ambition could sour. It was this that inspired his championship of the sailor and the surfman, of the carrier and the laborer, of the Indian, the Irishman and the Hebrew—of the downtrodden, friendless and persecuted whenever and wherever he found them."

Such was the testimony borne by a political antagonist, with whom during their many years' service together on the floor of Congress, Mr. Cox had often crossed swords.

Among Mr. Cox's papers was found, after his death, a little pocket manual of "instructions to mariners in case of shipwreck, with information concerning the life-saving stations upon the coasts of the United States." After the quoted words, on the title page, he had written, "for which thank God!"

CHAPTER XXVII.

"FOUR NEW STARS."

Mr. Cox was a thorough believer in the "manifest destiny" of the Republic, and stood ever ready to give consistent support to measures for the enlargement of the circle of the union of states. In his last session in congress, closing with the first term of President Cleveland on March 4, 1889, he spoke and labored with all the energy of which he was capable in favor of the admission of four new states—the two Dakotas, Montana, and Washington. It was a Democratic House, and there was a determined opposition to their admission on party grounds. That this opposition was overcome was conceded to be primarily due to the efforts of Mr. Cox.

"There is," he confessed in a speech made in the House January 15, 1889, during the last session of his service in that body, "a sort of glamor and fascination about the admission of states into our imperial federation. I am subject to influences of a romantic character. But they have not disturbed, and I think will not disturb, that discretion which belongs to congress when it votes to make complete the circle of our federal felicities.

"Mr. Speaker, as we approach the centenary of the life of our nation the mind becomes reminiscent. It would also be prophetic. In dim outline the ancient seers saw, through the mists of western seas, our hemisphere as the home of a race which rejoiced in a 'golden age.' These dreams take hold upon the imagination. They give an illusion to our 'discretion' on bills like these looking to future empire.

"The imaginary commonwealth of Plato was not altogether unsubstantial. Some of the visions upon the horizon of our early epochs have found realization. But a republic never imagined by Plato, nor dreamed of by Harrington or Sir Thomas More, has found its home in our hemisphere. Like all hope that has its fruition, this has come to us through toil, danger and heroism. These sacrifices have no parallel in the adventures of our race or upon our planet."

"This question of admission," he added, "is not a party question. In the nature of things it cannot be. The people of the territories are not wedded to any party. They are remote and isolated; preoccupied with absorbing local matters. They are easily molded, like the clay in the hands of the potter. As the wheel whirls, a little pressure here and a little pressure there, and out comes the graceful vase, irrespective of the rude and selfish manipulations of our Federal politics. If these territories be not admitted this session they will surely be admitted under Republican auspices in the next Congress, and their politics will take the reflection of the friends who give them their early nurture." Again he said: "Refuse to admit this

state and its territorial sisters? Why, sir, you may
enact that frost shall cease in the north and blooms
in the south, or try to fix the figure of Proteus by
statute, but you can not prevent the people of this
territory from their demand, and you must accede
to it; and if this Congress does not, we know that
the next Congress will. The spirit of this people
of the Northwest is that of unbounded push and
energy. These are the men who have tunneled our
mountains, who have delved our mines, who have
bridged our rivers, who have brought every part
of our empire within the reach of foreign and home
markets, who have made possible our grand
growth and splendid development. They are the
men who have made our national life. There is no
parallel in history to their achievements. You can
not hold them as captive to the Federal system.
You must give them self-reliant statehood.

"The historian of Rome draws a picture of the
proud Queen of Palmyra arrayed in purple and
loaded with golden chains to aggrandize the procession in honor of the conqueror of Asia. It
needs no such imagination to picture the condition
of our inchoate states in the West. They will
wear no golden chains. No, sir! They will march
in no procession of dishonor. Such exhibitions do
not belong to our country. Our people are not to
be led in fetters at the car of an imperial Congress. Why, such exhibitions were unfit even for
pagan Rome. So that in every possible equipment, whether divided or united, this remarkable
territory is ready to join that circle of felicity
which makes up the federal fraternity."

Anxious to testify their gratitude to him in person, the citizens of the newly invested States,

urged Mr. Cox, after the adjournment of Congress, to make a tour to their far off country. Accordingly, in June, accompanied by his wife, in response to their pressing invitation, he set out on his journey across the continent. Everywhere he was hailed as the father of the infant states. A continuous ovation it was. On the Fourth of July the announcement that he was to deliver the address at Huron, Dakota, sufficed to attract crowds from all available points of the new state. The address closed with these words:

"Standing upon the thresholds of these young states, and in the morning of another century, may we not have glimpses of the far future of their destiny? It may not be that of a Paradise regained; it may not be that of a New Atlantis rising from the wave, and where no frost congeals and no storm vexes; it may not be a Platonian ideal, where the abstract and the object are One, and that One is all beautiful with Truth and Virtue; it may not be some indefinite Utopia wearing its coronal of unreal happiness beneath Equatorial realms, but as men reason, is it not probable that in these new states, in the very heart of the continent, may be found the shining nucleus and the concentrated genius of the most miraculous progress known to human society? Already we may hear the cheerful music of requited toil, inspiring the builders of new homes and the founders of new commonwealths, with the incentive to and the fruition of the best human energy under the most favored institutions.

"Your celebration here and now is manifold in meaning. It combines Jefferson and the Declaration, Washington and the Constitution, Jefferson and Louisiana, and therefore Jefferson and Dakota. It embraces France with her revolution and our own, and France with Louisiana, Washington, Jefferson and Dakota, and all imbound in the golden rigol of republican institutions and human felicity. Said I not rightly, as men count the periods of time—it is a wonderful year?

"If other celebrations of this day be only the laudation of the historic past, then they will be a mere ostentation, which will die with the year. But your jubilee unites hope with history and advancement with memory.

"Yours, citizens of the Northwest, is a celebration that bids the glowing scenes of the future at distance, hail! No more the apprehension of the stealthy tread of the moccasin. No more the plash of the French trader's oar in your lakes and streams. Touch the pulse of our active age and you will feel the throb of the mighty mechanic movement which interweaves your interchanges with the world. Place your ear to the earth and you will hear the tramp, tramp, tramp of the coming generations. Stretch your vision from your dawning centenary eminence, and lo! Chaos and old Night roll away before an auroral splendor, 'far-sinking into splendor without end.'

"All hail! Sisters of the Northwest! As one not altogether unfamiliar with your territory and its inspirations, as one who has in the generation gone by endeavored to champion the rights and welcome the coming of the states, upon your southern and eastern border, even as the humblest of those accredited from the great entrepot of commerce to the National Congress—may I not be permitted to welcome you to the enjoyment of the privileges, advantages, immunities and guarantees which protect property, reputation, person, liberty, religion and life. Welcome to the Olympian race in which ye are about to start upon the course of continental empire! All hail! the promise of your superb morning, and may it be glorious to the end! Under favoring auspices may you so direct your destiny that the genius of your race and polity shall flourish beyond the imagination of man to conceive, or

'—Modern Homers
Sing, or smiling Freedom write
In their Iliads of Peace.''

A pathetic interest attaches to this journey and this address, as both were his last.

CHAPTER XXVIII.

Of his old campaigning days in Licking, Ohio,
Mr. Cox indulged to the full in reminiscence, in a
letter addressed to the chairman of the Democratic
County Committee of that county expressive of his
regret that illness forced an abandonment of his
engagement to speak in his old home, in the campaign of 1878. He was en route to keep his engagement when he was taken ill, and halted at
Pittsburg. "But," he writes, "as I 'lay sick of a fe-
ver,' all the old memories of campaigning in Licking thronged my mind, robed in many visionary
hues, and founded on many a serious and jolly
experience. I forgot for a time my trouble, and
the hum of the big city I had left; threw off the
coil of self interest, and lived again in the early
manhood. These memories were quickened by the
pleasing hope of renewing scenes of a score of
years and more ago. Since then, your fields, forests and houses have changed; but not so much, I
fear, as the good, jocund and wise friends of that
day. But the well known voices and faces came
trooping to my bedside, and I resolved, if I could,
to reproduce them on paper, if they did not escape
me on my memory. There are times when the
drums are unmuffled and they sound for the rally

and onset as of yore." And then recalling many
a person and many an incident of the days gone by
in "old Licking" he adds:

"Many lands have I seen since, redolent of associations, classic and romantic; but not in Van-
cluse, where Petrarch sung of Laura, nor in Scotland, where Burns sung of his Highland Mary, have
there been sweeter thoughts than I have had of
thy vale, sweet Cherry Valley! Other lands may
produce finer sheep, but give me Harrison and
Union, with their stock of Democratic shepherds,
like Colonel Alward, and another now dead and
nameless, who never allowed me to pass his house
without dedicating an eagle, with a flask to it, full
of "copper distilled" of his own brewing, which
(the eagle) received our special chrism in a wagon
shed near by. One hazelnut from the groves of
Fallsbury dissipates all memory of the oranges
and palms of Andalusia; a taste of the indigenous
peach from Hopewell, makes the apricots and nec-
tarines of the Mediterranean pall on the taste;
and the buckwheats, crinkled over with the dulcet
syrups of sorghum and Democracy, were made
sweeter by the relish I saw the bees take of the
purple flower as it bloomed in the fields of Burlington and Bennington. You may not, but others
may recall the procession as it came under the lead
of the most militant of militia captains from Hopewell and the southeast part of the county. It invariably had that same string band. Is the band
dissolved? I have heard many strange noises since
I have lived in this isle of Manhattan, and much
rare music, too. I have heard the weird songs and
tomtoms of Africa, listened to the tinkle of the
guitar and the clink of the castanet in Spain; have

listened to Tamberlik and Patti and all the stars
of operatic song; have held my breath before that
wonderful power which is evoked out of sound, by
the German skill of Gluck, Bach, Handel, Hayden,
Mozart, Beethoven, Schubert, Spohr, Mendelssohn
and Schuman; have been entranced, if not mys-
tified, by the transcendental genius of Wagner,
translating out of the inner soul the myths of the
past for the music of the future; and yet—yet, give
me the string band of the Flint Ridge boys and
their gallant captain. There was heart, soul and
patriotism in it. It was enough to satisy the sentiment as it pleases the memory.

"Men may come and go. Time with its chemistry changes even iron; the water drop in twenty
years will wear away the granite. These bodies of
ours, more easily affected than iron and granite,
change and go first.   They suffer many vicissitudes; but the indestructible memory of twenty
years ago in old Licking will never die. I live in a
town of twelve hundred thousand people, whose
factories make the big shafts and engines which
mate Neptune in his wildest tempest; but after all,
there is no stream, however small, like that which
dances through the memory of early days; no enterprise so interesting as that which identifies one
with early associations. Is there any thing dearer
to my heart than those farmer homes, where the
wooden latch lifted so easily to the touch? or
whose large open fireplace glowed so cheerily in
the autumn nights, and whose big feather beds
gave such delicious rest from the weariness of the
political arena? It is not what is big, but what is
dear that is remembered."

CHAPTER XXIX

A Western member had savagely assailed Mr. Cox for being a member of the Cobden club. In a speech in the House shortly after (May 17, 1888) on "The Surplus and the Tariff," Mr. Cox took occasion incidentally to pay his respects to his assailant, and to vindicate his own record. The following is an excerpt:

"Names are not much in a debate, but as the gentleman has spread my middle name—Sullivan —on the record, I must analyze that also a little in return, by saying that Sullivan is from the Latin "Sol" and "Levant." Sun Rise! (Laughter.) My ancestor came from the East. I went back as his reflux wave. (Laughter). I may mention confidentially that one of my ancestors carried a hod at the building of Solomon's Temple. (Laughter.) All I know of the family is that a recent ancestor came over from Ireland with Lord Baltimore. He was in 'noble' company. I need not enlarge further. There is another test of Celtic blood to which I may refer, as it is so pertinent to the Mills bill. The gentleman from Nevada will be pleased to know that his championship of the Tory protectionists of England indicates that he leans towards, if he does not belong to, the bluest blood

of the landed aristocracy of England.   Evidently
the speech of the gentleman was for the purpose
of prejudicing the Irish against the Democracy, by
reason of their dislike to their English oppressors.
But his arrow falls far short of the mark.   The
gentleman was pleased to say something complimentary of myself as a member of the Democratic
party, and referred to me as a representative of a
cosmopolitan constituency in a cosmopolitan city.
He spelled my name at full, and more than intimated that I became a member of the Cobden Club
because it was a 'nobleman's foreign association.'

"I am at loss how to discriminate.   I have no
special vanity, but I suppose the applause was intended for myself as a Democrat, author, wit,
humorist and representative (laughter), and that
the laughter was at the gentleman's expense for
associating me with noblemen—as such people run
nowadays in and out of divorce courts in England.

"Mr. Chairman, I am not altogether certain that
the gentleman should be laughed at for calling me
a nobleman.   I have had some sort of a decoration
given me by the successor of the Caliphs and the
Sultans.   But the nobility which I most admire is
not that of mere title.   I had almost forgotten my
honors abroad.   I did dearly yearn for the society
of you gentlemen.   (Laughter.)   All the pride I
have is to be a Commoner along with other common folks here.   (Applause and Laughter.)

"I do not care even for the courteous 'Honorable' in this House.   I have an ambition to be considered a good man and a faithful member.   I
have no special desire to be considered either
witty, humorous, or a litterateur.   Whatever the
House or the gentleman may have meant by their

laughter and applause, I would recommend to him
the verse of Tennyson, where he says:

> How e'er it be, it seems to me
> 'Tis only noble to be good;
> Kind hearts are more than coronets,
> And simple faith than Norman blood.

(Cheers).

"And certainly no one ever merited this tribute
of the laureate of England more than Richard Cobden, the yeoman's son, the friend of America, and
the defender of just economic laws. (Cheers).

"When the gentleman prints my name Samuel
Sullivan Cox in the Record, he indicates something
of my Celtic blood, but he indicates something better than my thought and service.

"I beg to say that I accept my middle name with
considerable pride; for among the best men of the
Revolution from New Hampshire were the two Sul-
livans, one of whom was governor of Massachusetts and the other a general in our army. Both
were the friends of Washington. The general was
not only the first to wrest Fort William and Henry
from the tory government of England, but, after
the Revolution was over, he signalized his bravery
and   skill   by   suppressing   the   Indians
in   Central   New   York   when   they   were
allied   with   the   Tories   with   which   the
gentleman   is   pleased   to   be   allied.   By
ancestry, by inclination, by virtue of long service
here, running through nearly thirty years, I never
had one thought for or sympathy with the Tory
leaders who sought to drive England to despera-
tion by their protective policies. The Tories of
New Jersey, from which state came my folk,
were in alliance with the Hessian and the red-coat

to drive the patriots of the revolution into ignoble
humiliation. They failed, but had they succeeded
and had the Liberals of England, whom the gentleman stigmatizes, failed, we might still have
been an English dependency, and the gentleman,
if he had lived at all, might have been engaged in
the constabulary force in Ireland to-day endeavor-
ing to suppress, under the orders of Tory Balfour,
the enfranchisement of the people of his native
isle who are seeking for home rule. * * * *
This little esprit of the gentleman, according to
the brackets in the Record, produced 'laughter and
applause.'

"It is well that the gentleman got in his laughter first. The incident reminds me of another
Irishman. He was in a meadow with a little
bovine. The bovine began to paw the earth and
tear up the ground with his horns and the Irishman laughed and laughed at the unique performance. (Laughter). But soon the little bull pitched
him over a fence. The Irishman got up and said,
'Isn't it lucky I got in my laugh first?' (Laughter.)
Before I finish with the history of this club and its
opponents and members the gentleman will be,
perhaps, not a little astonished to know where the
laugh comes in."

Later in the speech he paid a glowing eulogy to
Richard Cobden, in which he said:

"That night of English wrong was set thick with
stars—a whole constellation. Cobden among
them was shining resplendently as a star of the
first magnitude. Cobden was not a nobleman.
He was born of the people. He was the son of a
yeoman. He was brought up to trade. It was his

business training, together with observation
abroad, while a partner in a Manchester cotton
mill, that made him so cogent in debate and so
simple and earnest in his devotion to the cause of
the people and to the 'cheap loaf.'

"Mr. Chairman, I should be derelict as a member
of Congress, or as a citizen of the United States, if
I did not, even in this feeble way, vindicate the
splendid fame of Richard Cobden. He was not
merely a friend of the poor when they needed
friends, but he was a distinguished economist
when economy was thundered from the hustings
for the relief of the starving. More than all these,
by his speeches, writings, diplomacy, and parliamentary efforts, he has done more than any other
Englishman to hold up the institutions of our own
country, not merely for the indulgence of mankind, but for their imitation and admiration. Nor
were the enconiums which he had bestowed upon
our country born of a mercenary or trading spirit.
He had a genuine love for America. He twice
visited us. He denounced those who had depre-
ciated our character and slandered our people.

"In a volume of his writings, which I have in my
hand, there is a comparison between Great Britain
and America. With what fervor he turns to the
industrial, economical, and foreign peaceful policies of America, while with the live coal of a seer
on his lip he bids at distance our future, Hail!
He does this with a pride that knows no selfishness and with a humanity that regards no isola-
tion. England and America were, in his view,
bound together in peaceful fetters with the strong-
est of all ligatures that can bind two nations—

commercial interests and the destiny of representative governments. Every reform that England has made in the interests of her people, and for her colonial advancement, found Richard Cobden its friend, and his gifted speech its ally. And it comes with ill grace from an American, whether native or adopted. to blur the escutheon of this champion of America and this honest friend of the people."

CHAPTER XXX

Protection of our fisheries was one of the multifarious objects he sought through legislation. In a speech in the House May 12, 1884, on a bill to protect fish in the Potomac river, he displayed a wide knowledge of the entire subject. Incidentally he referred to his own experience as a disciple of Izaak Walton. We quote:

"I have made a pilgrimage to the tomb of Izaak Walton in Winchester Cathedral, and have made my homage to that 'grand old man' and rare old fisher. I found that his remains were under a large black slab, in a chapel in the south aisle called Prior Silkstead's chapel. It was evening when I endeavored to decipher the poetic tribute to the ancient angler—'crowned with eternal bliss.' The cheerfulness of his disposition and the serenity of his mind gave to him ninety years of felicity in the midst of great and good and yet sportive scholars and churchmen. I honor him as well for his pen as his hook and line; for his grace of diction as for his genial muse and his many colored flies; and, above all, for that lesson of equipoise which he teaches in his rambles after his favorite recreation. He teaches the contemplative as well as sportive quality of the art. But if any one think that the literature of fishing began with Izaak Walton let

him read classic lore. It is as full of the details
as it is of the fun and poetry of fishing.   Arion
rides upon a fish as easily as the bold Viking darts
out of the Norse fiord after his prey. But neither
the classic nor romantic past has any history or
fancy equal to the reality of our deep sea fishing
or of our artificial reproduction.

*   *   *   *   *   *   *

"I have had some experience in fishing. May I
be pardoned if I refer to the fact that I have fished
under the shadows of our Sierras in Tahoe, lake
and stream; that I have followed the mountain
rivulet Restonica in Corsica, where the waters
blanch the boulders into dazzling whiteness, and
the associations of the vendetta and the Bona-
partes give a ruddy tinge to the adventure; that I
have caught the cod in the Arctic around Cap
Nord, under the majestic light of the midnight
sun; that I have angled in the clear running Ma-
laren Saltsjon, which circulates healthfully amid
the splendid islets of stately Stockholm, and in the
Bosphorus, in sight of the historic Euxine and the
marble palaces and mosques of two continents;
that I have been tossed in shallops along with the
jolly fishers of the Bay of Biscay; that I have had
the honor of beholding the pillars near Iskender-
oon in the northwest corner of the Mediterranean,
erected by a grateful people on the spot where
Jonah was thrown ashore by the whale; and that
I have bounded through the league-long rollers on
the shores of New Jersey, along with my favorite
life-savers—to see and feel the 'bluefish wriggling
on the hooks.' But notwithstanding these wide-
spread endeavors, I am not prepared to say that
there has been any perceptible diminution in the
quantity of fishes in the waters of our star!"

CHAPTER XXXI.

"MAN OF WIT AND WISDOM."

One of his Congressional eulogists said of Samuel Sullivan Cox: "He was undoubtedly a man of wit, and I think regretted that he was such a man; but he was wise also." There is much force in this statement. The man of both wit and wisdom is in constant peril of seeing the former overshadow, in the popular estimation, the latter. As a rule, in a public orator, the wit is more eagerly waited than the wisdom. It was beyond question discomforting to Mr. Cox to discover that the wit of his discourse was oft remembered more vividly than its wisdom. That is one of the penalties all wits must suffer.

A close study of his speeches or his writings will serve to show that Mr. Cox's wit was only the hand-maiden of his wisdom. It sprang naturally from the subject in hand. Never seemed it forced or far-fetched. It was bubble and sparkle. In his speeches it came usually in repartee, and under conditions which forbade a possibility that it could have been premeditated. It was as involuntary as breathing. It used to be remarked by his Congressional colleagues that a witticism dropped from his mouth during a speech would convulse the House with laughter before he himself seemed to be aware of its perpetration. Mr. Cox did not court, and did not relish, a reputation as a wit. Fain would he, if it had been possible, have repressed this ever-present inclination to extract the humor from every situation. But in the words of one of his eulogists, Dr. Talmage, "he never laughed at anything except that which ought to be laughed at. There were in it no innuendoes that tipped both ways; nothing viperine." We have the authority of Douglas Gerold that "it is better to be witty and wise than witty and otherwise." Mr. Cox had a happy combination of wit and wisdom.

A significant illustration of the confidence reposed in Mr. Cox by his associates in Congress, political opponents as well as political friends, is afforded in the fact that Speaker Blaine, when charges of corruption of members by the Credit Mobilier filled the air, and a congressional investigation was demanded, called upon Mr. Cox to name the committee of investigation. Here at least was a member against whose personal integrity the whisper of suspicion had never been raised. Here was one who would be just and fearless in the selection of investigators of the damaging charges. To Mr. Cox, therefore, Speaker Blaine temporarily surrendered his chair, that he might name the committee to which reputations would be committed.

While Hayes was President, Secretary of State Evarts gave a dinner in honor of President Angell, of Michigan University, who had just been appointed Minister to China. Mr. Cox, Chairman of the House Committee on Foreign Affairs, was one of the invited guests. On Secretary Evarts presenting to him the guest of the evening, Mr.

Cox exclaimed, "Why! Jim Angell!" "Why! Sam Cox!" exclaimed President Angell in response. It transpired that the two had been college mates at Brown University a third of a century before, but had never meanwhile met, until this meeting under the roof of Secretary Evarts.

General Rosecrans, formerly member of Congress from California, to an interviewer once related this: "I remember one day some one on the other side, I forget his name, was making a strong pro-Chinese speech, winding up something in this way: "The Chinaman is clean, he is temperate, he is frugal, what fault have you to find with him?' Cox piped out: 'He wears his shirt outside of his breeches!' The House was crowded and that was the last of that orator and his Chinese speech!"

His impressions of those then great Liberal leaders of the British parliament, Gladstone and Bright, are given in a letter from London in May, 1881, giving an account of a visit to the House of Commons. "Gladstone," he wrote, "is a fluent easy speaker—not eloquent exactly—somewhat verbose and involved, with a happy audacity that, on party occasions, has a biting sarcasm. He looks somewhat like Daniel Webster about the head, and has much nobility of expression in his face. He is pale, thoughtful, and commanding, and never noisy. Mr. Bright is of another order, and reminds me somewhat of Thomas Ewing in his dignified, easy mode of stating questions."

Brimfull as he was of humor, Mr. Cox never lost sight of the proprieties of the occasion. He could be stern as the sternest, and severe as the severest, when sternness and severity were demanded. Often called to preside over the deliberations of

WASHINGTON RESIDENCE OF S. S. COX, 1889, NEW HAMPSHIRE AVE.

the House, he filled the chair with exemplary dignity, and ruled sternly and impartially. A stranger
would never have suspected in him the propensi-
ties for which the people really loved him best.
The following incident is related: While Mr.
Cox was acting speaker, during Speaker Kerr's
illness in the Forty-Fourth Congress, charges were
preferred against the Doorkeeper of the House.
They were based largely on a foolish and frivolous
letter the doorkeeper had written home to Texas,
in which, among other things, he had said, describing his own importance, that he was "a biger
man than Old Grant." The charges were referred
to the Committee on Rules, of which pro tem
Speaker Cox was acting chairman. Mr. Cox
wrote the report recommending the doorkeeper's
removal. His secretary, to whom Mr. Cox showed
his proposed report, laughingly remarked that it
seemed curious that one who himself so loved fun,
should condemn levity in others, the secretary add-
ing that since Mr. Cox had been occupying the
speaker's chair he had grown very serious and
stern. "I know it," spoke up Mr. Cox, with a
merry twinkle, "and if I don't get down on the
floor pretty soon and let off steam, I'll explode."

In addressing public audiences Mr. Cox quickly
sized the character of those before him, and
adapted his language, particularly his illustrations, to their grasp. No one could fail to be impressed with this fact who accompanied him on
his rounds of meetings in his Congressional District on the eve of an election. If they were Long-
shoremen he was talking to, there was no end of
nautical phrases and marine illustrations which
were at his command to point his argument. And

so all the way up the scale—his wondrous versatility enabled him to discourse to his hearers in a
vernacular best suited to their intelligence.

In his lecture on "African Humor" Mr. Cox gave
many a convulsing illustration of his subject.
Among others, one for which he was himself responsible:

"The African's religious views are peculiar. An
old negro expressed his faith in prayer, but he
said 'it depended on what yo' prayed for. I allays
notice,' said this Ethiopian philosopher, 'dat when
I pray for de Lord to send one of Massa Peyton's
turkeys fo' de old man it don't come; but when I
prays dat he'll send de old man fo' de turkey, my
prayer's answered.'" "Sunset" tells the following
in the same connection: "I remember one occasion
when my wife and I attended a colored meeting,
and they were trying to raise $16.50 to repair a
place in the ceiling of the church. After the box
had gone round once there remained a deficiency
of $6.87. They began to sing again and were
about to pass the box, when my wife and I decided
to make up what was lacking, and handed the
amount to a colored girl in front of us, who sang
like an angel and looked like the devil, who
proudly marched up the aisle and deposited the
money with the deacons. Then there was a shout
went up from the minister: 'Lock de door and shut
the winders. Glory hallelujah! Dere's angels
right here among us; let's raise $10.50 more while
we're about it.' They meant to make the most of
their opportunity."

In the freedom of social intercourse, as well as
in his private correspondence with friends, Mr.
Cox's humor was ever bubbling, like the perennial

spring. He was a born caricaturist, and many of his letters show pencilings worthy of a Nast.

Hardly a page of his correspondence with close friends that was not illuminated by flashes of his humor. A few random shots follow: To a friend who was a candidate for office in a "Salt" district: "If you are of the elect I shall —I know I shall—order a gurgling cocktail, and put salt in all my food for a year."

From New York in the fall of '83: "I have been speaking effectively—if my thorax is any index—in New Jersey and New York. I spoke with Ab-bett, McClellan, et al—et al will be elected. Look out for his returns!"

Referring to an impracticable proposition: "That would have been like the Irish mob, who hated a banker, and to spite him burned his notes!"

In response to a challenge to go to the Adiron-dacks: "If you mean by going into the woods for a fish, I'm your Izaak Walton. I'm no Nimrod, and don't know him from a ramrod."

Accompanying a pen-and-ink sketch of his party in a boat blue fishing: "You can see for yourself how we pursue the apostle's calling."

Near the end of the Congressional session of '76: "We are trying to close up. I get lots of instruc-tion on silver—enough for a temple in Cizco, or a full moon!"

Speaking of his summer outing in 1877 along the Jersey coast: "From Ocean Grove, where a Meth-odist whangdoodle was howling like the Dervishes of the East—to Long Branch where Boss Kelly re-posed under the red moon, as serene and gentle as a true man—which he is!"

Speaking of a political meeting addressed by him under the depressing influences of an Ohio defeat: "It was dull and dead; but we had a Sankey-monious (old) time, and the Moody fit passed by."

Acknowledging in London the receipt of a forwarded letter: "Yours has been to Egypt—had Cheops for breakfast."

From Manhattan Beach on an August day in '87: "I go to Sullivan county to-morrow, where I can catch fish and worship God like the Puritans—and correct proof, which was more than they did when they made rum out of Santa Cruz molasses."

Writing from Fire Island in June, '77, after having been selected for the Long Talk at the Tammany celebration: "I did not expect to be selected for the 'Long Talk,' 4th July. But I am; and here, after catching blue fish till I have got over the blues, and black fish till Fred Douglas seems white, I am anchored at my 'Talk'; and as I write Mrs. Cox copies. It looks so much better in MSS. after she copies, that I feel eloquent."

From Boston, November 21, '79, while on a flying lecturing tour: "I write you in Boston, under aesthetics! The air is redolent of the aroma of a refined and elegant cultchaw! But I lectured at Cambridge and Dartmouth, and had a full measure of success; and brought home ten days worth of gab. I levy on N. E. to pay my taxes! I have been through N. H. from the Canada line down to Concord; and ran only when the starry snowflake filled the circumambiency, as it were."

From Americus, Ga., in March, '77, while on a lecture tour, and referring to a reception at which

Congressman Blount addressed the honored guest: "We (Mrs. Cox and myself) have had since we left Columbia a floral procession, and such times! If you could have been along you would recognize what I never understood, the 'Sunny South' in its kindest sense of what they think is gratitude to a friend. Read Col. Blount's speech. It is rather steep, but I sweat it through."

At the close of the sesison of Congress, in March, '83: "It was a busy session for me. But am through it well. I send you a Washington paper. It has an article in it you will recognize; for it is mostly from one of yours; and a picture in it you won't recognize, for it is one of—me. Still gaze on it fondly for the good intentions."

From New York September 23, '84, on learning of the death of a political admirer: "I am very sorry to hear my old friend —— is deceased. I remember him very pleasantly. One of his odd ideas was—and I cannot put him down therefore as a crank—that I was considerable of a person and made a larger figure politically than I do physically. Perhaps in a better world, where things are measured by other standards, he has reversed his opinion, and may think I am a large man physically and otherwise not, for there must be different standards after the incorporealities have vanished."

On hearing of an addition to the family of a friend: "Mark Twain holds we were all babies once. I can't recall it, but I suppose it's so."

From a lecturing tour in the South in March, '77: "I have lectured at Rome, Atlanta, Macon, and last night here, to big crowds; and really am making money. Think of that! The noble pursuit of avarice!"

On hearing of the election of Hayes to the Governorship of Ohio in October in 1875: "Well, Ohio is gone! It makes me blue—for it makes 20 years work and waiting a doubt; 1876 is in peril. Am writing a book, 'Why We Laugh?' But I don't feel like answering that conundrum—in politics—as we don't laugh."

From New York, November 15, '76, amid the suspense following the disputed Presidential election: "We are in the mist, but the dawn is ours. But we won't count it till we see the peaks."

At the opening of a Congress: "I will order the Congressional Globe for you daily. You can so live as to 'die daily.' Grace Greenwood told my wife that she had read the 'Globe' of one day and felt like a 'She Atlas'—there was such heaviness in its rotundity to bear up."

From Washington, August 19, '88, in response to an inquiry from the agitated farmers of Pompey whether it was true that the Mills bill put potatoes on the free list: "Potatoes are not affected at all by the Mills bill. Put that down sure and salt it. They would have been affected if it were not for some stiff people who wanted starch, and starch, as you know, is made out of potatoes. The toothsome potato has the aegis of the government all over it. Every eye of the potato glistens with delight because it is protected."

From Washington a few days later: "I am glad that the potato question has been settled. It was a terrible strain on the Committee on Census, which organized all its forces and made a raid upon the Ways and Means committee room in order to make it an absolute verity so that Pompey could not sit down amid the ruins of Carthage and view vast potato fields grow to rot! What a beneficent government we are."

A new member, of large girth and pretentious wit, from Michigan, sought on one occasion, in the winter of 1880, to make Mr. Cox the butt of his ridicule. He not only spoke contemptuously of the New York member's stature, but more than intimated that his Committee of Foreign Affairs was engaged mainly in manufacturing witticisms. In his reply Mr. Cox pointed out the important measures which had originated in his Committee, and then turned his attention to the personal criticisms which had been hurled at him. "Why," said he, "should I be accused of mere play here? Have I not shown some fruits as the result of studious work? Did I not carry through here the Thurman bill as to railroads, the life-saving bill, the census, and many others which might be named? Is it not time to stop this constant depreciation of one who really cares little for being here, except to do something worthy? Where is the fun in such misrepresentation? Will my friend from Michigan bear with me if I give him a lesson in the matter of congressional debate? Humor is a large part of it. It should be ratiocinative, however. It should have a practical object. The point is to make your fun dialectic and rational. * * The gentleman from Michigan was also pleased to refer, in a pleasant way, to some volumes of travel I had written. Thankful for such notice, I fear he has omitted the one most apposite. There is a

volume in my desk and I will send it to him. It is
entitled "Why We Laugh." I send it to the gentleman with my regards, and with a view to ask
him to regard it philosophically, "why,"—not
"how," nor "at what" we laugh. It will show him
that nearly all great natures manufactured witticisms now and then, from Sir Thomas More to
Thomas Corwin, from Julius Caesar to the gentleman. But their wit had a rational purpose. They
were logical in their laughs. They used what
Aristotle knew to be the reductio ad absurdum,
and what Whately commends as the best means of
exposing fallacy and fraud. I wish I could read
an extract or so before I send my friend the volume.

"Now, in the view of these lessons for mirth, was
it logical for my friend the other day to call the attention of the House to my body? Suppose I am
little, was it logical, or parliamentary, or kind to
say it? It was done without malice, but it perme-
ated every one of my two million pores. Suppose
I had the gentleman's immensity of pores, where
could not the laughter extend? Then there would
have been need of some improvements, "because of
a loss of moisture." Why, sir, every sweat-gland
in my small body gave out its mortifying perspiration because they were so few compared with the
pores and glands of larger bodies. Now, sir, I
submit, was my size a subject for any gentleman's
logical laughter? I never claimed, because of its
smallness, exemption from the demands of courage or in the arena of debate. Laughter is health.
It oils the joints and the countenance, causing it
to shine. An animal that tries to laugh, like a

hyena, is specially despised; but a babe, when it
first beholds the sunshine, laughs! But where is
the point of making my small person—though I
carry the weight of the average man, one hundred
and forty pounds—the butt of his ridicule? Why
should smallness, in such an immensity of creation, and when everything may be reduced to
atomies, be accounted contemptible? When one
comes to consider all universal physical relations
—the size, say, of this dome and the goddess on it,
much bigger, even, than the gentleman, then of the
mountains of our earth, then of the sun, of Jupiter,
or the star Sirius, and then the constellations and
systems far beyond, pinnacled dim in the intense
inane, of creation, how contemptible a member of
congress seems! Therefore, where or what is the
humor of making a member of congress out to be
little, and laughing at his size? What is there to
boast of in this enormity of flesh and size? At the
best, Goliah did not reach more than twice as high
and was only one-sixth more than the size of some
gentlemen here. Lambert, with all his opulence
of oil, was only a poor, weak man, unable to grasp
what Isaac Newton knew—whose mother put him
in a quart cup when he was born. Sir Isaac Newton! Does the gentleman think he could get into
such a cup? Why then, why should the spirit of
mortal be proud? Proud flesh is not a sign of
health. I endeavor to debate here impersonally;
never refuse to yield; never invade another's right;
always consider my person almost an abstraction.
I am not proud of my appearance as some men are
who swell. Why, sir, I argued against making congress too big ten years ago. Two hundred and
fifty was enough. Had I known the advent of this

leviathan into our troubled waters, I should have favored two hundred as our number. But that is to be settled next year. Corpulency is not strength. Let us remember that!"

It is needless to add that Mr. Cox was not troubled again from that quarter.

As to Mr. Cox's methodical habits, his long-time friend and associate in congress, Mr. Holman, of Indiana, said: "No man in our period equaled him in readiness for any question that might arise. He was a man of the most precise method and order. His desk in the House was so methodically arranged, that even in the heat of an unexpected debate he could lay his hand at once on any paper which had been carefully laid aside for an emergency. Swift as a flash of lightning, the clipping from a newspaper, or a public document, or a carefully preserved letter would come forth to confound the incautious adversary. In those sudden emergencies, which have so often arisen in Congress, especially in times of public disorder in former years, when his party was fiercely assailed by the powerful majority, the eyes of his political associates always turned to Mr. Cox as one of their number best prepared to repel the assault."

Of the power he wielded by his oratory, one of his Congressional associates, Mr. Caruth, of Kentucky, said: "What a master of oratory he was! I have seen the House almost as tempestuous as the sea in a storm stilled to silence by the rising of his form from the midst of the tumult, the lifting of his hand with his familiar gesture, and the utterance of his 'Mr. Speaker.' I have seen the busy men of the House drop their pens and leave their desks to gather about him that they might hear what he had to say. I have seen the lobbies deserted, the cloak rooms emptied, even the seductive restaurant ignored, the seats of the chamber filled, because 'Sunset Cox' held the floor. I have seen the faces which were almost distorted with partisan passion, in the fierce hours of political conflict, smoothed to pleasant humor by the potency of his speech."

In a like vein, General Wheeler, ("Fighting Jo") of Alabama, said: "His humor always did good and never harm. He seldom used this faculty merely for the purpose of amusing his audience, but put it into play when it was evident that, by so doing, a desired, and frequently a very important object could be attained. We all remember how often he quelled a storm in the House of Representatives by some pleasant witticism, almost instantly changing the scene from one of angry dispute to one of most pleasant hilarity. It is a mistake to say that this detracted in any way from Mr. Cox's dignity or the great esteem which was universally felt for him. That he would have honored the presidency, no one who knew him would for a moment doubt. No one of his time was better equipped than he, with regard to all matters of government, and in general information and knowledge of politics and history the superiority of his attainments was remarkable. I doubt if any member of either House of Congress ever equalled Mr. Cox as a worker."

Senator Voorhees, of Indiana, in his eulogy, related an incident illustrative of the affection with which Mr. Cox was remembered by his old friends in Ohio. He had been recalled to Zanesville on a sad errand—the death of his father.

"During his melancholy sojourn of a few days at
Zanesville," said Senator Voorhees, "he concluded
to run down to Columbus, and it so happened that
Mr. Pendleton, Mr. Vallandigham and myself were
on the train with him. It was not generally
known that Mr. Cox was then in the State, and
least of all was he expected at Columbus that day.
When the train arrived, a concourse of people,
with music and banners, was at the depot to welcome those of the party who were expected. All
at once, as we emerged from the cars, an intent
look came into every eye in that multitude, and
then a jubilant, prolonged shout rent the air. The
brilliant Buckeye was discovered by his old neighbors and constituents, and in an instant everybody
was forgotten but him. It was his first return,
after going out from their midst, and taking up a
new home. He managed to get from the cars to a
carriage, but loving hands lifted him out of it. I
have witnessed many an ovation to popular party
leaders, but never anything like the intense personal devotion, affection and love, displayed on
this occasion. The last I saw of him, many hours
afterward, was as he stood bareheaded in the
street, surrounded by a surging multitude of men,
women and children, who were shouting, laughing,
crying, and clinging to him. His own eyes were
suffused, his face was pale, and his lips trembled,
though wreathed with smiles of rapture at his unexpected and wonderful welcome."

Many another like instance might be given,
showing the strength of the popular affection for
this tribune of the people.

CHAPTER XXXII.

With a rare gift of language were coupled in Mr. Cox, the ambition and the requisite energy to excel in the use of that gift. He wrote poetry, while in college, to improve his style. He allowed no opportunity for improvement or advancement to go by. We find him, even in his college days, an accepted contributor to the Knickerbocker Magazine, then the best of American periodicals. His interesting "Chapter on Fallacies," in which it was sought to show the influence of fallacies on morals, first appeared in the Knickerbocker, in 1847. In the same magazine, in 1851, appeared "Crossing the Border," a description of the borderland between England and Scotland, with a Sunday morning in the old York Minster.

In 1854, Mr. Cox, in response to the solicitation of the publishers, contributed to the Knickerbocker Gallery, a volume of choice miscellany, the proceeds from whose publication were to go for the erection of a cottage, on the banks of the Hudson, for the Knickerbocker's former editor, Lewis Gaylord Clark. "The Satanic in Literature" was the subject, and in it Mr. Cox recalled in his humorous way some of the notable shapes in which his Satanic majesty appears in literature.

If a man's rank is to be judged by the company

he keeps, Mr. Cox's place in American literature
was already, at that early day, well assured. The
galaxy of bright and particular stars in which his
star shone undimmed, included Irving (whose contribution was given first place), Longfellow, Hal-
leck, Boker, Bryant, Willis, Stoddard, Lowell,
Holmes, Curtis, Bayard Taylor, Donald G. Mitchell.
William H. Seward, Samuel Osgood, Epes Sargent
and John W. Francis—now nearly all gone.

But even before the publication of the Knickerbocker Gallery, Mr. Cox had produced the first
of his fascinating books of travel, with the title of
"A Buckeye Abroad." It consisted of impressions
of his trip, made after his marriage, through Europe.

In the preface, dated January 1, 1852, he writes,
hoping "that it may be read as it is written, more
for enjoyment than profit." It was not without
some profit, however, for in 1860 a seventh edition
was issued—the best evidence of the popular favor
with which it was received.

Busy years of Congressional activity followed.
It was a time for action rather than for writing,
and Mr. Cox's literary work took the form of writing speeches. With the close of the Civil War,
however, supposing his public life to be over, he
published, in 1865, his "Eight Years in Congress."
It was prepared at the request of his "constituents
in Ohio," to whom the book is inscribed "as a token
of esteem and gratitude." It consists of extracts
from his speeches and especially those on finance
and tariff; those that display the sedition and sectionalism of the North; those connected with questions of fugitives from foreign lands and the right
of asylum; those on foreign affairs; a eulogy on

Stephen A. Douglas; speeches on matters growing
out of secession and the war; a speech on the
amendment of the Constitution abolishing slavery,
and on the question of admitting the Cabinet into
Congress.

To the student of those times the book contains
much that is of interest as showing the views of a
representative citizen of the period who was not
an extremist of either party. They are the
thoughtful opinions of a conservative man, and
after a lapse of thirty years, it is, to say the least,
curious to see how nearly right, in the light of history, Mr. Cox was.

In 1868, close confinement to professional
duties, with failing health as a consequence, led
Mr. Cox to seek recuperation in a trip to the south
of Europe and North of Africa. His experiences
and observations under the title of "Search for
Winter Sunbeams on the Riviera, Corsica, Algiers,
and Spain," were given to the public in 1870. The
volume is dedicated to his "Constituents of the
Sixth Congressional District of the City of New
York." "These Sunbeams of Travel," he writes
"were made bright by your confidence and cheerful by your indulgence; without which I could not
have pursued them, into far and almost untrodden
paths—in search of the health so needed and I
trust, secured, for the duty which you have de-
volved upon me."

He spent pleasant, sunshiny days in Nice, in
Cannes, in Hyeres, in Mentone, and in Monaco—
that paradise of climate and beauty, and hell of
gambling. Then crossing the blue Mediterranean
he spent some time in Corsica, visiting the home of

Napoleon and studying the quaint habits of the people of this out-of-the-way island. From Ajaccio he returned to Nice and thence by steamer from Marseilles to Algiers.

A new continent with its ancient civilization was before him, and views of Arabic, Turkish, or Moorish life were opened to him. Notwithstanding the dolce far niente of the Orient he was active in studying the institutions and the customs of the people. He tells of the quaint architecture, the religious ceremonies, the theatres and entertainments, and the domestic habits of the people. He even extends his journey to the edge of the great desert, passing through the valleys of Kalybes, and learning on the way the mysteries of riding on camel-back.

Leaving the Arabs and their decadence, he turns northward and makes his way toward the Iberian peninsula, where the remains of the Moor in his greatness are found in such rich abundance.

He speaks of "a ring of cities, full gemmed," in his memory, and he saw them all—Carthagena, Alicante, Valencia, Murcia, Grenada, Malaga, Seville, Toledo, Cordova, Madrid and Saragossa. The Alhambra of Grenada, the Alcazar of Seville, and the aqueduct of Cordova are among the masterpieces of architetcure that he studied and admired. He listened to the music of the castanets and the guitar in Murcia, and when not occupied with the Cortes in Madrid, he walked the galleries of the Escuriel—the mausoleum of Spain's greatest heroes—looking at the rich paintings of Murillo and other famous artists of Spain, or else witnessing the bloody bull fights of the metropolis.

Malaga with its wine and its grapes, and Saragossa
with its history appealed to him as only can a well
digested meal to a bon viveur. He knew the
country from his extensive reading and enjoyed it
accordingly.

Spain, at the time of Mr. Cox's visit had but
recently sent her infamous Isabella across the
frontier and under the leadership of the distinguished Prim, was making her experiment with a
Republican form of a government. Our author,
who was in Madrid when the new Constitution
was adopted, takes advantage of the occasion to
express his views on the situation.

At the end of two months, warned by the summer's heat, he reluctantly left St. Sebastian, the
last of the important railway stations in Spain,
and crossed the Pyrenees into France. After a
brief rest at Biarritz on the Bay of Biscay, with its
health-restoring climate, he hastened to England
and then home.

The remarkable memory, coupled with the genius for compilation posessed by Mr. Cox is fully
shown in that most amusing book entitled, "Why
We Laugh." The purpose of the work is indicated
in the preface, which says: "The idea which
prompted this volume was to string such humors
as were illustrative upon some philosophic threads
which had been floating in my mind." It consists
essentially of amusing incidents and anecdotes,
chiefly American, grouped under various head-
ings, and for the most part from political or legislative sources. In the chapter devoted to early
American humor he introduces several stories that
go back to the time of the first Congress, and in-

deed from then on, no bit of humor that was ever
uttered in either branch of Congress seems to have
escaped his notice. The book was so successful
that in 1880 an entire new edition was issued to
which Mr. Cox added a chapter descriptive of Irish
humor.

Of Mr. Cox's published works, the next in chro-
nological order was a small square octavo, entitled: "Free Land and Free Trade. The Lessons of
the English Corn Laws applied to the United
States." It was published in 1880.

The shock of the financial crisis that came in
1873, and continued during the decade that ended
in 1880, gave rise to many discussions as to its
causes by the thinking men of the nation. Mr.
Cox's long experience in public matters and his
knowledge of political conditions led him to believe that a revision of the tariff laws was the pan-
acea that would cure the ills resulting from financial depression.

His contention was that "our amazing natural wealth is compelling us to alternatives of
yielding the policy of selfishness (i. e. manufacture
for home production only) or being choked with
our own abundance," and "we cannot sell without
buying," hence, the free entry into the country of
raw materials was essential so that we might sell
our manufactured products at the lowest price.

To prove this thesis he discussed the origin and
development of the Corn Laws in England, which,
by the way, was the subject of his prize essay in
the department of political economy, while he was
a student in Brown University—and further, taking the condition of Ireland as his text, he argued

that free land, accompanied by free trade was necessary to produce the best results.

His conclusions were that "the triumph of free land and free trade carries with it everywhere the blessings, and marks the boundaries of civilization," and finally "when that supremacy is accomplished the plough will be as free as the soil, and the land and all the inhabitants thereof will rejoice in that liberty which is the exaltation of individual and national life."

After several years of exacting attention to his duties in Congress, rest and change again became necessary. Early in 1881, therefore, he sailed for another trip to the Old World. The story of his travels is stold in two volumes, the first of which he called "Arctic Sunbeams, or from Broadway to the Bosphorus by Way of the North Cape." It was published in 1882.

The story begins with his arrival in Holland, whence, after studying the peculiar characteristics of the Dutch people, he goes to Denmark. At Copenhagen he takes the boat across the Sound to Malmo in Norway and is soon in Christiana. Still farther northward he goes and as the hot days of July come he is cool and comfortable within the Arctic circle. The most northerly point that he visits is North Cape, from which he looks out on the great North Ocean and watches the rising of the midnight sun.

Thence his journey is continued southward through Lapland and Norway again to Sweden. Reluctantly he leaves the Scandinavian peninsula and crosses the Baltic to Finland. From Helsingfors he goes to St. Petersburg by boat, and he devotes much time to the attractions of the

great capital of the north. The city of the White
Czar has for him a fascination, and he lingers con-
tentedly there until the time arrives to continue
the journey southward. Moscow, with its cathe-
drals and its memories of Napoleon, is a stopping
point on the way to Odessa on the Black Sea;
thence the swift steamer of the packet line takes
him to Constantinople.

The second volume, "Orient Sunbeams, or from
the Porte to the Pyramids, by way of Palestine,"
appeared in the same year as its companion.

After the long wandering in the harsh northern
climes, Mr. Cox was glad of the opportunity to
spend several weeks in resting. Part of his time
was occupied in visiting his old friend, Gen. Lew
Wallace, then American minister to Turkey. During this period he improved his opportunities by
making excursions in the vicinity of Constantinople and in noting the changes that had occurred
in the metropolis on the Golden Horn since his
first visit to it, thirty years previous. Having toward the close of his stay been presented to the
Sultan, he soon after passed through the Dardanelles into the Mediterranean on his way to Smyrna.
Short side trips were made to the classic city of
Ephesus, to Chios, and the Isles of Greece. Then
he journeyed southward to Damascus, with its
vanished wonders and glories, its walls and tombs.
Of course Jaffa, with its Biblical memories, was
not passed by. Three chapters are devoted to
Bethlehem, Jerusalem and Bethany, in which the
incidents of the birth, death and ascension of our
Lord, as related in Holy Writ, are recalled. The
pleasant days of the late autumn are devoted to
a brief visit to Egypt. In a week, all too short, he

travels from Alexandria to Cairo—the pyramids, the Sphynx, and the tombs of the oldest civilization that the world now knows, are visited. And so the journey ends.

These two volumes, word pictures, together constitute a series of entertaining, thoughtful and agreeable sketches of the interesting and historic places visited.

In 1883 there was issued from Washington a series of seven "Memorial Eulogies delivered in the House of Representatives of the United States by Samuel S. Cox, member from Ohio and New York, 1861-1883." These addresses formed an octavo volume of 86 pages, which was illustrated with engraved portraits on steel of the distinguished statesmen eulogized. The group included the records of men famous in the history of our country. The first, delivered in 1861, was on Stephen A. Douglas, the great leader of his party in the Presidential canvass that preceded the Civil War, and who died just as the new administration which his followers had hoped would be his own, was inaugurated. This was followed by an address on Samuel Finley Breeze Morse, who, persistent in his faith in the new science of electricity, overcame all obstacles until the electric message made communication between continents instantaneous.

Then came eulogies on two friends who were near and dear to him. The first was on Michael C. Kerr, a member of the House of Representatives from Indiana, and who for a short time served as speaker of the House. The other was on Julian Hartridge, a member from Georgia and a friend of his college days in Brown.

Mr. Cox was for many years a regent of the

Smithsonian Institution, and in its development
he took the greatest interest. It was therefore
eminently fitting that the memorial address in
Congress on Joseph Henry, its first Secretary,
should be delivered by one whose friendship for
science led to his close association with the Smithsonian. He told of Henry how "with unblemished
eye, like the eagle, his scientific ken gazed into the
sun itself for its revelation; and yet he nestled,
dove-like, amidst his human domestic affections,"
and that "his processes of thought were chastened
by his Christ-like life and heavenly faith; and he
has his reward in eternal bliss."

The next eulogy is on George S. Houston, a Representative from Alabama and long chairman of
the Committee on Ways and Means. Last of all in
this brief collection is a splendid eulogy of that
eloquent Georgian and Senator, Benjamin H. Hill,
whose magnificent courage in continuing at his
post when overcome by a fatal disease gained for
him the homage of his countrymen.

The next book from the pen of Mr. Cox was an
important contribution to the history of his time,
entitled "Three Decades of Federal Legislation,
1855 to 1885." In this elaborate volume he recalls and reviews the memorable events preceding, during and since, the American Civil War, involving slavery and secession, emancipation and
reconstruction, with sketches of prominent actors
during these periods. The book is a large octavo
volume of 725 pages.

The Republican party came into existence in
Pittsburg in 1855, and Mr. Cox was first elected to
Congress the year after. The first of his three
"decades" is therefore that from 1855 to 1865, and

includes the history of the events that led to the organization of the Republican party, together with a succinct account of the Civil War.

The second decade deals chiefly with the period of reconstruction and carries the reader from the death of the martyred Lincoln in 1865 to the beginning of the Centennial year, 1876. The outrages of the Ku-Klux-Klan and the abuse of power by the government formed in the Southern states by Northern adventurers, receive full consideration in his discussion of the events of this period.

The final decade deals especially with the results of reconstruction, closing with the beginning of a Democratic administration under Cleveland. The resumption of specie payments, the great census of 1880, and the initiation of civil service reform, are the leading issues that come under his review.

During nearly all of the time covered by the events described in this book Mr. Cox was active in public life. It was his fortune to mingle with public men of every shade of opinion, " men " as he himself says, "in every variety of public and private employment and every quality and grade of character." From these and from "decrees of state, and even the 'columns of the sepulchers,' as well as from the controversies of contending parties," he gathered the material from which he prepared this most valuable history.

Throughout his public career, Mr. Cox, as his ancestors for two generations before him, never changed his first unwavering trust in the principles of that party of which he was so able a representative, and throughout the book he endeavors to show and emphasize that which he says "he never ceased to believe," and which in 1885, as the book came from the press, seemed almost to be realized, namely, "that the party of constitutional limits, strict construction, state sovereignty, and federal unity would be found indispensable in the end to honest and united government." And finally he adds: "As this strange eventful period of history is concluding, that party is reascending to political prominence, by the inauguration of its recently elected chief magistrate, purified by the ordeal fires which only added to its invincible strength."

It will be remembered that with the advent of Mr. Cleveland's administration, Mr. Cox was tendered the diplomatic mission to Turkey. This honor he accepted and for two years Constantinople was his official home.

On his return to the United States, his ever facile pen found congenial employment in writing the "Diversions of a Diplomat." This work, which he dedicated by permission "To His Majesty Abdul Hamid II.," was published in New York in 1887 and covered 685 pages.

It is simply the written record of his impressions accompanied by pertinent comments and explanations. He tells of his journey to Constantinople, his reception by the Sultan, the social life of the Turks and their diplomatic conditions. The history of the Ottoman Empire—its origin and development—the various race influences that have brought it to its present condition, the many religions, including, of course, the Moslem, the Greek, the Armenian, and the work of the American Protestant Missions, the Turkish language and literature, its wit and humor, as well as the

stories of the East, or fables which are transmitted
from father to son, the life of the people, their diversions and pleasures, and their home life, including the education of children and the secrets
of the harem; all these and still others are among
the fruitful themes which he presents for the benefit of his reader.

He enters also into a philosophic discussion of
the political conditions of the Balkan peninsula,
the growth of Bulgaria, Servia, Roumania, and
other vassal states, the influence of Russia, and
the ultimate fate of Turkey. These problems are
discussed with the ripe knowledge of an experienced diplomat.

As a supplement to the "Diversions" last named
Mr. Cox wrote "The Isles of the Princes; or the
Pleasures of Prinkipo," recording a summer's experience among the Princes Isles, in the old Propontis.

"These Isles of the Princes," writes Mr. Cox, "lie
in sight of Stamboul and its splendors, and of the
Mountains of Asia, dominated by the Mysean
Olympus. They are glorious in physical loveli-
ness. They are still the 'Isles of Greece', although
under Ottoman rule. Out of their blue waters, at
morn and eve, the beauty of the Grecian myth
arises, to grace the isles with her smiles. Upon
them burn 'the larger constellations.' They are
fitly named 'Isles of Princes.' Upon them the palaces of the princes of old Byzantium were erected.
Here, too, were their monasteries and prisons.
The relics of these lines of civil and eclesiastical
empire are nearly all faded; but the monasteries
of the orthodox Greek church still hold here their

eminences, as well by virtue of their antique titles as by their superb situations."

Here, amid such surroundings, he spent the summer of 1886, and his book is a simple story of his excursions in and around these islands, as well as to adjacent places in Asia and Europe.

Like some of his earlier works, this volume bears a dedication. Mentioning that "it recalls our pleasant sojourn in those classic isles and the many courtesies bestown upon us—'strangers in a strange land,' "—he adds: "It is fit that to you, my dear wife, I should dedicate this volume, for if we have achieved any measure of success, socially or otherwise, in our island home, may I not say that it is due to those qualities of kindness and complaisance which you possess, and which have made our lives one in an ever increasing circle of felicity?"

In his tribute to the memory of Mr. Cox, Representative James O'Donnell, of Michigan, aptly analyzed his literary work as follows:

"All his books are interesting and instructive; his writings are entertaining, giving strength and knowledge. His industry, information and discrimination are apparent upon every page, and the clear, compact, and intelligent treatment of all questions, is observed in each chapter. He had the happy faculty of saying things in a striking way, and most of his publications are the product of conscientious study and research. The reader can not but note the admirable treatment of his themes, distinguished by a classic simplicity and lucidity, clear and graceful, denoting the intellect of the author, strong and full of creating force.

His historical works illustrate the experience and learning that embellish every page; the events narrated are excellently concentrated and condensed, and the author established himself as a clear and vigorous writer and thinker, delighting all with his extensive culture, discernment, and superior taste. His latest volumes exhibit the same polish, breadth, and thoroughness of preparation; the advancing years of the author show no deterioration in happy expression, terseness, and reliable statement. He exemplifies the saying of Milton, 'a good book is the precious life-blood of a master spirit embalmed and treasured up to a life beyond.' In several of his works there is a glowing style and general admixture of humor coupled with profound truths semi-humorously expressed. His name will have an honorable place in American literature."

CHAPTER XXXIII.

Mr. Cox returned to New York from Manhattan Beach a sick man. He failed rapidly to the end. His death occurred at half past eight o'clock on the evening of September 10, 1889—twenty days before he would have completed his sixty-fifth year. At that very hour he had engaged to deliver an address before the Steckler association on the "Wonderland"—meaning the Great West from which he had recently returned. It was another and a greater Wonderland to which he had gone. He passed away as one falling into a gentle sleep. Few knew of his illness until informed of its fatal termination. The sad intelligence as it sped with lightning rapidity throughout the great city and the country caused everywhere sincere mourning. From every quarter came expressions of tender sympathy for the stricken partner of the life that had gone out. Among the many came messages of condolence from ex-President Cleveland, Vice-President Morton, Gen. Sherman and Gov. Hill. Ex-President Cleveland wrote:

"On my arrival at home yesterday after an extended absence, I was shocked to learn of the death of your husband. I cannot refrain from the expression of my deep and sincere sympathy with you in your great bereavement, and my feeling of

personal sadness upon the loss of a talented friend.
Your husband's honorable career and the tribute
which his fellow countrymen will pay to his useful
life will not lessen the poignancy of your affliction."

The funeral was under the direction of the ser-
geant-at-arms of the House of Representatives,
and the following members were named to take
charge of the arrangements, to-wit: Messrs. Carlisle, Randall, Holman, Felix Campbell, Seney,
Heard, Muehler, Kelly, McKinley, Cannon, Reed,
Burrows and O'Neil. The honorary bearers were
Vice-President Levi P. Morton, ex-President Cleveland, Gen. W. T. Sherman, ex-Gov. Hoadley of
Ohio, Sumner I. Kimball, Superintendent of the
Life Saving Service, Col. John A. Cockerill, ex-
Chief Justice Charles P. Daly, John T. Agnew, Ed-
ward Cahill and Douglas Taylor of New York, S.
H. Kauffmann of Washington, and Milton H. Nor-
thrup of Syracuse.

The last rites were on September 13, in the First
Presbyterian church, Fifth avenue and Twelfth
street. The profusion of floral tributes from Letter Carriers and life saving stations attested the
affection in which the deceased statesman was
held. From the New York city Letter Carriers
came a mammoth "Gates Ajar," and a large floral
envelope, with "Our Champion" acrosss the face,
and, in the form of a post mark in the upper right
hand corner, "New York, 9-10-89, 8:30 p. m."—the
day and hour of his death. Brooklyn sent a scroll
of roses and violets, inscribed "S. S. Cox, champion." Philadelphia's floral expression was "1824,
Farewell, 1889. He was our best friend." The
Boston Carriers, by their offering, also testified,

."Our Friend." The Life Saving Service was rep·
resented by a life belt and muffled oar—on the
belt the words "Our Champion."

The services were conducted by the blind chap·
lain of the House of Representatives, Rev. Dr. W.
H. Milburn, Rev. Dr. Deems, of the Church of the
Strangers, and Rev. Dr. T. DeWitt Talmage, of
the Brooklyn Tabernacle.

No story of Mr. Cox's life would be complete
without a reproduction, at least in part, of the dis·
criminating eulogies pronounced over his bier by
Reverends Dr. Milburn and Talmage. Extracts
therefrom follow:

(From Rev. Dr. Milburn's Eulogy.)

Samuel Sullivan Cox, the humorist, the writer,
the speaker, a servant of the people, an officer of
the state, a most human-hearted man, has left us,
and we, the city, the nation, are the poorer for his
going. There was in him a vein of admirable wit
united to an excellent understanding and a rare
power of sympathetic speech, and these, with an
 indefatigablel industry and dauntless energy and
courage, early in life brought him to the front, and
throughout his days kept him there, in a position
of influence and power to which he was fully en·
titled. The country can ill-afford to spare, in
what should have been the maturity of his man·
hood, one so richly endowed by nature, labor, large
and varied experience, whose soul was wedded to
its honor, and to the happiness, interest, and wel·
fare of his fellow men. As his friends, we mourn
our irreparable loss, while the whole land sorrows
for the departure of one of its most faithful, val·
iant and devoted sons.

Sprung from a brave old Revolutionary stock,

COX'S RESIDENCE ON TWELFTH STREET, NEW YORK, IN WHICH HE DIED.

born in Ohio, one of a family of fourteen children,
taught from his earliest days to work with persist-
ence and energy, he gained a university education
as the fruit of his own toil, and then enlarged his
mind and quickened his sympathies by wide travel
making acquaintance with many climates, cities,
of men, and governments, and thus prepared himself for the work he was to do.   He first tried his
hand as a writer for the newspaper press and also
as the author of a book of travels, but soon entered
the Capitol of the nation as a member of the House
of Representatives, where his brilliant parts at
once gained him distinction.

Throughout his congressional career of nearly
thirty ears, he secured and maintained to the last
the kindly regard, the warm admiration, and personal friendship not only of his political associates
but of the members on the other side of the floor,
and in the bead-roll of his friends and admirers
there will be found as many opponents as members
of his own party.   Trenchant and powerful in debate, he used the weapons of research, clear statement, argument, keen wit, and an ever-present
humor, and wherever he inflicted wounds they
were always salved by kindness and mirth, and all
canker was removed.

Earnest in his political convictions and ardent
in their advocacy, he was yet more earnest and ardent in matters outside of politics that concerned
the happiness of his fellow men.   Notable illustrations of this are found in our Life Saving Service, of which he may be said to be the father, and
in his championship of the cause of the hard-
worked and underpaid clerks and carriers of the

postal service. His best and highest public utterances, which had the whole force of his character
in them, were in behalf of a larger toleration, a
sweeter and more practical humanity.

When one reviews his work in Congress, and
knows the immense labors he performed there, in
the profound study of all questions vital to the
nation's welfare, in committees, on the floor, and
at the Departments, it would seem enough to tax
any man's utmost strength and fill his whole time;
yet such was his unwearied industry and elastic
energy, that he managed to write book after book
which have instructed and delighted great bodies
of readers by their intelligence, vivacity, their wisdom, humor and wit.

I must leave it to others, to his colleagues in
Congress, to speak of his political services and the
debt of gratitude the country owes his memory.
This place is sacred to the consideration of character. How did he use those extraordinary talents
which he possessed? Were they for himself su-
premely? A less selfish man than Samuel Sullivan Cox has never appeared in the political life
of his country. He had a large heart, tender sympathies, a kind appreciation, and a power to inter-
pret the character of all with whom he came in
contact. Noble as was his head, his heart was
still nobler; and throughout his career he strove to
help, to cheer, to befriend those who were in need
of his friendship. There was a light in his eye, a
music in his voice, a grasp in the hand, a cheerfulness of speech, a heartiness of manner, which lifted burdens from the shoulders of those who came
near him. His honor was unstained. Although

he was connected with the politics of this city and
of the country in their darkest hours, when corruption ran riot and the infamous scramble for place
and pelf was common, the pitch never defiled him.
his good name was never assailed even by the
tongue of scandal.   He bore himself with a lofty
rectitude; his integrity was incorruptible.

Amid the dance of society, the roar of business,
the greed for office and money, we pause beside
this coffin in the stillness of this sacred place to
recall the form and features of one whose nature
was large enough to offer the generous hospitality
of recognition and sympathy to all sorts and conditions of men, whether they were Roman Catholic
or Protestant, Jew or Mohammedan; and who in
the battle of life ever struck with all his might for
the cause of the true, the right, the good.   One
who knew him best has assured me that his piety
towards God was as genuine, deep, and reverent
as his charity towards his fellow men was large,
unaffected and fervent.   He drew the inspiration
of his conduct and character from the truths and
faith of our holy religion.

This man bore himself to the age of three-score
years and five, not only untainted by the world,
but unworried with it.   No frown of discontent,
no scowl of misanthropy, was ever seen upon his
brow; no complaint of the emptiness of the world
or of its vanity was prompted by that cheery
heart.   He wrought for the welfare of others, and
in so doing found his own, for love is its own exceeding great reward.

(From Rev. Dr. Talmage's Address.)

"The nation weeps.   What a wide, deep, awful

vacuum the departure of such a man as Samuel S. Cox leaves in the world! We shall not see his like again. It will be useless to try to describe to another generation who or what he was like. He was the first and the last of that kind of man. He was without predecessor and will be without successor. What a genial, gracious, magnificent soul he was! And every year he lived made to the world a new revelation of his admirable qualities. Within the past few weeks I traveled in his wake across the American continent, and I heard everywhere of the ovations he had received and the superb impressions he had made, cities and territories and states casting their crowns at his feet.

"And while these tempests are raging on land and sea and the life-saving stations have rescued, within a few hours, the crews of thirty ships, we are called upon to perform the last office over the body of him who was the chief champion of that national benevolence for which every sailor on the seas feels thankful.

"And was there ever a truer friend? Tell me, ye who live in the high places of the earth, and the poor who last night, while his body lay in state, wept over this casket! There is hardly any one here to whom he has not done a kindness.

"Did he not speak for you a good word or write a generous commendation or give you the smile of encouragement in some exigency? How many people he helped; how many perplexities he disentangled; how many bright utterances he strewed in the pathway of others, no one can remember save God who remembers all.

"Firm as a rock, brilliant as a star, artless as a child, pure as a woman. God endowed him for a good purpose with a resiliency of wit, a faculty of impersonation, and an irresistible mimicry and a dramatic power that were inexhaustible. How much the world owes to such a nature we can not tell. It is often a greater good to cause a laugh than to start a tear. We all cry enough, God knows, and have enough to cry about, and we need no impulse in that direction. But he who can scatter our gloom by innocent merriment has been to us an emancipator. Solomon was right when he said, "A merry heart doeth good like a medicine." Wit is of two kinds, that which stings and galls and angers and makes the eye flash and the heart burn; the other is that which illumines, sets free, strengthens for another contest, puts us in good humor with the world and makes us renounce our follies. The one kind of wit is the lightning that rives, but the other is the dew that refreshes. Of that last kind was the wit of our departed friend.

"He never laughed at anything except that which ought to be laughed at. There were in it no innuendos that tipped both ways; nothing viper-ine; nothing that would have been discordant to recall if he had died the next hour. Prince of in-nocent pleasantry, sanctified reparteeist, our friend shall live in our memories like a sweet song too soon closed, like a banquet too soon ended, like a picture over which too soon the veil has dropped."

On October 10, just a month from the date of his death, the great hall of Cooper Union, New York, was filled with citizens of the metropolis, gathered to do honor to the memory of Samuel Sullivan Cox. The meeting was under the auspices

of the Steckler Association, before which body, it
will be remembered, Mr. Cox had engaged to deliver an address on "Wonderland" at the very
hour of his death. Julius Harburger, president
of the Steckler Association, called the great memorial meeting to order, and on his motion Hon.
Grover Cleveland, ex-President of the United
States, was chosen to preside. The ex-President,
on taking the chair, paid an appreciative tribute
to the character and services of the deceased, who
had, he said, "exhibited to the entire country the
strength and the brightness of true American
statesmanship." The chief address was given by
Hon. J. Proctor Knott, of Kentucky, long associated with Mr. Cox in Congress. "The name of no
man," said Mr. Knott, "was ever more widely
known or more lovingly revered among his countrymen than his. It has been heard wherever the
language of civilized men is spoken.   There is
scarcely a home in all this wide and wondrous
land, whether amid the busy haunts of the crowd-
ed city or in the solitudes of the far-off mountains,
in which it is not a familiar household word."
Mr. Knott's review of the memorable career of his
late associate in Congress, was singularly eloquent, analytical and to the last degree just.

Congress paid notable tribute to Mr. Cox's memory. Formal announcement of his death was
made to the House by Representative Amos J.
Cummings, on the 18th of December, and a resolution was adopted expressive of the "deep regret
and profound sorrow" with which the intelligence
was received. As a further mark of respect the
House at once adjourned. Saturday, April 19,

1890, was set apart for paying tribute to the memory of the deceased statesman. On like occasions the galleries and floors of Congress ordinarily present a beggarly array of empty benches. But on this day there were no vacant seats. The public anticipation that this was to be no idle formality but a heartfelt "recognition of eminent abilities as a distinguished public servant"—in the words of the resolution adopted—was realized. The eulogies that came from the lips of the most distinguished members of both political parties, were earnest and eloquent to a degree never surpassed in that historic chamber. Representative Cummings, who gave a most interesting and appreciative review of Mr. Cox's eminent career, was followed by Gen. Banks, of Massachusetts; Roger Q. Mills, of Texas; Ben Butterworth, of Ohio; Col Breckenridge, of Kentucky; Richard P. Bland, of Missouri; Buckalew, of Pennsylvania; Benton H. McMillan, of Tennessee; Col. Grosvenor, of Ohio; Outhwaithe, of Ohio; Lawler, of Illinois; Dunnell, of Minnesota; McAdoo, of New Jersey; Chipman, of Michigan; Covert, of New York; Stone, of Missouri; O'Donnell, of Michigan; Carruth, of Kentucky; Washington, of Tennessee; Maish, of Pennsylvania; "Fighting Jo" Wheeler, of Alabama; Yoder, of Ohio; Quinn. of New York; McClammy, of North Carolina; Turner, of New York; Hansbrough, of North Dakota; McCarthy, of New York; Sherman, of New York; Morrow, of Califorma; and Geisshamer, of New Jersey. Together these tributes constitute a notable volume.

Memorial day in the Senate was July 8, 1890.

The resolutions of the House having been reported, Senator Hiscock, of New York, offered resolutions which were adopted, expressive of the Senate's "profound sorrow," and suspending business
to give opportunity for "fitting tributes to the
memory of the deceased, and to his eminent public
and private virtues." Eulogies no less earnest
and eloquent than those which fell from the lips of
the deceased statesman's own colleagues, of the
House, were made, to a full Senate and overflowing galleries, by Senators Hiscock and Evarts, of
New York; Voorhees, of Indiana; Sherman, of
Ohio; Vest, of Missouri; and Dixon, of Rhode
Island.

All concurred in recognizing the super-eminence
of his ability as an orator and statesman, his mas-
terly grasp of all public questions, and his invalu-
able services to his country. With the Reverend
Doctor Talmage, they said: "We shall not see his
like again. Without a predecessor, he will be
without a successor." This, we believe, is likely
to stand as the judgment of history.

GRAVE OF S. S. COX, GREENWOOD CEMETERY,

As Decorated by the Letter Carriers.

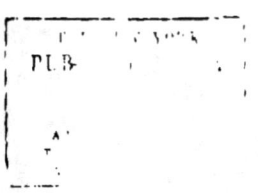

APPENDIX.

Laws Affecting Letter Carriers Enacted through
Efforts of S. S. Cox.

THE ANNUAL VACATION LAW.

Chap. 126.   An Act to grant letter carriers at
free delivery offices fifteen days leave of absence
in each year.

Be it enacted, etc. That all letter carriers at free
delivery offices shall be entitled to leave of absence
not to exceed fifteen days in each year, without
loss of pay; and the Postmaster General is hereby
authorized to employ, when necessary, during the
time such leave of absence is granted, such number of substitute-cariers as may be deemed advis-
able, who shall be paid for services rendered at the
rate of six hundred dollars per annum.

[June 27, 1884.]

THE "FIXED SALARY" LAW.

Chap. 14.   An Act to extend the free delivery
system of the Postoffice Department, and for other
purposes.

Be it enacted, etc. That letter carriers shall be
employed for the free delivery of mail matter, as

frequently as the public business may require, at every incorporated city, village, or borough containing a population of fifty thousand within its corporate limits, and may be so employed at every place containing a population of not less than ten thousand, within its corporate limits, according to the last general census, taken by authority of State or United States law, or at any postoffice which produced a gross revenue, for the preceding fiscal year, of not less than ten thousand dollars:

Provided, this act shall not affect the existence of the free delivery in places where it is now established. And provided further,

That in offices where the free delivery shall be established under the provisions of this act, such free delivery shall not be abolished by reason of decrease below ten thousand in population or ten thousand dollars in gross postal revenue, except in the discretion of the Postmaster General.

Sec. 2.   That there may be in all cities which contain a population of seventy-five thousand or more three classes of letter carriers, as follows: Carriers of the first class, whose salaries shall be one thousand dollars per annum; of the second class, whose salaries shall be eight hundred dollars per annum, and of the third class, whose salaries shall be six hundred dollars per annum.

Sec. 3.   That in places containing a population of less than seventy-five thousand there may be two classes of letter carriers, as follows: Carriers of the second class, whose salaries shall be eight hundred and fifty dollars per annum, and of the third class, whose salaries shall be six hundred dollars per annum.

GEO. T. ESTES, LYNN, MASS.
Oldest Letter Carrier (from 1864) in the Service.

Sec. 4.   That all laws inconsistent herewith are hereby repealed.

[January 3, 1887.]

THE "EIGHT HOUR" LAW.

Chap. 308.   An Act to limit the hours that letter carriers in cities shall be employed per day.

Be it enacted, etc. That hereafter eight hours shall constitute a day's work for the letter carriers in cities or postal districts connected therewith, for which they shall receive the same pay as is now paid as for a day's work of a greater number of hours.   If any letter carrier is employed a greater number of hours per day than eight he shall be paid extra for the same in proportion to the salary now fixed by law.

[May 28, 1888.]

CONTENTS.

	PAGE
Ancestry	9
Boyhood	29
College Life	40
Choosing a Career	61
His Marriage and Trip to Europe	67
As An Editor	70
Enters the Arena of Politics	76
Elected to Congress	78
Eight Years an Ohio Representative	80
Removal to New York	96
Returns to Congress	98
Race for Congressman-at-large	102
Spurns the "Back Pay"	106
Again Returns to Congress	108
From North Cape to the Pyramids	114
Again at His Post	126
As Minister to Turkey	128
A Retrospect	153
Mr. Cox and the Electoral Commission	159
"Free Cuba"	163
Our Debt to Ireland	172
The Persecuted Jews	177
Champion of American Commerce	181
"The Letter Carriers' Friend"	185

Father of the Life-Saving Service...........201

"Four New Stars".......................217

Old Campaigning Days in Ohio.............223

Member of the Cobden Club................226

A Disciple of Izaak Walton................232

"Man of Wit and Wisdom".................234

As an Author and Traveler................249

His Death and Burial.....................264

Appendix: "Letter Carrier" Laws...........275

ILLUSTRATIONS.

FACING
PAGE

Samuel Sullivan Cox, frontispiece.

General James Cox........................ 10

"Box Grove"............................. 16

Judge and Mrs. Samuel Sullivan............ 22

Maria Matilda Sullivan Cox................ 26

Cox's Boyhood Home...................... 30

Muskingum Court House................... 34

E. T. Cox, wife and ten children............. 38

First paper mill West of Alleganies......... 46

Buckingham Mansion, Zanesville........... 66

Cox's first Columbus residence.............. 74

Dr. Henry Bennett in his garden, Mentone.... 98

North Cape group.........................114

U. S. Legation on the Bosphorus............134

Mehemet, Cox's Turkish guard..............138

Nile party, a cosmopolitan group...........142

Decorations conferred by theSultan.........146

Five photographs at different periods.......156

Little Ethel Sullivan.......................186

Cox statue, Astor Place....................192

Group of Officers, N. A. L. C...............194

A Life Saving Station......................202

Vase presented to Mrs. Cox................210

Supt Kimball of Life-Saving service.........214

Cox's Washington residence................236

His New York residence....................266

His tomb.................................274

Oldest Letter Carrier................Appendix